AF071299

REVENGE COMES IN MANY COLOURS

TED TAYLER

BOOKS

Vinci Books

vinci-books.com

Published by Vinci Books Ltd in 2026

Copyright © Ted Tayler 2017

The author has asserted their moral right to be identified as the author of this work in accordance with the Copyright, Designs and Patents Act 1988. This work is a work of fiction. Names, characters, places and incidents are the product of the author's imagination or are used fictitiously. Any resemblance to actual persons, living or dead, places and incidents is entirely coincidental.
All rights reserved. No part of this publication may be copied, reproduced, distributed, stored in any retrieval system, or transmitted in any form or by any means, including photocopying, recording, or other electronic or mechanical methods, nor used as a source for any form of machine learning including AI datasets, without the prior written permission of the publisher.
The publisher and the author have made every effort to obtain permissions for any third party material used in this book and to comply with copyright law. Any queries in this respect should be brought to the attention of the publisher and any omissions will be corrected in future editions.
A CIP catalogue record for this book is available from the British Library.
Paperback ISBN: 9781036700577

The EU GPSR authorised representative is Logos Europe, 9 rue Nicolas Poussion, 17000 La Rochelle, France
contact@logoseurope.eu

By Ted Tayler

The Phoenix

The Olympus Project
Gold, Silver and Bombs
Nothing Is Ever Forever
In the Lap of the Gods
The Price of Treachery
A New Dawn
Something Wicked Draws Near
Evil Always Finds A Way
Revenge Comes in Many Colours
Three Weeks in September
A Frequent Peal of Bells
Larcombe Manor

The Freeman Files

Fatal Decision
Last Orders
Pressure Point
Deadly Formula
Final Deal
Barking Mad
Creature Discomforts

Silent Terror

Night Train

All Things Bright

Buried Secrets

A Genuine Mistake

Strange Beginnings

Dead Reckoning

A Normal November

Into the Sunlight

Tame the Storm

One True Friend

Whispered Truths

A Morning Murder

Quick to Anger

Red Herring Season

Gathering Clouds

Still Standing

Chapter One

Sunday, 29th June 2014

"Good to see you again, Phoenix,"

"You too, Biggles," replied Phoenix.

"So, we're off to Bonnie Scotland this evening then, I gather?" asked Les Biggar, the pilot Olympus had on speed dial for urgent flights around the United Kingdom.

"Yes, and Rusty is coming along for the ride. He's parking the van. I've left him to carry the equipment over to the chopper on his own. Rusty will let you know how he feels in a few minutes."

"There's never a dull moment with you two," said Les.

The rear door of the helicopter flew open, and a bag got shoved into the luggage compartment. The helicopter rocked as the door slammed. Rusty Scott, the rugged, red-headed agent who was Phoenix's best friend, clambered on board.

"Travelling light?" asked Biggles.

"His lordship needed a few essentials for this job. He

forgets, sometimes, just how heavy they are. It's his age," muttered Rusty.

"Neither of us is getting any younger," said Biggles, "okay, gents, if you're ready, we'll be on our way."

"How long do you think it will take, Biggles?" asked Phoenix.

"Two hours in these conditions. It's a pleasant enough evening."

Rusty checked his watch. It read six forty-five.

"Relax," said Phoenix, "our pick-up is for nine o'clock. If we're early, we can get coffee. If the weather closes in, the Glasgow team will sit and wait until we land."

"What's the mission, lads? Can you tell me?" asked Biggles.

"A lot less dangerous than the last one we used you on in Ireland," said Rusty.

"Good, I still get the odd twinge and a few flashbacks, but it goes with the territory."

"I guess you won't be in a rush to return?" asked Phoenix.

"Been there already. I've ferried a few racegoers to meetings at Cheltenham and Newbury and then home again. Apart from a few drunks, there's been no problem. Afterwards, either get back in the game straight away or check out. I chose to keep flying. I'll go wherever the money is, Phoenix."

"Well, this Glasgow trip will be easy enough. It was a direct result of our Manchester mission a few weeks ago," said Phoenix. "We cleared out a fair number of the Grid's gang members based in the Bent Triangle."

"Where's that when it's at home?" asked Biggles.

"The area containing Beswick, Hulme, and Cheetham Hill," replied Phoenix. "The whole place is rife with people for whom law and order is only the name of a TV programme."

"Drugs were being smuggled to Scotland by car or train, using couriers from the region," continued Rusty. "We passed the information gathered by the Lancashire and Merseyside Olympus agents to our colleagues over the border. They had to follow up on our leads."

"The fact you're travelling north suggests progress has stalled somewhat then, am I right?"

"Yes, and no. Our agents acted on the leads we provided, and the noose has tightened," said Phoenix. "The whole network in Glasgow and Edinburgh has now been identified. Zeus sanctioned direct action to eliminate the leading faces in the organisation, but resources are stretched to the limit by other demands around the country."

"Sometimes, Olympus should avoid getting caught in the media headlights," added Rusty, "and let the authorities take the credit."

"This mission aimed to expose enough of the network that even the police can uncover and clean it up," said Phoenix.

Biggles laughed.

"Am I right in thinking an anonymous phone call will be your last act before I fly you home?"

"We're so predictable," groaned Rusty.

The rest of the trip proved uneventful. Les Biggar landed at Glasgow Airport at eight forty.

"Leave your gear in the storage compartment, Rusty," said Biggles. "Follow me, we can get checked in, and then I'll start scheduling our flight plans for the return flight. Do you have any suggestions on timing, Phoenix?"

"First light in the morning, Les," he replied, "I don't intend hanging around up here any longer than necessary."

"Fair enough."

"Will we have time for that coffee?" asked Rusty.

"We'll make time," said Biggles.

They were checked in and drinking a mug of coffee by nine o'clock. Phoenix kept a weather eye open for movement on the tarmac outside the window. The single-storey building stood on the airfield perimeter, and pilots of helicopters and small private planes used it. They were the only people in the place tonight.

"Here they come, right on time," said Phoenix.

A black van motored towards Les Biggar's helicopter. It stopped, facing the building, and the driver turned his headlights off and then on again. Ten seconds later, he switched off the engine, killing the lights. The area around the parking bays was bathed in a dim amber glow from lamps high overhead. It felt eerily quiet.

"Not a bad night for it, Sunday," said Rusty, "it's peaceful."

"We still need to be off this airfield as quick as we can," cautioned Phoenix.

The three men emptied their coffee mugs, carried them to the sink, and swilled them under the hot tap.

"Can you tell we've been house-trained recently?" laughed Rusty.

"Leave them to drain," said Biggles. "I'll pop back and tidy up once you've left. Then get to sleep for a few hours, so I'm ready to fly you south at around a quarter to five."

"I'll call you if there's a delay," said Phoenix. "Although, there's not much room for anything to go wrong on this trip."

"Famous last words," muttered Rusty.

The night was warm outside the building, and the breeze was no more than a whisper. The driver's door opened as they approached the van, and a short, stocky man stepped out.

"Jimmy McLean, as I live and breathe," exclaimed Rusty, "how are you, my friend? It's been a long time."

"I volunteered for this gig when I heard who was coming," the man replied, "our team leader Greg is in the passenger seat. Apologies, but he's on the phone with our lads on the other side of the city."

Phoenix walked around to introduce himself.

"You two have met before then?" asked Biggles.

"We trained at Hereford together on both occasions," replied Jimmy. "When we applied to join the SAS, then again in 2005 when we formed part of the first intake for the Special Reconnaissance Regiment. I left in 2008, the year before Rusty had a difference of opinion with a superior officer."

"He thought he was proficient," said Rusty, "I told him he was a bleeding liability,"

"OK," said Phoenix, returning with Greg, the Glasgow team leader.

"If you two have caught up on the old days, we'll get moving."

"We're off to Barrhead first," barked Laidlaw, "get your kit stowed, and climb in."

Greg Laidlaw was a tall, angular man in his mid-thirties accent pure Glaswegian. Rusty reckoned he had been born and raised no further than five miles from Govanhill. He knew how rough that district was and had a degree of respect for a man who dragged himself up from there to a senior post in Olympus.

Biggles smiled as he watched Phoenix offer to help Rusty carry the heavy bag. Rusty patted his arm away and slung the equipment over his shoulder. The pilot knew the score. No way would he let his old SAS comrade McLean think the years had caught up with him.

"I'll see you guys in the morning," said Les Biggar, "good hunting."

Phoenix and Rusty raised a hand in acknowledgement as the pilot trudged towards the building. They got into the van, and Jimmy McLean drove away from the airfield. They were soon leaving the motorway and heading along the A76.

"Another fifteen minutes, and we'll be there," said Jimmy.

"What's at Barrhead?" asked Rusty.

"A town that has seen better days, with a population of twenty thousand," said Phoenix. "The gang leaders selected this place for its variety of industrial estates. Plus, it's accessible by road and rail from Manchester, with none of the risks associated with being spotted in the heart of Glasgow. So they rented several units across the town, and most of the face-to-face meetings needed were in a bar in Cross Arthurlie Street, just up from the railway station."

"Thanks for the history lesson, Phoenix," said Rusty.

"My pleasure," Phoenix replied.

"We're coming up to our first warehouse just now," said Laidlaw, "so let's park, and I can go through the layout with you."

"Who's running this outfit?" asked Rusty.

"Gregor McGrath," replied Greg Laidlaw. "He's quietened a touch as he's grown older, but he was a wild one in his teens. His reputation with a blade has left him untouched for forty years. Nobody has threatened his position as the head of the organisation covering Glasgow and Renfrewshire and lived. Yet there's nothing to suggest McGrath's laid a finger on anyone in the past three decades.

On the contrary, he has a loyal crew of enforcers who carry out his orders without question."

The four men sat in the van one hundred yards from the warehouse that was their target. The building was in darkness, just what you might expect, late on a Sunday night. There was no sign anyone was on the premises, let alone that it was a potential hive of illegal activity.

"Do we have a backup team in place?" asked Phoenix.

Laidlaw nodded and unfolded a drawing that showed the ground surrounding the building, plus the layout of all three floors.

"We have a van here and on the far side. Each vehicle holds six agents. It doesn't take a genius to work out why we can't see signs of activity because we're looking through the windscreen at a two-floor warehouse building. The drawing shows the layout of the basement. That's where the workers are grafting away, converting the product transported from Manchester into a street-ready product. It's a slick operation, and quality control is variable by design. They put every kind of rubbish into the gear to sell to junkies and cut the crap content the further they move up the social scale; they've got the process off to a fine art. Stocks of every grade match demand to the ounce. They never hold excess stock. Just in time and continuous improvement were management tools in the Nineties; now these buggers have taken it to a new level."

"Kanban, and Kaizen," said Phoenix.

"Those names sound more like sumo wrestlers," said Jimmy McLean to Rusty Scott.

"Watched that every week, didn't we?" replied Rusty, "did they ever fight that Hawaiian giant, The Dump Truck? Davy Glass was a big fan, I remember. What happened to him?"

"He came out of the mob and returned to Edinburgh. That was three years ago. His wife and kids had moved south within six months. He found it difficult to adjust. She couldn't handle his moods. The last I heard, he was living on the streets. I keep meaning to look him up, to see if I can help,"

"Damn shame, he was a good lad," said Rusty.

They sat silently for a few minutes, reflecting on the times the three had lived, fought, and socialised together. Along with the rest of the regiment they had served in, how things had changed. The spell broke when Laidlaw issued an order.

"Time to move in," he said into his mouthpiece.

The action against the Grid's gang members was underway on the far side of the warehouse. Eight heavily armed Olympus agents burst into the ground floor and descended into the basement. Laidlaw ordered Jimmy McLean to drive to the right-hand end of the building.

Phoenix and Rusty could hear flashbangs, smoke bombs, and brief bursts of gunfire.

"The best point of entry for the teams was at the opposite end," said Laidlaw. "We should see activity here in a tick."

Phoenix and Rusty were out of the van and grabbing their gear from the bag. McLean and Laidlaw had already moved to within ten yards of the building.

"Cover the far door and subdue anyone who tries to escape," shouted Laidlaw. "Once we finish that part of the exercise, we'll head inside. You're aware of the layout now. The stairs on the left take you to the basement and bring you into the rows of storage racks. Not every gang member carries a weapon, but you must be careful as you progress. The other team will inform me of how much resistance these guys offer. We can adapt our tactics from 'subdue' to 'eliminate' as required."

The metal door was suddenly flung open, and two men ran out onto the ground. McLean and Laidlaw overpowered them in seconds. The bright light from the doorway showed Phoenix that the men were only teenagers from Southeast Asia.

"McGrath seems to be an equal opportunities employer," said Rusty.

"I doubt they were born and bred in Barrhead," said Phoenix. "I guess they were trafficked in and set to work long hours for little or no pay."

"Well, it keeps the profit margins high, which will please the Grid's hierarchy," muttered Rusty.

"We need to get inside," shouted Laidlaw. "Our lads have dealt with another half dozen kids like these. As many again remain with handguns keeping them occupied. We've suffered no casualties so far, thank goodness. Let's give these gunmen something to think about."

The four agents edged towards the open door; McLean led the way inside. The hallway was empty. He signalled to the others to follow as he descended the stairs one at a time. Rusty moved ahead of Phoenix and Laidlaw to join his former colleague.

"Just like old times, Jimmy," he whispered.

They crept past the first rows of roof-high racking. There were cartons dotted here and there but plenty of gaps, which gave them a chance to look across the whole width of the building. There were no gunmen near the back wall yet.

Jimmy indicated to Phoenix and Laidlaw to replace them.

"We'll make our way across to the far wall," he whispered.

"Take care," said Laidlaw.

As he and Rusty moved from one stack to the next, they checked the gangways for any sign of opposition. Halfway over, the sound of automatic weapons caused them to stop and hit the floor.

"That was our lot, opening fire again," said McLean, "but I've no idea where."

"The low ceiling in this basement and the metal racking are causing every sound to echo," said Rusty, "but we're no help lying here. So let's head for the far wall, as planned, and make our way forward. Keep Greg and Phoenix well behind us. I don't want us to engage with the enemy simultaneously if they move past us towards the exit. It might get hairy."

"Agreed," said McLean, and they set off at a run, crouching low. Finally, they reached the relative security of the far wall. McLean contacted Laidlaw and said they were moving forward.

"We've had two agents hit in the past few minutes," Greg told McLean, "only flesh wounds, nothing terminal. They've eliminated two shooters. There are three to sort out, and they're in the centre of the room, just beyond the final row of racking."

"All received," said McLean, and he and Rusty inched forwards.

"There," said Rusty, grabbing his friend's left arm and bringing them to a temporary halt.

He could see the three gunmen through the gaps in the racking. They were shielded from the other teams by a forklift truck and steel cabinets that housed electrical equipment. The two agents could see the rest of the layout as

Greg's plan had shown. In the distance was the racking for the Inward Goods. There were tables for the preparatory work and then the final assembly. Nothing was left to chance. It was a lean, mean production plant.

The gunmen were still concentrating their attention forwards where the initial attack had started. They weren't expecting an attack from the rear.

"Let's finish this," said Rusty.

"Permission to eliminate the threat, boss," McLean asked Laidlaw.

"Affirmative," replied his team leader.

"Here goes nothing," cried Jimmy.

He and Rusty stood up from their crouching position and burst into the open. They skirted the rows of racking, firing as they ran. The gunmen half-turned, aware of the danger at last; it was far too late. They fell in a hail of bullets.

"Clear," Jimmy McLean called to his team leader.

Phoenix and Laidlaw emerged from the other side of the racking, and four other agents joined them. A final sweep by two colleagues soon confirmed that each of the three warehouse floors was under Olympus' control.

"How are your wounded?" asked Phoenix.

"Embarrassed," came the reply.

"They live to fight another day, unlike the Grid's casualties," said Rusty.

"We've got a group of Vietnamese teenagers to hand over to the authorities," said Laidlaw. "I'll start the ball rolling on that later. But, for now, we need to clean up in here. Then, my crew will dispose of the bodies."

The agents looked around them. A clean-up crew would soon dispose of the bodies. But the explosions and the gunfight had disturbed much of the product the warehouse was handling. The air was full of white particles, and the floor looked like a carpet of snow.

"What's the plan?" Rusty asked Phoenix.

"Any scrap of information within these walls to help the police track the source of the drugs backwards to Manchester and the distribution network onwards will be accessible to them. The young lads will be next to the tables they were working at, awaiting their arrival. Trussed up like chickens, perhaps, but alive and well. Greg's men will leave as few clues as possible that we were here. The anonymous phone call will hint at a turf war. The workers don't know any different and pose no threat to Olympus. Our best bet is for McGrath to believe this was a police operation driven by a tip-off of the illegal immigrants. The uncovering of a drug network was a happy coincidence."

"Let's hope he swallows that," said Laidlaw. "If we can dispose of the bodies and spread misinformation on the whereabouts of the gang members within the police system, then we buy ourselves valuable time."

"It's a ploy that's worked well for Olympus over the years," agreed Phoenix.

"We had better make a move," said Jimmy McLean, "you guys need to transfer to your next target site. Greg will look after the wounded here and make the call when the place is shipshape."

With a quick nod of gratitude to Greg Laidlaw, Phoenix and Rusty followed Jimmy McLean outside. They crossed the open ground to the van quickly and quietly. Once they had stowed the gear, Jimmy started the engine, made for Glasgow on the M77, and then took the M74 towards Edinburgh.

"Sit back and enjoy the ride, lads," said Jimmy. "We'll be there in less than forty minutes."

Rusty checked his watch; it was still only twenty-five minutes past ten. Time flies when you're enjoying yourself.

"Have you prepared a history lesson for me about our destination, Phoenix?" asked Rusty.

"A thumbnail sketch," replied Phoenix. "What do you expect? I'm a past master at turning over every little detail in case it affects the outcome of my mission. If you're sitting comfortably, then I'll begin. Coatbridge lies ten miles east of Glasgow; it's a working-class town, twice the size of the place we've just left, and is called Little Ireland. It has great transport links via road and rail. In recent years it's become Scotland's inland container base."

"That sums the place up," said McLean. "The container aspect gave the town ample opportunity to develop the trafficking of drugs, women for the sex trade, and illegal workers. It wouldn't surprise me if those Vietnamese teenagers we uncovered didn't arrive through that route."

"It sounds just the place to settle down and raise a family," said Rusty.

"As if," scoffed Jimmy McLean. "I can never remember you chatting to a lassie, let alone having any intentions of getting settled."

"Times change," said Rusty. "I needed to find the right girl, and I did. We live together at Larcombe Manor."

"Good for you, mate," said McLean. "Jessie left me while I was in Kosovo. There were no kids. When I threw my lot in with Olympus up here, I didn't think it fair to lumber a woman with the worry of whether I'd be coming home at night. Jessie had enough of that to bear while I was in the SAS."

"There's still time, Jimmy," said Rusty, "and it's good to

have someone to come home to after a mission. It makes the fight worthwhile, believe me."

"You'll get no argument from me," said Phoenix. "My wife and daughter keep me sane. If I had nothing else to occupy my mind except the criminals out there and the depraved nonsense they get up to, I'd go crazy."

"I'll bear it in mind, Rusty," said Jimmy. "If you find a girl looking for a vertically challenged Scotsman, the wrong side of forty-five, tell her to call me. Right, lads, this is your stop."

Jimmy had turned off the motorway and was nearing the ubiquitous industrial estate. Phoenix thought their footprints were so similar these days that you could be anywhere in Europe. Only the local road signs and the weather set one place apart from the next. Truckers from every corner of Europe used the motorway systems these days, and the estate they were entering had vehicles from Germany, Norway, Poland, Netherlands, and Spain, parked up overnight.

"Who are we meeting here?" asked Rusty.

"The Edinburgh team Greg was talking to when you met us at the airport. Their leader is Hugh Fraser, an ex-Captain in the Scots Guards. Hugh earned a reputation as the Army's supreme logistics man. When Greg took us through tonight's small skirmish, he showed us the floor plan, issued basic instructions, and then relied on our training to know what to do when the action started. Fraser gives each agent under his command a detailed, colour-coded file containing every step of the mission. It's all rather anal if you ask me, but his success rate is off the chart, and his men never complain, not in public, at least."

Jimmy was soon driving onto the Monklands Industrial

Estate. In front of them was a single black van with tinted windows. It was facing the estate road exit.

"I think that's Fraser's crew," said Jimmy. "Hard to tell whether they're inside the van or already on the ground."

"Did Laidlaw say what time Fraser was hitting the warehouse?" asked Phoenix.

"There's something you need to know about Fraser," chuckled Jimmy. "When he thinks he has the same window of opportunity, he's off like a rat up a drainpipe. He likes to lead from the front and isn't one for waiting around for backup. When I got out of the van to talk to Rusty earlier, Greg had a few words with our Hughie. Unfortunately, he never did fill me in on the outcome of that conversation. We were too busy with our work after that."

"I'll walk over and have a word," said Phoenix, "you two cover me in case it's a trap."

"No problem, Phoenix," said Rusty.

He and Jimmy got out of the van and collected their weapons. They watched as Phoenix wandered across the lorry park towards the van. As he drew near, the passenger door opened, and a tall, distinguished-looking man stepped out.

"Phoenix, I presume?"

"You must be Fraser?"

"I have something for you," said Fraser, handing a blue folder to Phoenix.

"What's this?"

"My report on tonight's direct action. In brief, my four agents and I entered the building at 21.50 hours. We overpowered the four criminals we found. They're in the warehouse's canteen, for now. I've indicated where the relevant documentation was so it could go to the police. We found information on the entire trafficking network from Asia through Central Africa, Southern Europe and beyond. I think you'll find the report comprehensive enough for the authorities to take immediate action to cripple this damnable human trade."

"There's little to do, then?" smiled Phoenix.

"Sorry I didn't wait for you. Time was of the essence. The criminals could have left by ten o'clock. Instead, they used this building as a transit site after the human cargo arrived. Men, women, and children were shuttled through here overnight, with none staying long. Then transport arrived to distribute them throughout Scotland. On the outside, the firm looked like a building trades supplier. But it held a far darker secret."

"Does your report suggest how we proceed regarding your prisoners?" asked Phoenix.

"Of course," said Fraser, somewhat surprised at the question, "it's unlikely the police will rouse themselves tonight. So I'll arrange a call in the morning. One of my men is standing guard. Once the police are on their way on the approach road, I'll tell him to get off home. He knows the escape route."

"He has a blue folder, too?" asked Rusty.

"Naturally," replied Fraser. "Look, if there's nothing more, I'd prefer to get off home. I suggest you read the report at leisure, and then you can head back south. Our work here is as good as done. We'll tie a neat bow on matters first thing tomorrow."

"Right," said Phoenix, "well, thank you, and good to meet you."

Fraser turned on his heel and got back in the van.

"White was the colour in Glasgow," said Phoenix, "blue seems to be popular in Edinburgh."

Phoenix and Rusty stood and watched as Fraser's driver

pulled away. Jimmy's van was now the only vehicle in the lorry park.

"Back to the airport, guys?" he asked.

"We might as well get some shut-eye with Biggles and then head home at first light," said Phoenix. "I can't help feeling cheated. I was looking forward to the action."

Rusty smiled. That was typical of Phoenix. He liked to take the troubles of the world on his shoulders. So much so that he had been stressed in recent months. When someone gave a helping hand, he took umbrage.

Jimmy McLean dropped the two agents at the airport building.

"It was grand to meet up with you again, Rusty," he said, "keep in touch. A pleasure working with you, Phoenix."

"Thanks, Jimmy; I'm sure we'll be back this way before too long."

They heard loud snoring from the room's far end as they walked through the building door. Phoenix sat in the nearest chair and read the report Fraser had handed him. Rusty found a comfortable chair and hoped to get some sleep before sunrise.

Biggles never stirred.

Phoenix reckoned it would be a long night.

The upside was that Fraser was everything Jimmy McLean had said. The man was meticulous; never a bad thing as far as Phoenix was concerned.

Chapter Two

Wednesday, 2nd July 2014

The journey back from Glasgow had been uneventful. Les Biggar had woken up at four o'clock without an alarm. Finally, he was ready to fly after a cold shower and changing clothes. Phoenix and Rusty were tired, dirty, and uncomfortable.

"A good morning for it," Biggles had shouted as they took off.

"If you say so," Rusty had replied.

"Everything went to plan last night, I suppose? I didn't hear you return."

"I'm not surprised with the racket you were making. Yes, our involvement was limited, and both crews will apply the finishing touches in an hour or two."

"We could have stayed at home," Phoenix had said. "By the way, I've asked for someone from Larcombe to collect the van from Bristol airport. I hope you don't mind?"

"Not a problem."

Biggles had then taken them straight home to Larcombe Manor, touching down on the lawns at the far end of the grounds. Long enough for them to gather up their kit and jump out. Phoenix and Rusty had run at a crouch towards the ice-house and watched as Biggles lifted and powered away. He signed off with a swish of the helicopter's tail as he flew over the manor house and back to base. Several people sleeping in the main building, and the staff quarters, were now wide awake. It was a few minutes before seven,

"That will go down like a lead balloon," Rusty had said.

"I didn't fancy driving through the morning traffic from Filton back to Bath. I need a shower and a decent breakfast before I start work. There's plenty to get done."

"Artemis is already at work in the ice-house. I doubt she realises we're back. I might grab a bite, too, before the nine o'clock meeting. See you there later."

The pair had crossed the lawns to the house and gone their separate ways to their apartments.

The next forty-eight hours had seen activity, both north and south of the border. An anonymous call about the illegal immigrants working in the warehouse in Barrhead offered the Glasgow police a terrific start to the week. The paperwork they found opened several lines of enquiry, and the elaborate production set-up raised eyebrows but brought a rare smile from the Chief Constable. At last, they had good news to deliver to the public.

In Edinburgh, the police were also seeing a more positive future, as news from Coatbridge filtered through from their Glasgow colleagues. They found four men with known links to organised crime at premises on the Monklands Industrial Estate.

Data gathered from the offices showed a well-established global trafficking network, with items offering them the chance to identify how this warehouse linked to one of the most famous gangsters in Scotland. A man who had been untouchable for decades and known to be involved in drug supply the length and breadth of the Central Lowlands.

It was early in July and seasonably warm, but there would have been no cold hands in police headquarters even if it had been January. Every senior police officer in Fettes Avenue was rubbing his hands with glee.

Further south, in Manchester, enquiries remained ongoing. Activity had been high since the night of the incidents in Beswick, Hulme, and Cheetham Hill. The news from Scotland only added extra fuel to the frequent requests for overtime. There were smiling faces everywhere.

Except in the home of Gregor McGrath and those of his fellow gang members. They were trying to stem the flow of damaging information. Scapegoats were selected. There was an inevitability this would end with somebody ending up in prison.

McGrath and his senior colleagues determined it wouldn't be them.

Within every organisation, some are expendable. In the criminal underworld, it's no different. If your name came up, you hoped the gang looked after your family while you were inside taking one for the team.

Two things bothered Gregor McGrath. First, who had notified the authorities of the Vietnamese workers in the first place, and then where had the police taken the men running the drug operation in Barrhead? The guys arrested in Coatbridge assured him they weren't in Glasgow. He was awaiting news from Edinburgh. Inevitably, someone there knew their whereabouts. McGrath planned to call a Grid colleague in Manchester to check whether they had gone there if all else failed.

Gregor McGrath needn't have worried about the Barrhead gang members. The police also wondered where they were. They couldn't imagine the Asian teenagers running the show alone, but they were clueless about who their bosses had been. Or why they left their workers alone without supervision.

Greg Laidlaw could have told them both not to worry. The gangsters enjoyed the rural views from the forested hillsides in several country parks between Glasgow and Edinburgh.

At Larcombe Manor, Athena had been full of admiration for the success of the Scottish missions.

"Apart from giving Hope and me a rude awakening when you returned on Monday morning without warning," she had said to Phoenix, "we couldn't have hoped for more."

"Everything went as planned," Phoenix had replied.

"Do you think we've got the Grid on the run now?"

"Let's not count our chickens yet,"

"Resources are thin at present," Athena had said, "but our meeting on Wednesday will be a happier one now despite that. It's always good to report successes to Zeus and the others rather than excuses for lack of progress."

At dawn on Wednesday, Phoenix and Athena had driven north to Manchester. They arrived at the conference centre in Fountain Street at a quarter to nine.

"Maria Elena was half-asleep when she arrived, wasn't she?" asked Athena as they took the lift to the second floor.

"Hope won't have woken up for at least two hours. Maria Elena will be wide awake by now. I expect Hope is wondering where her parents have gone, though.

"I don't enjoy leaving her," sighed Athena, "but we both must attend these get-togethers."

The lift doors opened, and the two senior Olympus agents walked along the corridor to the conference room reserved for their meeting.

"I agree," replied Phoenix. "Look who's here before us. Zeus, and Hera, there's never any question of either of those two taking a holiday."

They exchanged greetings. Hera was keen to take Athena to one side to ask how little Hope was progressing. Phoenix and Zeus discussed the weather and the latest news headlines. It didn't take them long to exhaust those topics. Zeus knew Phoenix wasn't a great conversationalist. He was more interested in action than words; he switched focus to Olympus-related matters.

"You might imagine we have enough on our plates, Phoenix, but you can rely on the authorities to give us even more work. An announcement of a major review of allegations of historical sex abuse across every area of UK society is imminent. The Home Office's failure to act on allegations that a paedophile ring operated at Westminster in the Eighties prompted this decision."

"Another review into a cover-up, you mean; will it have any teeth, or is it destined to be another whitewash?"

"Well, the police are to get emergency powers to access phone and internet records, as I understand. But, unfortunately, the government have had to rush them through after the European Court of Justice overturned the existing legislation."

"Worst day's work we ever did, throwing our lot in with Europe," muttered Phoenix.

"You'll get no argument from us on that one," said Hera as she and Athena re-joined their husbands.

"Is there a specific time frame for this review, Zeus?" asked Phoenix.

"It will take a while to set terms of reference and choose a figurehead to lead it," replied Zeus. "Experience tells me the former will take many months, and the latter will be such a poisoned chalice the list of people they will need to approach will grow and grow."

"So, the finished report will be due some time, never."

"Ever the optimist," said Athena.

"I believe we should check what the review uncovers and take direct action without delay. One thing is vital. If Westminster figures still alive today were guilty of offences thirty years ago, they must be dealt with immediately. There's nothing to gain by wasting valuable resources on dead men."

"I agree," said Athena. "Ah, here come the others."

As usual these days, Heracles and Aphrodite entered the room together. It wasn't long before the eagle-eyed Hera spotted the Duchess's left hand as she brushed her ash-blonde fringe from her forehead.

"Elizabeth, darling," Hera cried, "congratulations. James, you old romantic. Congratulations to you both. What wonderful news."

Phoenix strolled across to the side table to fetch himself a soft drink. He knew he might as well make himself comfortable for a while. This meeting would get nothing done until the women had gushed over the size and quality of the ring Heracles had bought.

Although he wouldn't admit it, he was pleased for Heracles. Sir James Grant-Nicholls was one of the Olympus hierarchy for whom Phoenix had a lot of time. Aphrodite was from the nobility, extremely wealthy, and with her big heart in the right place. Phoenix accepted her as a staunch supporter of the Olympus Project and its ideals. But he could never imagine inviting Elizabeth to Larcombe Manor and chilling out on the patio with her over a few beers. The gulf between their social standing would always be far too wide.

Phoenix sat and watched as Zeus, Hera, and Athena surrounded the happy couple. Apollo and Dionysus had arrived, had a brief chat with Zeus, and came across the room to join him.

The newcomers, Achilles, Daedalus, and Ambrosia, were present today, ready for their first meeting. They looked uncomfortable as they stood to one side, confused by what they saw.

"Good morning, Phoenix," said Apollo, "it's good to see you again."

Dionysus nodded a greeting. Sir Malcolm Dunseith had earned respect through his civil service career and his role on the Privy Council. He was as eager as Phoenix to cut this pantomime short and get into the meat of the meeting.

"Let's make the three new gods welcome," said Phoenix. "I checked the seating arrangements as I collected my orange juice. Each of us has one of them sitting next to us. If we introduce ourselves and usher them to their seats, it might persuade the others we need to start."

Phoenix had recognised Achilles at once. Ludovic Tremayne's bearing showed him to be every inch the military man he had been before leaving the British Army to create a successful business empire. He offered his hand.

"Welcome, Achilles; I'm Phoenix."

"Ah, Phoenix, I look forward to working with you."

Phoenix guided the ex-soldier to the oval table.

"We're here," he said and sat next to where he hoped his wife would be very soon.

His companions had joined them, and all six were now seated. Zeus spotted the flurry of movement around him and realised it was time to move.

"Right," he said, "perhaps we can begin," and he took his place at the head of the table. Hera sat on his right-hand side; Athena sat on his left, next to Phoenix, as the others filled the remaining seats. Phoenix glanced towards the vacant twelfth chair. There would be no place for Aurora, not now nor in the future. They had avenged Dawn Prentice's death even if her position within Olympus had never materialised.

As he reflected on the events leading up to her death and the subsequent action he and Rusty had taken, he sensed somebody watching him. At the far end of the table, next to Dionysus, sat the diminutive Piya Adani, now known as Ambrosia.

Phoenix smiled. Ambrosia gave no sign she had noticed; her eyes had shifted to Athena.

"Ah, she's giving each of us the once-over," thought Phoenix, "weighing up the opposition."

The successful young businesswoman had great ambition. She hadn't transformed her father's modest family business into a global phenomenon by being afraid to make tough decisions.

Phoenix anticipated her having designs on reaching the summit of the Project. Zeus would step aside one day. Athena was next in line for the top job, with Phoenix by her side. How long before Ambrosia mounted a challenge against that eventuality, he wondered?

Zeus checked everyone had switched off their mobile phones and confirmed that the venue had been swept for bugs by Olympus staff before the gods arrived. Security was essential.

"Today marks the start of a new era as we progress to regaining our optimum number of twelve gods. Our three newcomers provide us with far more than the money they have agreed to commit to the Project. They bring valuable commercial experience, military intelligence, and in Ambrosia's case, youth. These qualities will be essential to Olympus's future."

Over the next ninety minutes, he gave them an update on the Project's progress in many countries worldwide. He described the significant commitment of agents in hot spots on four continents and the drain on financial resources this represented. Athena and Phoenix listened as Zeus praised them for their successful actions at home since the last meeting.

"The Grid is far from being beaten," he cautioned, "but, week by week, we have dealt telling blows on their network, thanks to Phoenix and his teams. We removed their leading figures, and as the summer ends, we will receive a welcome addition to the number of agents at our disposal. Perhaps, you can expand on that, Athena?"

"The first intake of new operatives will finish their training at Larcombe Manor by September," Athena said. "The first batch of agents withdrawn from duty overseas are four weeks into their six-week reassessment programme. Our two teams of trainers have been superb. They have proved to be an excellent choice. The speed of training and re-training may be slower than we wish, but when the agents start active duty, they will be ready."

"How many agents will that be?" asked Ambrosia.

"We can only train fifty new agents yearly," replied Phoenix. "The re-training exercise is for the one hundred agents we repatriated. We are handling a dozen agents on this course. So far, their physical and psychological tests haven't eliminated anyone as unfit for active duty. That may not be the case with later batches. We hoped for an eighty per cent success rate. Early signs are good for bettering that, but it's impossible to predict."

"Will a twenty-five per cent increase in UK-based agents be enough for Olympus to carry out the missions we need?" asked Achilles.

"With only five hundred agents available, it stretches our resources," said Athena. "An extra one hundred and thirty will not be unwelcome."

"Recent events have shown that as we step up the direct action against the Grid, we will experience losses," Phoenix added. "Two men were injured on Sunday night in Scotland, as you have heard. When the 2015 intakes take up their posts, they might only replace men and women who have lost their lives in the fight against the Grid. Unless there's a sudden cut in the number of volatile spots around the globe, then we cannot count on any agents arriving for re-training for the foreseeable future. If we lose people in actions abroad, we will need to replace them. So, we must understand that not everyone training at Larcombe will end up on assignment to a UK-based team."

"Maybe, we need to think outside the box," said Ambrosia, "because operating from hand-to-mouth could lead to cutbacks in the services we offer. One only has to look at every other organisation in the country at present to see what damage that does."

"If you have any suggestions on how to do things better during this period of austerity, then please, share them," said Athena.

Phoenix could feel the tension in the room as the two younger women crossed swords for the first time. He was not alone; Mother Hen came to the rescue.

"I think it's time we took a break for refreshments," said Hera. "There's much for everyone to take in. Our newcomers haven't met everyone around the table yet. I suggest we relax, socialise for thirty minutes, and then tackle the second half of the agenda."

Zeus didn't need to be told twice. He marched off to the refreshment table at once.

Phoenix and Athena followed him to the side table together. They collected a plate of food each and refreshed their drinks.

"Let's find somewhere quiet," said Athena. "I don't feel like socialising today."

"I know what you mean. I prefer people-watching too," said Phoenix. "Did you want to call Maria Elena to check on Hope?"

"Would you mind?"

"Don't be silly. You get off outside and see if you can get a signal."

Athena left the room, and Phoenix stood against the side wall and absorbed the surrounding scene. Zeus and Hera stood with Ambrosia, Heracles, and Aphrodite. The Indian pocket-rocket seemed to lead the conversation. Phoenix doubted the subject was the recent engagement or forthcoming wedding.

Apollo and Dionysus listened intently to Achilles while Daedalus was on his own, a few feet away. Finally, he noticed Phoenix was alone and joined him.

"Bonjour, Phoenix," he began, "I'm Daedalus; this is awkward, no?"

"Absolutely, yes," grinned Phoenix, "I don't do small talk either. Athena will soon be back. She's checking in with our nanny. Hope is only six months old, and leaving her for longer than an hour or two is hard. Athena copes at Larcombe, but today is a trial."

"Family is important to you, yes?"

"It's everything, Daedalus."

"Then that is why you do what you do,"

Athena re-entered the room, and her face lit up with a big smile.

"Hope's well-behaved, as usual," she said, "Maria Elena says she hasn't once asked where we are."

"Typical," said Phoenix.

"Daedalus, at your service, Madame. Good to meet with you, at last."

"It's a pleasure to welcome you to your first meeting," Athena replied, "do you have any first impressions you wish to share?"

"The provisional financials for the year's first half were rather boring, n'est ce pas? I was keen to hear more news about the missions. I am a man of action."

Phoenix bit his tongue. The Frenchman had been under suspicion because of his unconventional marriage. Until Minos and Alastor confirmed Jean-Paul St Clair was not cheating on his younger wife, his elevation to the Olympus hierarchy had been on hold.

"Perhaps you can design us a robot agent that only needs programming, not twelve weeks of training," said Phoenix.

He glanced across the room to Ambrosia, who was still clinging to Zeus. She wasn't going to let him out of her sight.

"She's an impatient one, that one," said Daedalus. "The design process doesn't allow for that much emotion. I always found it more helpful to take small steps and test each stage until I was confident to continue to the next. It's costly if you get it wrong. You did not pick the training schedules out of the air. They are what is necessary, oui?"

Phoenix knew he would get on well with Daedalus. It was good to find a potential ally. Athena might overlook the changing dynamics within the group, but Phoenix could sense it this morning.

When the half-hour was up, they re-took their seats.

"The vacant chair will be obvious to everyone," he said. "Before our next meeting, I want to have three, maybe four candidates to choose from to fill it. If any of you have a name to put forward for consideration, then Hera and I would be glad to hear it."

"Rusty would be terrific," whispered Phoenix. "I'll tell him to buy a lottery ticket. Otherwise, he might get excluded for lack of funds."

Athena kicked his ankle.

"We need another female," she said, "there's a seven, four split at present."

"I believe it's more important that *he* should be young," said Apollo.

"I agree," said Dionysus.

"So, we're looking for a wealthy young man, who is intelligent and has a social conscience," Hera concluded.

"That counts out our professional sportsmen and pop stars," Phoenix muttered.

He had moved his feet this time; Athena missed his ankles.

"We meet again in London in October," said Zeus. "Please inform me of your proposals, with the necessary background checks, between now and then. We must resolve this matter at that meeting."

"We are fishing in a shallow pool," said Phoenix. "You know that from the small number of candidates we uncovered in the last sweep. It appears we have made good choices. I enjoy lively debate. Today's events suggest we have much more to anticipate."

Daedalus chuckled.

Ambrosia sat up straighter in her chair but remained silent.

"It's good to see that you're on better form today, Phoenix," said Zeus. "If only we could unearth the right person to help you at Larcombe Manor. Athena has mentioned on more than one occasion that you take on too many responsibilities. The potential burn-out of our most important asset is something Olympus cannot contemplate."

"You needn't worry about finding someone, Zeus," said Phoenix. "I've saved you the trouble."

Athena looked puzzled. She had no idea what her husband meant.

"Rusty and I worked with the ideal person on Sunday night, up in Scotland. Hugh Fraser is fifty-one years old and an Olympus team leader. He was a Captain in the First Battalion of the Scots Guards, based at Catterick. Fraser was a supreme logistics officer and has carried those skills into his new role. I want him released from his post in Edinburgh and re-located to Larcombe Manor by the end of the month."

"That's wonderful news, Phoenix," said Zeus. "I'll leave it to you to sort out the details, shall I, Athena?"

"Of course," Athena replied, "I can't wait to meet him."

"You'll need a bigger desk in the administration office for all the reports he will write," said Phoenix.

Zeus rattled through the last few items on the agenda and confirmed the date for the next meeting on Wednesday, the eighth of October. Phoenix wanted to escape as soon as possible so he and Athena could play with Hope before Maria Elena put her to bed.

As people made their way to the door, Heracles cleared his throat.

"Ahem, if you could hold on a second, please? Elizabeth and I don't intend to have a long engagement. We have set a date for Saturday, the sixth of September."

Elizabeth's cut-glass voice sliced through the general buzz of the noise of congratulations.

"We shall marry at the castle. A small, private family ceremony," she said, "and then we honeymoon in Martinique. James and I would be most happy if you could join us for a party at the Dorchester. Now we know the date of the next meeting. I suggest we make arrangements for the evening of the eighth of October. We will fly home to Scotland by the first of the month."

"That sounds terrific," said Athena.

"Why don't we bring Hope to town with us?" said Phoenix. "We can drop her off at your parent's home. They will enjoy spoiling her rotten, and we won't have far to stagger back to Belgravia. The Dorchester is fifteen minutes from Vincent Gardens."

"I'll need to check they're in the country. You know those two."

"Well, if we want them to change their plans, we can work on them next month when they are at Larcombe for Hope's christening."

"Very devious," laughed Athena, "it's becoming a habit. When were you going to tell me about this chap, Fraser?"

"If Zeus hadn't mentioned the matter, I would have ignored it for as long as possible. I know I've been pushing it too hard of late but handing things over to someone else is tough. I want everything to be right, and so far, the only way to ensure that is to do it myself. On Monday morning, as I read through his reports, I realised he's more meticulous in his preparations than I am, and his success rate is as good, if not better. It was too good an opportunity to miss. Honestly, I hadn't decided on a course of action until Zeus posed the question."

While they chatted, the room had emptied. Phoenix spotted Zeus and Hera saying a final goodbye to Ambrosia. They waved as they left, and the young woman came towards them.

"Is it permitted for me to visit you at Larcombe, Athena?" asked Ambrosia. "I want to run an idea past you regarding the recruiting of agents. I'm concerned that we will not have enough bodies to complete the fight against the organised crime network strangling the UK."

"We don't encourage visitors," said Phoenix. Ambrosia gave him a stare.

"What my husband means, Ambrosia," said Athena, "is that Larcombe Manor is the home of the Olympus Project charity to the outside world. People might question the purpose of those visits if we had frequent visitors other than the Charity Commissioners and their inspectorate."

"I understand that," said Ambrosia. "I believe my cover story will suffice to deter questions. I became an Ambassador for the Veterans Association UK earlier this year. My presence would be natural, don't you think?"

"Well, in that case, yes, I don't see a problem," said Athena. "When do you want to visit us?"

"I'll be in Bath first thing on Monday," replied Ambrosia. "I'll see you then."

With that, she turned on her heel and left Athena and Phoenix open-mouthed.

"She doesn't let the grass grow, does she?" said Phoenix.

"At least we've got the weekend to get the house ready for inspection," said Athena.

"She's not royalty," said Phoenix.

"Maybe not, but she's ambitious. I want her to see what she's facing. I don't want her leaving Larcombe thinking I can't bring up a family, keep my home spotless, and run Olympus."

"Multi-tasking is your middle name, darling. I've always known that. It will be a breeze."

"Time to get home," said Athena, "we need to get started. You can help me plan the menus for Monday and organise a detail to tackle the lawns, gardens, and vegetable plots. I'll get the staff to sort out the reception rooms and bedrooms. The trainers will need briefing too. The stable-block, transport garage, and workers' cottages will need a fresh coat of paint and a deep clean. They can handle that. The ice-house is off-limits. No matter how grand she thinks she is, she's not getting clearance to go there."

"I love you, Athena," said Phoenix. "You always take things in your stride. You never overreact. It's your greatest quality."

Athena chased him along the corridor to the lift. As the lift doors closed behind them, he gathered her in his arms and kissed her hard.

"We're a great team, aren't we?" he said as they stepped onto the ground floor. "Together, we're a match for anyone. Everything will be in tip-top condition by Monday morning, don't worry."

In the car, as they began the journey south to Bath, Athena called Maria Elena.

"Can you kiss Hope from Mummy and Daddy? Tell her

we'll be home in time to bath her and tuck her up in bed, please?"

"Will you tuck me up in bed tonight and read me a bedtime story?" asked Phoenix.

"No chance," Athena replied. "I know you. We've got far too much to do in the morning. We need a full night's sleep."

Chapter Three

Sunday, 6th July 2014

Nobody in the village noticed anything remarkable about their arrival.

These days, limousines and luxury SUVs are commonplace in the leafy suburbs near Oxshott, Surrey. One by one, under Hugo Hanigan's express instructions, the vehicles entered the car park of the exclusive country hotel in nearby Stoke D'Abernon. Then their passengers made their way quietly to the front door.

Management at the upmarket venue had welcomed the influx of so many guests on a late mid-summer weekend evening. However, the generous sum of money offered for the drawing-room for a meeting scheduled to last only two hours had been obscene — an amount not to be dismissed.

The sun set at ten past nine. Twenty minutes later, their visitors could begin to arrive with impunity. Staff learned what had to be available within the room. Their presence after that was not required. They were well-drilled in melting into the background, allowing clandestine assignations to occur in this area. Nobody would call the media with a possible headline in the morning. Discretion became a vital ingredient in every employee's curriculum vitae.

In the semi-darkness, figures slipped inside the building and made their way into the drawing-room. Meanwhile, Hugo Hanigan, leader of The Grid, sat in the rear of his Rolls Royce and watched from behind tinted windows. He mentally ticked off the various gang leaders as they passed.

Hugo smiled; this was the perfect setting for a diverse collection of nationalities. They fitted this part of suburbia like a glove. Something one could never have dreamed of a decade earlier.

As the property boom played out, large country houses and city penthouses fought for headlines. Behind the scenes, the term 'suburbia' no longer covered the properties enshrined in the capital's orbital motorway boundaries. After a decade of growth, the best areas had earned the dubious accolade of 'Superbia'.

When the Crown Estates released land for building after the war, executives who worked in finance and business services congregated in the corridors of wealth leading from London into the countryside. Houses in the old stockbroker belt now attracted international buyers - Middle Easterners, Russians, Asians and Europeans, and sporting superstars and celebrities. In the middle years of the last century, the original houses were built, thrived, and matured. With the monied newcomers in recent years, they often demolished them and replaced them with modern monstrosities.

Tasteful was not the overriding impression one gleaned from the transformation, thought Hugo. He was happy, however, that he had chosen this venue well. The Grid's leaders came from each of the four corners of the country, and their international flavour was a perfect match for the owners of properties surrounding this hotel. Moreover, there was no suspicion over why they convened a meeting at such short notice.

Hugo looked at his watch. Five minutes to ten o'clock. He left his car and walked toward the front door. He would be the last to arrive; his checks had confirmed that. Fifty-eight men now waited in the drawing-room. Many of them, if not all, were armed. The banker stood in the hotel foyer to collect his thoughts and listened to the low hum of conversation behind the drawing-room door. The minute hand on the clock in the deserted reception area clicked forward to twelve as Hugo threw open the door and swept inside.

"Good evening, gentleman," he said, "thank you for coming. Let us get straight to business."

The Grid's leader stopped at the head of the table, turned and faced his audience. Every man in the room looked towards him. Hugo took his seat, and the others took their place at the tables arranged in a large oval in the centre of the room. Four men remained standing. They were Hugo's bodyguards. As the leaders arrived, they performed the role of drinks servers and ushered each criminal to their reserved seat.

Now the bodyguards occupied the room's four corners, ready to respond if someone dared draw a weapon and threaten their employer. Fergus Mallon gave a brief nod to Hugo. That confirmed that every mobile phone and recording device was off. The room was swept for any listening devices before the guests arrived. Nothing said within these walls must go any further.

"I felt we needed this meeting to lay to rest misconceptions that arose in the past three months," Hugo began. "Since April, the Grid has not entirely been in control of matters across the country. That is not how we envisaged our joint enterprise would operate. Anyone who opposes us by not joining forces with us, or betrays us from within, must be eliminated. The stranglehold on criminal activities on these shores must be total."

"Are you accusing one, or more of us, of having betrayed the Grid?"

Hugo knew this voice belonged to Artem Klimenko, the East Anglian gang master. Only thirty-three years old, the Ukrainian had facilitated the smuggling of hundreds of illegal immigrants into the region since 2010 to pick fruit and vegetables. His reputation was a ruthless thug, and he controlled the one hundred gang members in his organisation with an iron fist.

"You live in the countryside, Artem," Hugo replied, with a wry smile, "you may have missed the significance of events since mid-April. The authorities received a message. A message designed to demonstrate we could strike anywhere in the country at will. The police and the security forces never linked the killings. They were too preoccupied with meeting targets, promoting political correctness, and attempting to cover more crimes with fewer resources."

"You underestimate my thirst for information," Klimenko sneered. "We were aware of the pattern of killings and the message you meant to convey, even in the Fens. Perhaps the source of the Grid's problems began with the murder of the jurors in the O'Riordan case. Was that not too parochial? It endangered all of us, yet the only gang to benefit would have been his own in Kilburn. The link between you two stretches back to childhood. Did you ignore the wishes of the many to satisfy the thirst for revenge of a few?"

"Our friend from the Fens has a point," said Gregor McGrath. "The attempted murder of the High Court Judge before sentencing proved a step too far. Who thwarted that attempt? Not one of the local gangs or you would have weeded them out and got rid of the bodies by now."

Hugo paused for a moment. McGrath was a senior leader north of the border; he had held sway in the city of Glasgow for decades. Not a man with whom to cross swords.

"That was my decision," Hugo answered. "I was disappointed the authorities hadn't recognised our hand behind the rash of killings a fortnight earlier. I felt we had to make an example. We handled the initial attacks with precision; someone intervened at the airfield. That someone will pay with their lives. We have yet to identify them. I suggest we pass the word on to our junior members. The offer of a reward of one hundred thousand pounds should loosen a few tongues."

Hugo heard the murmurs as they rippled around the room. Money was an excellent motivator for criminals. One voice rose above the rest; it was Klimenko again.

"I hope this money will come from your pocket and not ours. You accept responsibility for the decision to attack the Judge and his family, so it's only right you clean up the mess it left. What of those men here who lost valuable personnel since that ill-fated decision? Were the same people responsible for the London deaths in Selhurst and Park Royal? What of Handsworth, Solihull, Manchester, and Portsmouth? Is this a series of one-off attacks on the Grid by rogue elements from the criminal fraternity, or is a separate highly organised group responsible?"

"Aye," muttered McGrath ", it stinks. The next question hangs over what occurred at Rayleigh. Almost on your doorstep, Artem. Who killed Tommy O'Riordan, and the others? What happened to the one man who survived?"

"Simms?" said Hugo. "He was a loose end, hired to help spring O'Riordan from the prison transport vehicle. He never worked for me. Sean Walsh put that team together. Walsh was O'Riordan's brother-in-law and former second-in-command. I had Simms picked up for questioning, but he saw nothing. Their car was struck from the side, trapping him against a dry-stone wall. The first gunman killed the driver and front-seat passenger. Tommy O'Riordan got out of the rear door and died at the hands of a second shooter. Why they left Simms alive, I have no idea."

"You said Simms *was* a loose end?" asked McGrath.

"He's in a home of his own now," said Hugo. "If you're travelling back via the M1 later, he's stood in the footings of one of the bridges they replaced last week."

"I'll remember to wave," said McGrath.

A new voice emerged from the far end of the room.

"Excuse, please? Where is Walsh? Who is running the gang O'Riordan led?"

"Shabbir Shah? You operate out of Cardiff, don't you?" said Hugo. "You have family in Tower Hamlets, no doubt?"

"You are well-informed, Mister Hanigan."

"When O'Riordan went to prison, Walsh took charge. He was an excellent second-in-command but wasn't keen on stepping out of his brother-in-law's shadow. In recent weeks, Walsh surprised me with his grasp of the bigger picture, but this business with the prison break proved too much for him. He drank heavily. As a result, O'Riordan's wife did most of the planning. Colleen O'Riordan came to terms with her husband's death far quicker than I thought possible. After his escape, she ordered her brother and his family to the Dominican Republic, her husband's proposed destination. She reasoned Walsh could crack under questioning when the police came calling."

"Another loose end?" asked Klimenko.

"If it proves to be a problem, I will handle it," said Hugo. "It's early days in the police investigation into the attack on the prison van and the subsequent killings. They are scratching around for leads. I understand that Colleen O'Riordan has had a visit from them and played the grieving widow well enough. Whether they will return to question her further, I don't know. The widow has since gone to ground. I hadn't seen or heard from her since before her husband died. I rang to congratulate her on the successful engineering of his escape. She had the funeral to arrange, which took place last Friday."

"Who told you the police questioned her?" asked Klimenko.

"The buffoon Sean Walsh selected as his number two after Tommy O'Riordan went to jail; one Seamus McConnell."

"So, he's in charge of the Kilburn gang now?"

"No, Artem, he is not," replied Hugo. "Somehow, everything is running smoothly in that borough. I don't yet understand who's in charge. There may be a power struggle between the O'Riordan, Walsh, and Kelly clans. McConnell is due to report back tomorrow morning."

"The sooner it's sorted, the better."

The hairs on the back of Hugo's neck bristled. That gruff voice was a rare sound. It belonged to Michael Terence Quinn, known to everyone from London as Mighty Quinn. At sixty-three years old, Quinn was a hard bastard who had spent as many years behind bars as he had on the outside. He was a man of few words, but it was wise to listen when he spoke.

"McConnell is due in my office at nine o'clock, Michael," said Hugo. "Everything will become clear before ten."

"Word on the street is that Tommy's widow has run the show for the past fortnight, mate," said Mighty Quinn. "Whether she had a funeral to arrange or not. I don't see many birds sitting at these tables, do you? It needs sorting. It stands to reason. I thought you had your finger on the pulse. Kilburn's only around the corner from your gaff, and you're in the dark."

Hugo sensed the mood in the room change. He needed to nip this in the bud and fast.

"I'm sure the Kilburn problem can get resolved to everyone's satisfaction. There are less than twelve hours between now and my meeting with McConnell. You know you can trust my judgement. I've laundered your money through the Glencairn Bank for the past few years at a favourable commission. None of you could have handled your affairs better."

He nodded to Fergus Mallon, and the four bodyguards distributed files. Eyebrows raised as each man noted that a personal copy reached them with unerring accuracy. Hanigan's men knew precisely who sat where despite the lack of identification on the table or their person. Hugo stood and paced the width of the room. He began to relax. The focus of the meeting had switched.

"You can see the performance of your portfolios in these reports. Each of you has profited from our joint enterprise. Your stocks are bucking the national trend and are giving you greater returns than you could hope to receive anywhere else. The bonus is that with the Grid, you have greater security. Left to your own devices, many of you would fritter the profits on luxuries. My programme helps you invest in your future while providing you with the cash to indulge yourself now and again. If you decide to retire, you won't be scratching around trying to survive on a state pension. Without the Grid's governance, you would have to cleanse your money in shoddy, back-street businesses that would alert the authorities in no time. Few of our number have spent time in prison in recent years for financial irregularities, for which I'm sure you, and your families, are grateful. Have these figures checked by a friendly accountant if you wish? I've simplified the language as much as possible, and for those whose first language isn't English, I hope the translation is accurate."

The silence that followed suggested nothing amiss. Hugo breathed easier.

"This is all well and good," said Klimenko, who wasn't swayed by Hugo's diversionary tactic, "but let's get back to O'Riordan. Who does his widow blame for his death? Not her brother, that's obvious. She spirited him away to a place of safety in the Caribbean. One with no extradition treaty with the UK. She blames you, maybe?"

"It's true I withdrew my protection from Tommy as soon as he went into Belmarsh. He was damaged goods and unlikely to come out, but I had no reason to kill him. Why call Colleen and congratulate her on engineering his escape if I planned to have him killed within hours?"

"Because you're a devious bastard, Hanigan," said Quinn, "most of us here have done something similar. You would have given the woman a false sense of security. Then got rid of a loose end. The longer Tommy rotted inside, with no prospect of parole, the more chance of him trying to broker a deal in return for details of our organisation."

"Well, that potential loose end is no more," said Hugo, "but I had no part in it. The reward offer will throw up a name in time. As for Colleen O'Riordan, and her status in the gang structure once run by Tommy, and her brother, Sean Walsh, I will confirm in the morning."

Quinn, McGrath, Klimenko, and the others quietened for a moment. Hugo had quashed the disagreements for now. He determined to bring matters to a swift conclusion.

"You can enjoy the facilities here for a while longer. My men will keep the bar open until two o'clock. Then you should return to your people, in whichever corner of the country you represent. Relay the message that the Grid is still on course to gain total control of organised crime on these shores. Our strategy is sound. We recently suffered a few minor setbacks, but the net is closing on those opposing us. Victory is within our grasp. As senior men in the organisation, you will enjoy the fruits of that victory. Keep the faith."

With that, Hugo collected his things and swept out of the room. He sat in his Rolls Royce and began the twenty-mile drive back to his penthouse thirty seconds later.

Fergus Mallon and his team started pouring drinks and handing out cigars. Fergus spotted a few gangsters chatting with colleagues and thought they looked set to squeeze as many free drinks out of Hugo before two o'clock arrived.

The others soon prepared to leave and went outside to the car park. There weren't many close friendships in the world in which they made their living. Some had arrived with guns because it was second nature to them. Others, because they didn't trust their near-neighbours around the tables. It wasn't unknown for business rivals to eliminate the opposition on these occasions. Socialising with gang leaders from the largest cities in the country was not on their agenda.

Fergus ensured his team kept their eyes and ears open. He would report back what they learned to Hugo at lunchtime tomorrow. The small cluster of men, drinking, smoking, and deep in conversation, made strange bedfellows. His team needed to overhear as much as possible without drawing attention. He wandered around the room, collecting glasses, straightening chairs, and moving closer with each step.

Their voices were hushed. Fergus found it impossible to pick out specific words and phrases. One thing was sure. This group did not accept that Hugo had given them satisfactory answers to the O'Riordan situation. The explanation offered by McGrath seemed logical; it was a rival gang in London that O'Riordan and Walsh had clashed with in the past. During Walsh's search for personnel for the escape bid, someone had talked, and the rival gang seized an opportunity for revenge.

Klimenko and Quinn favoured the idea undercover cops had been behind the killings and the fire-fight at Denham airfield. It was Shabbir Shah, the diminutive Bangladeshi gangster from Cardiff, who neither drank alcohol, nor smoked, who caused the others at the table to burst out laughing.

"I believe we are under attack from a secret government unit," he began. "A security force not known to exist by the public. They appear from nowhere and then vanish like smoke. They are too well-organised to be a small rival gang. The deaths of Grid members were too widespread. No individual gang has that reach."

Fergus approached the table and collected empty glasses.

"Can I get you a refill, gentleman?" he asked. "Perhaps you would appreciate food? I'll get one of my lads to chase up the management if you're hungry,"

"Not for me, son," growled Mighty Quinn, "it's time we got home. Our friend from Cardiff here is away with the fairies. He's overtired and coming up with stupid theories. Nothing will get sorted tonight."

Nobody argued with Quinn. If he was leaving, everyone was going.

"I'm away home too," said McGrath. He stood up and stretched. Klimenko ferreted in his jacket for his mobile phone' the Scotsman shook his head.

"Don't let those things run your life, laddie," he said. "Mine's off until morning. I don't want my beauty sleep interrupted on the long drive north. I need my wits about me. Someone's been leaking information to the police on my patch too. I can feel the law's hot breath on my neck. I don't believe Hanigan has gotten the answers to our problems by a long way. For now, I can't worry about what's going wrong here in London. I'm concentrating on my city and saving my arse."

Fergus watched the four men as they headed for the door. A nod from him indicated the two bodyguards behind the bar should follow outside and make sure they left without incident. The other man joined Fergus, and they started the clean-up. Every surface was wiped clean within twenty minutes, and every item the gang masters had touched cleared of any telltale fingerprints. It was as if they had never been here.

When they had finished, the four men had a final drink of their own. At last, they could relax. They had needed to be on constant alert during the previous three hours in case of trouble.

"You know, it's odd," said Fergus, "the boss got these rival gangs to put aside their differences to form a country-wide alliance. The Grid is highly profitable and moving forward daily; yet, at the first hint of trouble, they revert to type and bicker over minor issues that shouldn't concern them."

"What's he like, the boss?" asked one bodyguard.

"He sounded like Churchill, with that rousing final speech," said another. "I thought we would be fighting them on the beaches next."

"He's highly intelligent, a financial genius, and as ruthless as they come," replied Fergus. "After the meetings I've had with him over the past eighteen months, one thing stands out above the rest."

"What's that, Fergus?"

"He's as mad as a box of frogs," replied Fergus.

It was time to leave. Fergus switched off the lights in the drawing-room, and they walked into the deserted reception area.

"If I heard what the Cardiff boss said correctly, I'd better pass this suggestion on to Hanigan tomorrow lunchtime when I'm due to meet up with him. A secret security force might sound fanciful to Michael Quinn, but it makes more sense than the other options they've considered."

The black SUV they had travelled in from London was the only vehicle in the customer car park. Everyone else had long gone.

"Right, let's get you lot home to bed," said Fergus as he climbed into the driver's seat. "Buckle up, gentlemen."

Fergus switched on the ignition.

The van exploded into flames.

Inside the hotel, guests got rudely awakened from their slumber.

In his room, the night manager wondered whether the substantial financial gain from the meeting outweighed the negative publicity a bomb blast brought.

As for Fergus Mallon and his colleagues, it was as if they had never been there.

Chapter Four

Monday, 7th July 2014

Hugo Hanigan awoke early. He fretted over his meeting with Seamus McConnell as he travelled back to London last night. Seamus would be here sometime after nine; the thought kept him awake half the night. He knew the usual Monday morning pattern. The big lummox would shuffle into the penthouse with the same tired list of excuses for being late, and he'd be stinking of the weekend's Guinness and worse.

Hugo would have learned what the Mighty Quinn professed to know when their limited conversation ended last night. The identity of the person running the South Kilburn gang, now that Tommy O'Riordan, lay six feet underground.

Hugo dreaded confirmation Colleen was in charge and everything was going smoothly. He looked at the clock, daring it to tell him it was before eight. He groaned. It was a quarter past six. Who gets up at this unearthly hour?

Hugo showered and dressed. Then made his first coffee of the day and thought about breakfast. Cereals or croissants? He checked what was available. Ah, well, it had to be cereals. He sat and ate a bowl of something that tasted of cardboard but whose packaging screamed super healthy. It was still only a quarter to seven when he turned on the TV.

Hugo set the cereal bowl aside. His coffee in the mug grew cooler. The breaking story concerned the massive explosion in the car park of an exclusive country hotel in Stoke D'Abernon. A burnt-out shell of a vehicle gave no clue as to its make or model. The police gave little away in their comments. Hugo sat forward in his seat and listened.

"The explosion occurred just before one o'clock this morning. Staff from the hotel tried to put out the flames, but nothing could save the occupants. It's believed that three or four people were in the car. They were not guests of the hotel but attended a private meeting in a function room on Sunday night. There's no indication at this stage that this was a terror-related attack. We are continuing with our enquiries."

The police spokesman walked away with a blank expression on his face. He looked as confused as Hugo felt. The news report wound up with the standard requests for information and details of whom to call. Hugo was already contacting Fergus Mallon. The number was unavailable.

"What the hell's going on?" he shouted to anyone prepared to listen.

Hugo paced the floor of his apartment, deep in thought.

If this was an attack on the Grid, anyone attending last night's meeting might have been the target. Yet, how could news of the conference have leaked to give their enemies time to organise such an attack? Hugo couldn't accept that.

So, had last night's get-together inspired this possible car bomb? Did one of those men whose voices spoke against him grasp an opportunity to threaten his leadership?

It might be the type of sneaky trick Klimenko might carry out.

McGrath and Quinn would have been more direct. They would target Hugo himself and wouldn't be shy in telling him what they thought of him before they killed him.

As for Shabbir Shah, he was a new breed of gangster that had moved into the country. Hugo's impression last evening had been of a quiet, thoughtful man who didn't seem dissatisfied enough to commit a vicious assassination despite the questions he raised.

Despite the positives of Grid membership, rivalries still festered. Perhaps it was one of the gang bosses who stayed in the background last night. If they had a long-standing dispute with a neighbour, maybe they took advantage of them sitting around the same table the previous night.

Who might that indicate? Hugo imagined each of them capable, and unwittingly, he'd handed them their opportunity on a plate. In his darker moments, Hugo wondered whether the wreckage on screen was what remained of the SUV he bought for his security crew. If so, he needed to organise a replacement and four new men to ride in it. Why, though, would anybody, inside or outside the Grid, target his security team? What did they hope to gain? Their deaths made no lasting impact on either Hugo himself or the Grid's hierarchy.

Hugo was perplexed; and, in truth, somewhat scared.

When Seamus dragged his weary body through the lift door at ten past nine, Hugo drained the last drop of a tumbler of Bushmill's. It was his second large glass since he switched off the television.

"Good morning, boss. I'm running behind today."

"Forget that, McConnell," said Hugo. "Get over to Fergus Mallon's place. Get him out of bed and ask him what happened last night."

"What's up, boss? Did I miss something?" asked a bemused Seamus.

"While you were in a drunken stupor, someone blew up a vehicle in a car park. I left an hour earlier. That bomb wasn't for me, but Fergus and his crew should have kept the place safe for everyone in attendance last night. I want to know what went wrong. Get moving and report back. Once we've cleared that up, we'll hear what you've got to tell me about what's happening in South Kilburn."

"Okay, you're the boss," said Seamus and shuffled off to the lift.

Hugo watched him leave. Oh, for the days when Sean Walsh was his Monday morning guest, he thought, and before him, Tommy O'Riordan. But, of course, things would never have got this bad in their day.

In her luxury apartment, Colleen O'Riordan finished breakfast. She had adapted quickly to her new surroundings; the daily chore of cooking an Irish breakfast for Tommy was a distant memory. As soon as he went to prison, she began a new regime. The bowl of fruit, nuts, and yoghurt was far healthier; the fresh orange to drink was its perfect companion. After she read the morning newspaper, she allowed herself a small cup of decaffeinated coffee serviced from a top-of-the-range machine. Times had changed.

Friday's funeral had been the ordeal she expected. Tyrone and Rosie rushed off as soon as was decent. Colleen had enough to do without sorting their lives out too. They knew it was time to stand on their own two feet.

As for the family, especially those at the heart of Tommy's gang, she had called them together a week before the funeral. She explained the reasons behind her brother's absence and that of his family. Naturally, there were disapproving looks, but they accepted her decision with no firm opposition.

Colleen sensed this was her moment. With Tommy and Sean out of the picture, Seamus McConnell would never gain the respect required to assume command. So she played her trump card.

"A man from Portmarnock could never become your leader," she told them. "We've known each other since childhood, and our heart lies in the bosom of the seven streets of our home city. So your leader must originate from there. We think alike, have the same values, and share the same blood. So I offer myself as your leader. I have the credentials. Will anyone stand against me?"

Nobody objected. Whether it was the common-sense approach, the prospect of continuity offered, or the steely gaze noted by anyone who dared meet her eye. Colleen was happy that she had their full support.

"Well, now that's settled," she said, "we can move forward. I won't disappoint you."

Only days after the funeral, Colleen exercised her influence over the day-to-day affairs of the gang. The changes were subtle, but even hard-nosed lieutenants on the streets admitted profits rose rapidly. They then received an order to separate the wheat from the chaff.

That necessitated punishment for the worst-performing soldiers. Those guilty of lining their own pockets at the expense of the gang were brought before Colleen and her lieutenants at midnight in the borough's social club.

Two days before Tommy's funeral, Colleen watched as two men had three fingers on each hand removed to underline that she was not afraid to take extreme action. Thin Lizzy on the club's jukebox drowned out their screams.

A young man, Conor Key, a twenty-two-year-old tearaway, appeared before the tribunal. His head bowed; he was a snivelling wreck. He witnessed what had taken place. Conor was also aware his offences were much more severe.

"Do you have anything to say?" asked Colleen.

"I'm sorry," yelled Conor, "it won't happen again, I promise."

"Oh, I'm certain of that," whispered Colleen. "Take him away. Leave him where the others who work for us can see him. Let this be a warning. Skimming a percentage off the top is one thing but using large quantities of our product without payment is also unacceptable."

On Friday evening, as the guests at the wake left the club, they saw Conor's body hanging from a lamp post. His face had been blown away by two bullets delivered to the back of the skull.

Nobody breathed a word. They made their way home; the message was delivered. Conor Key's body disappeared by morning; whereabouts unknown.

Two days later, Colleen finished reading the paper, her coffee cup empty. Conor Key and the other two men didn't trouble her conscience one bit.

She wasn't surprised there was nothing of interest to read this morning. The events of the early hours would have been far too late filtering through to make the morning headlines. The news reports covering the capital, and the

Home Counties, would be far more revealing. She switched on her television.

Colleen viewed the same bulletin as Hugo. They saw the same raw data. Hugo struggled to make sense of it. Colleen turned her head away from the sight of the burned-out vehicle and looked through her window. Below, in that apartment block, sat her mortal enemy. She held the high ground. That was a dominant factor in her hunt for a new place to live when she sold the family home.

As for the assassination of Hanigan's security detail, she wanted the man to be preoccupied. The longer he spent worrying about who killed Mallon and the others and why, the more time she had to cement her place at the head of the Kilburn gang. Hugo was going nowhere. She could torture him a while longer.

One hundred miles away on the outskirts of Bath, Piya Adani drove towards Larcombe Manor. It was a beautiful morning. She felt relaxed and looked forward to meeting Athena again. They had much to discuss.

Life in the old manor house and its surrounding buildings had been hectic in the past four days. Athena was true to her word. Phoenix received a dig in the ribs at seven o'clock on Thursday morning.

"Shower first, then breakfast," Athena ordered, "when you've done that, I have a list of things you need to delegate before the nine o'clock meeting."

Even the daily meeting was shorter. Athena quickly debriefed the Manchester conference and then asked Giles, Henry, and Minos whether any urgent matters needed sorting out before Monday.

The three men looked at one another and decided that

discretion was the better part of valour. Alastor was absent. Minos had heard Athena going through his revised duties for the day as he left his apartment earlier. Best to ride out the storm.

The hive of activity that followed had quietened now. As Ambrosia turned her car between the stone pillars at the end of the driveway, Athena performed her final checks on the results of their combined handiwork. Inside and out, the old building looked spotless. The lawns were immaculate; every flower that even threatened to need deadheading had disappeared from the borders.

Phoenix was by her side, and when they visited the walled garden, he reckoned the carrots stood to attention. He looked back over his shoulder as he left. Had his eyes deceived him? No, each plant had received a haircut. There wasn't a yellowed leaf or untidy piece of greenery in sight. It reminded him of the array of prize vegetables at a village fete.

"I feel like a judge from the Gardening Guild," he muttered.

Athena gave him the stare.

"Did you make sure the outbuildings are as good a shape as this?" she asked.

"I did, and I almost wish I was still living in the old stable block. It was never that clean when Rusty and I were neighbours. Those trainers and their trainees don't know they're born. It will be even better when the faint smell of paint fades."

Athena was too busy checking her list to react to that one. Her mind had moved on to other matters.

"Daddy rang back last night while you cleaned up the orangery. They are ecstatic over the prospect of having

Hope stay with them even if it's only for twenty-four hours."

"You never know, if we let our hair down at James and Elizabeth's party, it could be longer. Neither can drive back until we're sober, with our baby on board."

"Heaven's; is that the time?" Athena yelled and dragged Phoenix into the house through the side door and the kitchens. They ran along the corridors to the main hallway and arrived just as Henry escorted Ambrosia through the front door.

"Athena was expecting you," Henry said, "they'll be along in a minute, I'm sure. Ah, here they come now."

"Thank you, Henry," said Athena. "Good morning, Ambrosia, and welcome to Larcombe Manor. Excuse me, are you alright?"

Ambrosia dabbed at her eyes with a damp tissue. She was distressed.

"I was fine until I negotiated the long driveway," she replied, "but I suffer from hay fever. I know to avoid exposure to grass and weed pollen in the summer months. That's why I've lived in the city since I was a small child. You've just mowed your grass, and my eyes and nose started streaming before I parked my car."

"I'm so sorry," said Athena, "if only we had known."

She took Ambrosia's arm and led her away from the open door towards the relative sanctuary of their apartment. The guided tour of the gardens was on hold.

Phoenix told Henry Minos would chair the meeting this morning as he and Athena entertained their guest. Henry looked at his watch.

"I might as well stay in the building. The meeting gets underway in twenty minutes."

Henry nodded after the disappearing Athena and Ambrosia.

"It's unusual to receive a visit from one of our senior people. She seems young. What a shame she suffers from an allergy such as that."

"Is it?" said Phoenix. "I thought it was reassuring to learn she wasn't perfect. That's the impression she has tried to give everyone since I met her. I wonder whether she has an aversion to the smell of fresh paint. If so, we could spend her entire visit indoors. Such a pity after the effort everyone's made."

Phoenix trailed along the corridor after the two women. Henry Case scratched his head as he watched him walk away. He admired Phoenix and what he'd achieved since arriving here, but there were days when he couldn't make him out. Why would another person's discomfort cause the man to have the widest smile he'd seen on his face in months?

When Phoenix reached their apartment door, he heard Athena introducing Ambrosia to Maria Elena. He entered the room, and Hope gave him her full-beam smile. Life didn't get much better than this, he thought.

"Hello, sweetheart," he said, gathering his daughter in his arms.

"Maria Elena is taking Hope for a walk in the garden, as it's such a lovely day," said Athena, "so don't get too comfortable."

Ambrosia's mood seemed to lighten at the news of Hope's imminent departure. Phoenix knew she had never married. Had her father tried to arrange suitable marriages for her, and she'd dismissed them out of hand? He couldn't remember. He would check with the Two Amigos later.

Perhaps her maternal instinct hadn't kicked in; if so, he

might have sympathy for her. Piya Adani didn't know what she was missing. He handed his daughter back to her nanny and watched as the two of them headed for the gardens. Maria Elena collected Hope's buggy on the way, and Phoenix sighed. He would rather be outside in the sunshine.

This upcoming session with the ambitious Ambrosia promised to be a lecture on recruiting agents, not an exchange of views. That was the Larcombe way, and he preferred it.

"Are we ready to get started?" asked Athena.

"I'm ready," said Phoenix.

Ambrosia blew her nose.

"Things are settling down, thank goodness," she said, "thank you for allowing me the chance to visit — what a beautiful area. I would love to spend time in Bath itself. It has so much history, and yet it's very much a modern city too. The university is well-thought-of, and you have a famous men's rugby club and the ladies' netball team."

Phoenix knew of the university, but the sporting references came as a surprise to him. These things had never been on his radar. He tried to keep up with a few highlights for those long journeys with Rusty. Otherwise, the conversation dried up fast. Rusty wanted to chat for as long as possible because he knew Phoenix would fill the silence with his brand of rock music. For some strange reason that Phoenix couldn't fathom, Rusty wasn't a fan of Iron Maiden and Judas Priest.

"We have a good selection of Indian restaurants, too," he said, "other nationalities are available, of course."

"I'm sure," said Ambrosia, her dark eyes flashing her annoyance.

Phoenix knew he had crossed a line, but he wasn't taking a backward step with this woman. He was his own man. In the past four years, Athena rounded off a few of his sharp edges, but the rebel in him lay only just under the surface.

"In Manchester, you intimated that you had a more inventive proposal to speed up the pace of recruitment and training of additional agents," said Athena.

"When I sold my business last October, I looked for areas where my wealth would do the most good. I researched my local community of Leeds and got invited to join the Board of Trustees for a homeless charity in the city. That was the first of several groups I became involved with, and then I was approached by a national association. When you no longer spend fourteen hours a day from Monday to Friday running a business, you have spare time on your hands. I had nobody to share my weekends with, so the first seventy hours were extended by those I spent writing reports and researching the opposition."

"Can I get us a coffee?" asked Phoenix.

It felt like the start of a long morning. Both women nodded their appreciation, and he disappeared into the kitchen.

"This may have been what led the Olympus Project to my door," Ambrosia continued, "I believe in everything you do. My money will help in the fight against evil. I still stay in touch with my local charities. It's apparent from my experiences with them that one group of people might prove to be a valuable resource."

"I brought chocolate biscuits, too," said Phoenix as he backed through the kitchen door with a tray.

"Thank you, darling," said Athena as she picked up her cup.

"He's very domesticated, isn't he?" Ambrosia said to

Athena. "My father never made a cup of tea or coffee for my mother in forty years of marriage."

She looked up at Phoenix, who moved back to his seat opposite her and Athena.

"It's difficult to equate the image of the man of action I had from how Zeus describes you with the husband and father I see in his home surroundings. How can you separate the two?"

"This is the real me," replied Phoenix. "Circumstances throughout my life have forced my alter ego to the surface. Evil doesn't exist within the boundaries of Larcombe Manor; therefore, I can switch off as soon as I drive through the gates. When I go on a mission, it's for a crime the system has failed to identify or punish. That's when I transform into a stone-cold killer."

Athena shivered. Ambrosia hesitated and found it hard to continue.

"Please, take your time and carry on Ambrosia," said Athena.

"My work in Leeds encouraged me to look across the country to gauge the true scale of the problem. Homeless charities estimate seven thousand ex-servicemen and women are living on the streets. Men and women who have served their country in Kosovo, Iraq, and Afghanistan are living rough; in desperate need of a roof over their heads. But instead, thousands of empty properties are going to asylum seekers. It's not right."

Phoenix almost choked on his digestive biscuit. This girl spoke his language.

"They introduced the Armed Forces Covenant two years ago to tackle this problem," he said.

"I know, and the Community Covenant was to operate at a local level," agreed Ambrosia. "It was supposed to ensure our heroes took priority on affordable housing. Ninety-seven per cent of local authorities signed up for it. The Department for Communities and Local Government doesn't even know how many armed forces veterans need or have received housing in the UK."

"This goes back to the housing associations, doesn't it?" asked Athena.

"Local authorities have handed the affordable housing problem on to a third party," sighed Ambrosia, "they pass the buck. Only a dozen associations from the register of over fifteen hundred signed up to the Covenant. That means they have no binding obligation to help veterans."

"You are aware of our charitable status here at Larcombe," said Athena. "We pass off fully fit ex-servicemen as veterans suffering from post-traumatic stress disorder. In no way do we belittle the condition, and our financial support in that area is well-documented. We know that veterans with mental illness can wait two years to get medical help and therapy through channels approved by the authorities. By the time they receive help, a number have attempted suicide; a significant number are successful. These are men and women scarred by the horrors of war. They deserve far better."

"What I saw in Leeds shocked me," said Ambrosia. "Life on the streets is the gateway to a downward spiral into addiction and crime. These people came home after years of brave service in defence of their country. Whatever help the government is offering is ineffective. I want to give each of them a roof over their heads, a purpose in life, and, where necessary, get them treatment for their PTSD."

"The Covenant's wording needed to be specific," added Phoenix. "It should have read that social housing 'must' rather than 'should' go to veterans. We have the most dedicated, professional troops globally, and how we treat them once their military service is over is a disgrace. What I wish to hear, Ambrosia, are your ideas on how you would find these homes for heroes?"

"First, we need to identify where they are," she replied, "and then determine how many need urgent treatment for PTSD. It could be as high as forty per cent. Charities can increase the lobbying of the authorities for action to redress the problem. I aim to concentrate our attention on the remaining four thousand veterans. I propose we find them accommodation in their region. It might be a flat, a hostel, or even a bunkhouse — anything that gets them off the streets and eligible for benefits. Olympus would offer financial support in the short term to prevent them from slipping back into homelessness in return for their help. Did you read Sherlock Holmes when you were a child, Phoenix?"

"I can't say I did," he replied, "I studied Shakespeare, and Milton, while at school. My mother forced me to work as soon as I was old enough. I never found the time to read for fun after that."

"I think I can see where this is heading," said Athena, "you're referring to his Baker Street Irregulars."

"Exactly," Ambrosia said, with more enthusiasm, as she sensed Athena warming to the cause, "the street urchins led by the older boy, Wiggins. Holmes paid the gang a shilling per day, plus expenses, to collect information for his investigations. With an extra guinea prize for a vital clue. They knew the streets of London like the back of their hand and every dirty deed on them."

"Four thousand veterans spread across the entire country, with a grudge against the system," said Phoenix, thinking through the possibilities. "Men and women who feel abandoned by their country. We must act fast to capture their hearts and minds before extreme factions step in and twist their arm. They might take the wrong road. In return for our help in getting them back on their feet, they could continue to play the role of living rough and become our eyes and ears on the streets. It will involve a ton of work, but it's an ingenious plan."

"How will they get away with pretending to be homeless when they're not?" asked Athena.

"Are you serious?" asked Phoenix. "Beggars in every major city leave their pitch with their dog and jump into a BMW with the cash they've collected. It's just playing a role."

"So, how do we manage that subterfuge?" Athena asked.

"It won't be difficult for old soldiers such as Rusty, Bazza, and Thommo, to show them the ropes and train them in what to say if challenged. We train undercover agents on how to survive in the field every day."

"I knew I could rely on Larcombe to devise systems under which our Irregulars could operate," said Ambrosia. "The trick is to convince sufficient numbers to work for us without eroding the overall security of the Project."

"Good point," said Athena. "Four thousand extra personnel sounds manna from heaven, but they would be inactive for much of their time. Then, after settling in, they would only get paid for information received."

"OK, are we both agreed the basic idea is sound, Athena," said Phoenix.

"Yes," she replied.

"Good, then I suggest we involve the entire senior staff here at Larcombe. Ambrosia can give us support throughout the process. Giles and Artemis will begin identifying where these veterans live. Minos and Alastor will begin the hunt for suitable accommodation. Athena will communicate those with Zeus and urge him to release the necessary funds when costings are available. As for the vetting procedures and the training, that will be the responsibility of Henry and Rusty. We will meet one month from today to discuss progress."

"That's wonderful," said Ambrosia. "I'm so happy."

"I think we've earned a rest," said Athena, "do you feel up to a tour of the building? After lunch, perhaps we can show you our beautiful gardens and the other facilities at our disposal?"

"I can't wait to see everything," replied Ambrosia. "I have only one request; do you have a tissue I can borrow, please?"

Phoenix heard the door opening and the sound of laughter. It was Hope as she tottered alongside Maria Elena. As she accomplished those early steps, the squeals of delight brightened the day even more. Despite his reservations about Ambrosia, Phoenix had to admit things were improving.

Chapter Five

Tuesday, 8th July 2014

Athena, Phoenix, and Ambrosia were satisfied with the results of their meeting yesterday.

As she drove back north, Ambrosia felt as if she had formed the basis of an alliance. She was younger than her two fellow gods and newly appointed, but other colleagues at the head of the Project were elderly and coming to the end of their tenure.

Her ambitious nature encouraged her to aim for the top. Her late father drilled this into her from an early age. He also said the best way to achieve your goal was to keep your opponents as close as possible. You learned more about their strengths and weaknesses that way. You learned nothing if you operated as a lone wolf.

The three had enjoyed an excellent meal with fresh vegetables and fruit from the garden. Of course, the senior team at Larcombe Manor didn't live in the lap of luxury and squander money the Project provided, but they pulled out the stops to ensure she was impressed.

Perhaps they already feared her; it was early days. If they didn't, then in time, they would come to realise the threat she posed. Her ambition was overall control of Olympus. Nothing less would satisfy her.

Phoenix and Athena had stood on the steps of the old manor house with little Hope and waved goodbye to Ambrosia as she drove away.

"That turned out better than I dared hope," said Athena.

"We needn't have done so much cleaning," said Phoenix. "Her allergy prevented her from seeing much outside this building. I've had to change my opinion of her massively. Her Irregulars proposal was a surprise. That has legs. I can't wait to get people started on identifying possible candidates around the country."

"Let's enjoy the sunny afternoon and sleep on it tonight," suggested Athena. "We can put the ideas forward at tomorrow's morning meeting."

"Good idea," Phoenix agreed. "What do you say, Hope? Shall we play ball on the lawn?"

Hope's chubby little hands came together in a semblance of a clap, and a big smile showed her first two teeth on her bottom gum.

That should be fun, she thought; Mummy and Daddy haven't seen the weather forecast.

"If we agree, then let's go," said Athena.

Storm clouds gathered before three o'clock, and Hope and her parents were driven indoors by thunderstorms before teatime. It was fun while it lasted.

The Tuesday morning meeting got underway as usual at nine o'clock.

Athena heard reports from Henry and Giles on life in the ice-house. There was no shortage of crime across the country; the Grid was still active in every quarter. The police in Scotland ticked the necessary boxes before any real action on the fallout from work carried out by Phoenix and Rusty.

"The wheels of justice grind exceedingly slow," sighed Phoenix, "we gave them enough of a head start. The whole sordid network could be behind bars by now."

"Maybe, we should have eliminated more than we did?" asked Rusty. "They seem to be wary of accepting gifts. The police think walking in to find half a dozen criminals after an anonymous phone call is too easy. There must be a catch, somehow. So, they check and double-check everything in case the whole thing turns out to be a prank, and they look foolish."

"They don't need help on that score," said Alastor.

"Anything we can do, Giles?" asked Athena.

"We sprinkled a fair amount of misinformation in the forty-eight hours after the mission, Athena," he replied. "I don't believe there's much to gain from further distribution."

"Fair enough, we have a new search for you to undertake, one that must take priority."

Athena ran through the highlights of their meeting yesterday with Ambrosia and allocated tasks to the ice-house crew and Minos and Alastor.

"That should keep everyone busy for the rest of the week," said Athena. "Any questions?"

"You remember my request for the weekend off, Athena?" asked Henry. "I want to leave soon after lunch on Friday."

"Don't worry, Henry," said Athena, "we haven't forgotten. Give our love to Sarah, and have a lovely weekend."

"Jolly good," replied Henry, breathing more comfortably.

"Let's hope the weather is better than today's," said Giles. "There are more thunderclouds out there."

"Don't be such a pessimist, Giles," said Athena, "did anyone have any other business?"

"There's been a disturbing increase in a different type of crime over the past weeks," said Artemis. "Most of it has occurred in the north of England. Some of it is in Ambrosia's town of Leeds. I don't know whether she's been affected."

"It didn't crop up in conversation yesterday," said Phoenix. "What type of crime?"

"Hate crimes," said Giles. "We're recording increasing amounts of attacks on immigrants in general, and Muslims in particular. It's not always clear whether the perpetrators are part of a wider organisation or just idiots acting alone."

"The Grid is in no way responsible for orchestrating these attacks, I take it?" said Phoenix.

"No, there are no links with organised crime."

"There's been an increasing presence of right-wing groups strengthened by the ongoing effects of the government's austerity policies," said Minos. "The English Defence League grew from the football supporters' scene and has voiced opposition to militant Islam for the past five years. So it was easy for them to gather support from marginalised and disadvantaged white working-class communities."

"The marches they've held have caused short-term trouble," said Rusty, "but the numbers they attract aren't great, are they? Trouble flares because an equal number of anti-fascist supporters turn up simultaneously. It's your typical football fan mentality. It's Saturday afternoon; so-and-so is in town. Let's break a few heads."

"The EDL and its off-shoots claim to be fighting for race and nation and want to stop immigration and start repatriation," added Phoenix. "Individuals commit most acts of race and religious hatred, don't they?"

"What form do these attacks take?" asked Athena.

"Nasty verbal, physical, and emotional attacks against Muslims occur regularly," said Alastor. "In some areas, this has escalated from spitting, and abusive language to arson, serious assaults, and even murder."

"We must monitor this situation closely, Giles," said Athena. "We cannot allow this to fester and grow in strength while our attentions focus on the Grid. Keep an eye on the Government's response and bring this matter to the forefront of your future reports if matters deteriorate."

Giles and Artemis nodded. Their hands were full recording the activities of the Grid. Now Athena added two more tricky problems to the list to tackle. Within the hour, they were below ground in the ice-house. They assigned crews to the intelligence-gathering duties, and the fun began.

Wednesday, 9th July 2014

Solomon Hussain was a seventeen-year-old law student; his classmates missed him. He was always smiling and happy. Solomon didn't arrive at college this morning; his close friends tried to contact him on their mobile phones. Their attempts went straight to voicemail.

The police in Newcastle knew why. They held his phone and other personal items at their city centre headquarters. The owner of a kebab shop dialled 999 late last night; a group of young men had attacked Solomon outside on the pavement. He suffered severe head injuries and died early this morning at the Royal Victoria Infirmary.

When the police arrived on the scene, the paramedics were working on Solomon. The pavements were empty. A handful of concerned people gathered nearby. There was no sign of the attackers.

"Solomon was one of our regulars," the shop owner told the officers who attended, "he was friendly; he didn't drink or smoke, but he enjoyed our food. As he chatted with my staff, half a dozen lads entered. Not much older than Solomon, eighteen or nineteen, and very drunk. These youths asked what he was doing there. Was he an illegal? Then they began pushing him, goading him into a fight. The abuse got worse; Solomon tried to ignore them. My staff and I shouted at them to stop, to leave the boy alone. Then Solomon ran out into the street. They chased him and caught him. As soon as he was on the ground, I made the call. I could see he was in danger. One lad kept kicking and kicking him. It was horrible."

"Did your staff try to help?"

"The boys warned us to stay out of it; they threatened to torch my shop. I've never seen these boys before. I was scared for my family; my wife and four children live upstairs with me."

"Do you have CCTV?"

"I have cameras, yes, but they are not working. I can't

afford it now. Takings have dropped. Customers don't have the money to spend on takeaways these days."

The police viewed CCTV images from cameras near the shop, but the closest was too far away to capture the incident. They only had grainy shots of groups of youths moving around the city centre. Identification of the attackers would be nigh on impossible.

The descriptions given by the shop owner and his staff could have fitted any teenager in the country. They wore trainers, jeans, and a hooded jacket. They wore baseball caps, and most of them had tattoos.

Everything they heard convinced the police the attack was racially motivated. A male and female officer informed Solomon's parents of his death before lunchtime. The press was notified simultaneously and told there would be a uniformed presence in the area from tonight to reassure the public.

Solomon's college friends and tutors heard the news as it filtered through that afternoon. Tears fell for the popular young man. On social media that evening, messages were posted. Many carried tributes to a promising student whose life had been cut short.

Fingers pointed towards young men on the streets last night who disappeared when trouble broke out — comments mentioned their affiliation with the English Defence League. The rumours spread. By midnight, names circulated online for those responsible, and the police personnel monitoring social media traffic took notes.

Earlier that afternoon, Jack Ferris left school in Bradford at half-past three. He wandered home. Nobody would be in, so he could take as long as he wished. Unfortunately, it hadn't been a good day. It was a little over a week away from the summer holidays, and his tutors were disappointed with his work.

The headmaster asked him to consider whether staying on in the sixth form had been the right choice. Perhaps, his parents would come in for a chat? I don't think so, thought Jack. They hardly talk to one another, and as for going somewhere together, you can forget it.

Jack saw the evidence of deprivation everywhere he looked on the streets on his way home. Places where he knew homeless men and women would sleep rough later — boarded-up shops. The unemployed, standing on street corners yards from their homes, with despair etched in lines on their faces — nothing to do and nowhere to go.

Jack could see his future, and it didn't look bright. He was in the city's heart, where the immigrants lived, while he headed further out to the outskirts. White people had to live in the suburbs. The city that his grandfather grew up in had gone.

His namesake, Jack Ferris, was wounded in North Africa and never lost the limp in his left leg that shrapnel from the Panzer shell inflicted. His grandfather didn't like the changes in the make-up of the city's population since the war. He instilled mistrust and dislike of foreigners in his three sons. When he died ten years ago, Jack was seven years old.

His dad Gary, and his uncles were football fanatics; they followed their local team from their early teens, home and away. No game was complete without running fights before and after the match. Saturdays were more fun if the grounds were well-established and didn't have the barriers and security systems of the newer stadiums. Running along the terraces, causing mayhem among the opposing fans, became their afternoon's highlight. It's what they lived for from week to week.

Gary settled down later than his siblings. The fourteen-year age gap between him and Jack's mum, Michelle, was significant when they married on her twentieth birthday. It was a chasm now.

There was no shortage of Union flags or the Cross of St George on the avenue where Jack lived with his parents. They left you no doubt about which area of the city they represented. Dad joined his mates on the streets on the weekends.

The cost of a match ticket had priced him out of going for years; that, and the police banned him from most of the nearby stadiums for violence. Dad didn't want to sit, anyway; that was for wimps. He wished to stand where he liked, chant the abuse he chose, and taste blood on his knuckles.

Last year, his Dad and his mates joined others on marches. They were putting Britain first and fighting back. Jack trailed behind them one Saturday afternoon to see what went on.

There seemed to be around a hundred hard-core individuals involved. Most of the chants were anti-Muslim. Jack remembered what his grandfather had said about them. He decided this was something he wanted to be a part of, something to make his grandfather proud. It might help things improve around here for white youths like himself. Nobody else did anything to help.

Last winter, one such march attracted opposition. The police were out in force; they had a helicopter circling overhead. Jack saw banners and placards calling the people his Dad marched with Fascists. Jack had studied that at school. He couldn't see the link. Jack believed his Dad walked to argue that we wanted our country back. It was in danger of being overrun by foreigners. Areas in the centre of Bradford were already a no-go area for non-Muslims.

Today, as he turned the corner onto Manningham Lane, Jack passed the shops and restaurants that antagonised his family members. Every other shop front carried a foreign name. His grandfather called it League of Nations Lane. His Dad's language was far worse.

Two women came out of a shop doorway in front of Jack. One carried a large shopping bag. An older woman pushed a buggy with a young child. Both women had their faces covered with a niqab. Their laughter told Jack they were happy and content with their lot.

The stress of his school situation and prospects, his home life, and the racist language he was exposed to from an early age at his grandfather's knee burst to the surface.

Jack Ferris snapped.

"Where the hell do you think this is? This is England. Why can't you dress like normal people?"

Nilima Thakur, the young woman, turned to face him. Her accent honed on the streets of a Yorkshire city.

"I was born in Bradford, mate. My mother has lived here for over thirty years."

Parveen Chowdhury had pushed the buggy a few yards away; she stopped and called to her daughter in Bengali. The baby began to cry. Parveen didn't want trouble.

"Yeah, right," Jack Ferris seethed. "Thirty years, and she ain't bothered to learn the language."

Staff from the shop gathered by the door, and passers-by slowed their pace. They stopped by the shop's plate-glass window to stand and stare. Jack was fired up and didn't want to look foolish. This girl had a lot of nerve, facing up to him. Except she wasn't facing up to him, with it hidden behind that bloody scarf.

"That can come off too," shouted Jack, grabbing the niqab. Nilima screamed as Jack caught hold of her hair. They struggled on the pavement, and Nilima fell to the ground. Jack's right foot lashed out and landed on her stomach.

The small crowd was horrified. Two Indian shop workers rushed forwards to grapple with Jack.

"You're going nowhere," one said, "we called the police."

Jack Ferris was strong and agile; he broke away and dashed up Manningham Lane. He glanced over his shoulder and could see the blue lights flashing. A police car was a hundred yards away. He darted into the next turning and escaped into the maze of side roads and back alleys with which he was familiar. Jack stopped running. Other students walked on the surrounding pavements, returning home after another dull school day. His breathing slowed.

He pushed his jacket hood off his head. Thank goodness, I don't wear a school uniform now, he thought; they'll struggle to identify me. Even if they had CCTV on the street, I could hear what they'll be telling the cops now. They all look alike, officer.

Jack arrived home to an empty house, just as he anticipated.

As he lay on his bed listening to his music, he thought of what he had done. He had no remorse or shame. He was putting us first and fighting back. He thought these people had the council and the law in their pockets. Ten years from now, Bradford won't have a white face if we don't fight back.

Jack hoped his grandfather would be proud of him.

Thursday, 10th July 2014

Before first light, Newcastle police teams raided addresses in Byker, Cowgate, and West End. They arrested five youths on suspicion of the murder of Solomon Hussain. The community rallied around and did the first part of the police's work for them. The public now had to rely on them joining the dots, getting the case to court, and hoping for the correct result. It wasn't guaranteed, though, not with the slippery legal system in operation in this enlightened, modern world. There was always a chance they would escape justice.

In Bradford, the police studied CCTV images. Two cameras captured the ugly incident on Manningham Lane. The irritating thing was neither gave a clear picture of the attacker. He was tall, well-built, and in his teens. They had little more to go on than that.

When officers arrived on the scene outside the carpet shop yesterday afternoon, they found one young woman in tears, with a torn niqab on the pavement beside her. She complained of a bruised midriff. The palms of her hands and her knees were scuffed and bleeding.

The officers called an ambulance. Nilima Thakur went home later that evening.

The older lady, who they now knew was Nilima's mother, was agitated but unable to communicate with the officers. Neither of the officers spoke Bengali. A toddler in a buggy was crying, and several women tried to soothe the infant. The shop owner offered to take Mrs Chowdhury and the child to the hospital. Police interviewed the pedestrians and shop assistants and collected various descriptions of the attacker.

As the officers drove up Manningham Lane, they saw half a dozen youths who might have been responsible for the attack. None of them was spooked by seeing the car. Nobody ran away, inviting a chase. It looked like a dead end. The vehicle returned to base until assigned to its next callout.

This morning, the prospect of a result looked even more remote.

"I'll get us a coffee," said a young Detective Sergeant.

"Thanks, I'll skip through these CCTV images once more," said the female constable working with him. "If nothing turns up, we'll have to leave this and move on."

The DS left the room; a phone rang. The constable answered; it was the desk sergeant. An elderly lady had arrived to help. Mrs Chowdhury waited at Reception.

"Do we have anyone in the station who speaks Bengali?" asked the constable.

"I'd be surprised if Deb Sengupta doesn't," said the desk sergeant, "one of the Community Support Officers. He's in his late forties and moved here with his family ages ago. Deb's your best bet. I'll check if he's at the station and get him to bring Mrs Chowdhury to you."

"That's brilliant, thanks."

The DS held the door open with his backside and tried to manoeuvre through the opening without spilling the coffee. He managed it with ease.

"Years of practice," he said as he sat on a chair, "any luck?"

"Maybe, the mother's outside, and we may have an interpreter."

Deb Sengupta arrived two minutes later with Nilima's mother. Within five minutes, the old lady had given them a description of her daughter's attacker that was as good as a photograph. She saw his face. The CCTV camera angles caught nothing but a hooded jacket.

"That's excellent," said the DS, thanking Mrs Chowdhury.

She nodded and carried on chatting with the PCSO.

"Hang on, boss," said Deb, "she knows his name. It's Ferris. When she first came to Bradford, her late husband ran a corner shop further out of the city. There was aggravation back then; they had graffiti on the shop door and verbal abuse. One man was at the centre of it. Jack Ferris. She says his sons should be known to us; they were football hooligans back in the day. Mrs Chowdhury reckons this young lad is the old man's grandson."

"She doesn't want a job, does she, Deb?" said the DS, with a grin, "come on, constable, let's go make an arrest."

There was nobody at home when they visited the Ferris house. A neighbour told the DS the mother worked at a local school as a lunchtime supervisor and would be home by two-thirty. The father was a delivery driver and could be anywhere. Young Jack should be at school.

The constable drove them across the city to the sixth-form college. Jack Ferris was escorted to reception by a teacher. The DS read him his rights and asked for a phone number to contact either of his parents. Late in the afternoon, Jack was interviewed, under caution, with his mother in attendance as his responsible adult. She wasn't happy.

Jack was gutted. He had been so sure he'd get away with it. Just as his grandfather said, the cops bend over backwards to help the immigrants, refugees, and asylum seekers. Yet, if a white person whose family has lived here for a thousand years needs a helping hand, they go to the back of the queue.

Gary Ferris got home from work at a quarter to six.

Dinner wasn't on the table. Michelle explained they had just arrived and why; Gary had hit the roof. Michelle cowered in the corner. Jack lay upstairs in his room.

Michelle didn't need to worry this time. Gary's anger wasn't aimed at her or Jack. It was Muslims in Bradford in general. He phoned his older brothers.

"We need to do something," he told each of them. "I'll meet you later tonight."

Three dark-clothed figures left the bar at closing time. It was where the Ferris brothers had drunk together since they were old enough to get served. Before that, their father carried the drinks into the beer garden on summer evenings. They were hardened drinkers ready to strike a blow for the cause they supported.

They stole a nondescript Toyota from a nearby car park. The three men travelled to the city centre. A carpet shop on Manningham Lane was their first target. The slogans 'No Surrender' and 'EDL' were spray-painted across the plate-glass window. Poppies strewed in the doorways.

Bricks were thrown through the windows of solicitors' offices further up the street, where a bronze plaque indicated the practitioners bore Indian names.

Gary Ferris drove the Toyota towards White Abbey Road. Their last call was to the local mosque.

"It's time this place got a makeover," he cried.

"Let's do this," his brothers Terry and Duncan shouted.

Farhad Kirmani was an imam at the mosque; he was fifty-seven, a gentle, soft-spoken man, and a pillar of the Muslim community. His fellow worshippers had left. The fifth stage of Salah ended at ten o'clock. Prayers were now over for the day.

Many of his community would return tomorrow. Friday was always a busy day. Farhad wanted to tidy up and prepare for an early morning start. He enjoyed the peace and tranquil atmosphere in the building when empty.

He heard noises from the entrance hall. Farhad was sure everyone had collected their shoes and made their way home. Who could be out there now?

As he opened the door to the hallway, he faced two men. They were almost as old as him and drunk and angry.

"What are you doing?" he asked, "this is a place of worship. You should leave."

The men stopped what they were doing. Cans of petrol in their hands continued to drip their contents onto the mosaic floor. The smell that greeted Farhad told him their cans were almost empty already.

The Ferris brothers laughed at the imam as Gary appeared behind him. He had broken in through a rear door and discarded the empty petrol cans inside.

"You ever been to a pantomime, Muzzie?" sneered Gary.

"He's behind you," cried Terry and Duncan.

The frightened imam turned and threw an arm up to protect himself from the baseball bat aimed at his head. It was no use. After several hefty blows, he crumpled to the floor, fracturing his skull.

"I'll meet you at the car," said Gary. He ran back to the rear door, lit the cloth he had prepared and cast it into the room. The fabrics on the walls, soaked in petrol, caught fire quickly, and the rear of the building was soon ablaze.

Gary ran along the side of the mosque and out onto White Abbey Road. The Toyota's motor was running. He jumped in the back. The front of the mosque billowed smoke, and an orange glow shone through the narrow windows.

"Drop me off at home," said Gary. "I'll drive out to Lister Park and meet you there."

The Toyota was abandoned and reduced to a burnt-out shell before the three Ferris brothers reached their beds. The emergency services arrived at the mosque thirty minutes after the fire broke out.

Early enough to save the building from destruction. Too late to save Farhad Kirmani.

Chapter Six

Friday, 11th July 2014

Athena brought the morning meeting to a close. They debated the alarming events of the last forty-eight hours in the North-East of England and sanctioned direct action at the earliest opportunity. Phoenix and Rusty were already heading to the orangery to prepare their response and discuss other issues raised during the week.

Henry Case walked across the lawn to the stable block. Anyone who observed him on this sunny afternoon would have remarked on his progress. But, today, it was more a 'skip and a whistle than a stroll or a world-weary trudge after a stressful week.

Henry was off for the weekend.

The Reverend Sarah Gough had invited him to tomorrow's summer flower show. He was staying at the Hurtwood Hotel for three nights. Henry couldn't wait to see Sarah again, but his first treat this weekend was driving to Surrey and finding the delightful venue for his temporary stay. It sounded quintessentially English. The hotel was in Walking Bottom, Peaslake, just three miles from Sarah's parish.

As soon as he had packed his bag, Henry decided to visit the canteen in the workers' cottages. A light lunch was all he required today — something to fortify him for the two-and-a-half-hour drive ahead of him. No alcohol, of course; that fortification would need to wait until he arrived.

Henry was nervous. This weekend promised to bring a significant shift in their relationship. Sarah had promised him an evening stroll through her parish followed by a meal at the Royal Oak. There was much to admire in the village. The road which inspired Summer Street in Forster's 'Room With A View' was hidden somewhere nearby, and the village had strong links with Beatrice Webb, the social reformer.

Sarah Gough had written of these landmarks in her letters, and to his eternal credit, Henry tried to feign interest. Tucked away in his bag were scraps of paper with handwritten notes. They held what he hoped were appropriate responses to Sarah's comments as they passed these points of interest.

Henry was desperate not to upset her by revealing his ignorance of the literary and political world in the first half of the twentieth century. In a quick background check on the good lady Sarah had mentioned and her husband Sidney, he discovered they loved one another and loved justice.

At last, he had found common ground. Henry was all for justice.

Henry threw his bag into the back of the car he collected from the transport section at two o'clock. As he pulled away from the stable block, he wondered whether Athena had given the chief mechanic licence to issue a classier model for the occasion. He opened up the limousine along the A303 as he sped towards the leafy gardens of Surrey. Henry eased back on the accelerator after a while. A speeding ticket and points on his licence would put a black mark against his name. The next time he wanted a weekend off from Larcombe, Athena might not be so cooperative or generous.

The first-floor bedroom at the rear of the hotel in Peaslake was well-appointed and promised to be quiet. Henry unpacked his bag and called Sarah to tell her he'd arrived safely. She was keen to see him.

"Can you drive over straight away, Henry," she said. "I've finished writing my sermon, ready for Sunday. My evening is free. Let's spend as much of it together as we can. There's plenty of time before we're due at the pub."

Henry drove the three miles to the vicarage. In truth, he could have floated there; he was that happy. As soon as he pulled up outside, Sarah rushed to greet him. She kissed him on both cheeks and hurried him indoors.

A trifle formal thought, Henry. He had hoped for more.

Sarah saw the confusion on his face and laughed.

"My parishioners are inquisitive and would be shocked if they saw us kissing in public."

With the door firmly shut behind them, Henry received his reward for his patience. Several minutes later, Sarah came up for air.

"This won't do, Henry," she said, "we're wasting this lovely weather. Let me show you the sights."

Henry held on tight and gazed at the flushed face of the woman he loved.

"This is the sight I have waited weeks to see," he said.

"Easy, tiger," said Sarah, squeezing him, "everything comes to he who waits."

The happy couple then strolled, arm-in-arm, past the church that gave the village its full name.

"St Mary's is only one of four parishes I cover. I'm happy here in the country. There's so much for the locals and visitors to enjoy. The surrounding hills are popular with walkers, cyclists and horse-riders. There's no shortage of activities to occupy one's leisure time."

They continued their tour, and Henry noted the village green, pond, and well. All standard features on the tick-list for the English village.

"It's like stepping back into an Agatha Christie novel, isn't it?" said Sarah.

"What can I look forward to tomorrow at this fete-cum flower show?" Henry asked.

"What you might expect, I suppose," Sarah replied. "Stalls of home-grown vegetables, fruit, flowers and plants. Inside the marquees, there will be displays of floral art, handicraft, and photography. Of course, there will also be an ample supply of baked goods."

"Ah, good," said Henry. "I love a good cake."

"Neither of us needs fattening-up," chided Sarah, "but I freely admit to a sweet tooth. Anyway, I believe the true measure of the endurance of the village depends on shows such as these. Critics say places like this are full of commuters, second homers and locals who can't afford to leave. While that may be true, those elements of friction get set aside on a day like tomorrow. There will be activities for young and old. The hog roast, ice cream parlour, beer tent, bouncy castle, and dog show will attract families from all walks of life. If there's still a fete every spring and summer, with maybe a bonfire night and carols in the pubs at Christmas, then the village will keep its soul intact."

"You've fallen in love with this place," said Henry. "I can see why. Could you ever leave, I wonder?"

"Henry was that a proposal?" asked Sarah.

Henry was flustered. Sarah came to his rescue.

"It's alright, my love. I know what you meant. Well, there are village parishes throughout England. I'm sure if my superiors wished to move me to a place where they thought I could be of more use, I would settle soon enough."

The rest of the evening passed quickly. The meal at the pub was excellent, and the pair found that conversation still posed no problems. As Henry escorted Sarah back to the vicarage after closing time, he spotted fellow pub-goers, dog-walkers, and love-struck teenagers scattered around the main street. He and the Reverend Sarah Gough seemed to be the centre of attention.

"You see what I mean, Henry?" said Sarah, "you can only walk me to my door, then drive back to your digs. Tongues would wag if I invited you in, if only for coffee."

"If a kiss on the cheek is my limit," said Henry, "then I shall carry the memory of that kiss into my dreams tonight."

"You old romantic, come here," said Sarah, leaning in for a kiss as they paused in the shadows by the high hedge in front of the vicarage.

"Until tomorrow," said Henry.

He drove back to Walking Bottom, walked upstairs to his room, undressed and got into bed. Before he dropped off to sleep, Henry reflected on Sarah's question. Had that been a proposal? Was it possible to prevent her from discovering the true nature of his role at Larcombe Manor? If so, he would wish to spend the rest of his life with her. But were the chances of a broken heart worth the risk?

While Henry had been motoring towards his weekend getaway, Phoenix and Rusty were tucked away in the orangery. It was another long session discussing issues raised during that week's meetings and deciding which should become their priority assignment.

"Do you believe someone's orchestrating the flurry of racially motivated attacks in the past forty-eight hours?" asked Rusty.

"Not one bit," replied Phoenix. "I'm convinced they're random acts. The locations aren't surprising, though. If you recall, at the end of June, the far-right used the murder of Lee Rigby last year to push their racist ideology. Leeds saw one of the largest turnouts the English Defence League managed. They marched through the city to the war memorial. While they were mobilising, the Unite Against Fascism crowd were already en route to lay their tributes, calling for unity in the face of far-right fascism."

"Both Islamist extremists and EDL were their targets, weren't they?" asked Rusty.

"That's right," said Phoenix. "The police moved in to keep the two groups separate, the EDL laid their wreath, and apart from a few minor scuffles, the groups dispersed in an hour."

"Much ado about nothing?" asked Rusty.

"Neither group has shown signs of capturing the hearts and minds of enough of the public to make a real impact. There are internal squabbles in the EDL, and as with many of these organisations, they centre on whether they should adopt the path of peaceful protest or violent confrontation. The authorities won't ban the marches while conditions remain as they were in June. Even if there were rumours of EDL members outside a pub near the city centre verbally abusing an Asian woman."

"So, where does the danger lie, do you think?"

"With the anti-fascists. If they proactively build a grass-roots movement amongst the working class. Then, we might expect to see more violent militancy erupt on our streets."

"How do we tackle that problem?"

"I think we leave that to the authorities. Our focus must be on the loss of life in two of the most recent incidents. The killers of Solomon Hussein, and Kirmani, the imam last night, must face justice. We will need Giles's help to identify the attackers, and the call for action sent to Zeus for final approval."

"Who's likely to be selected for direct action in that region?" asked Rusty.

"Unless something requiring our skills sends us elsewhere, Rusty, we'll have a day out in Yorkshire and Tyneside. I haven't been up that way in a while. I have fond memories of my time in Durham four years ago."

Neil Cartwright, the man who had murdered Phoenix's daughter Sharron had been released from Durham Prison at nine in the morning on the day in question. He had served a miserable ten years inside the high-security prison before he somehow got parole. As Cartwright walked towards the station concourse to board a train bound for his hometown of Newcastle, Phoenix killed him with two bullets to the chest from a silenced gun.

"A penny for them?" offered Rusty.

"Happy days," said Phoenix, "let's move on. I've been reading this report from Minos on anti-Muslim hate crimes.

There's nothing unusual about the main culprits; most are white males between twenty-five and sixty — the incidents occur in public spaces. On the streets, on footpaths, in parks, for instance. It's common for a mosque or Muslim community building to be somewhere in the vicinity. A few of those responsible belong to organisations such as EDL, but many are ordinary working-class people with no link to any group whatsoever. Minos noted that there had been a significant increase in online abuse. The victims are as likely to be Muslim women as men in that case."

"Why don't the social media sites do more to stop this abuse?" asked Rusty.

"My gut feeling is they remove offensive material wherever they spot it, but something crops up on another thousand pages within seconds. Unless they had to filter every posted comment, image, or video before release, they don't have many options left. But, of course, the whole point of these sites is their immediacy. Legislation to slow it down would face stout resistance. I doubt either side has the appetite for spending months tied up in the courts."

"So, what's the way forward for Olympus?"

"We ask Giles and Artemis to locate the frequent offenders online and decide the appropriate direct action. Then, we delegate that to the nearest local team. Our intervention must be untraceable but will ensure those targeted learn a harsh lesson. It must be clear there are no further chances."

"One more strike and they're out," Rusty nodded.

"Exactly," said Phoenix. "Game over."

Phoenix and Rusty continued to work until it was too dark to see.

"Shall we pick this up again in the morning?" asked Phoenix.

"We might as well," agreed Rusty. "Artemis will be in the ice-house with Giles and the team, chasing down the exact location of your Irregulars. I'll be at a loose end."

"Fine, I look forward to it. We need to move fast on the veterans' situation. Sleeping rough, even in July, is no picnic," said Phoenix. "I aim to help Ambrosia get as many of these people as possible indoors before the autumn. They mustn't have to spend another cold night outside. Nobody who fought to protect their country should ever suffer so shamefully."

"And yet you keep me slogging away until it's too late to have any fun," said Rusty.

"Artemis will be home by now," said Phoenix.

"Shattered after a full day's work, as am I; neither of us will want to do anything except sleep tonight."

"We live in hope, mate; we live in hope."

The two friends walked back to the main building. Rusty could see lights shining in both his and Phoenix's apartments. Artemis was still awake. He said goodnight and made for the doorway.

Phoenix continued walking towards the far entrance, which took him via the kitchens, to the stairs, and up to the awaiting Athena. Rusty was only just through the door, perhaps with a foot on the bottom step when the light in his apartment went out.

"Unlucky, mate."

Saturday, 12th July 2014

In his warm bed at the hotel, Henry Case awoke to a bright and sunny morning. He, too, was living in hope. First, the weather stayed fine throughout the day. A flower show in the pouring rain was no place to spend a Saturday afternoon.

Second, he prayed Sarah never uncovered his awful secret.

Third, he hoped that before he returned to Larcombe Manor, they could spend more time together, alone. It was fine bowing to the sensitive nature of her parishioners, but Sarah's letters had promised so much more.

Henry could recite every line. He recalled the comments from Giles and Artemis as they walked to morning meetings minutes after he had read one of her letters.

"Have you been running, Henry? You look flustered."

Henry checked the clock. It was a little after eight o'clock — time for a shower as cold as he could stand it. Then there was a heart-stopping full-English breakfast to look forward to downstairs.

In the vicarage, Sarah was already busy. She was puzzling over what clothes to wear. Could she be daring and don a summer dress accentuating her well-upholstered figure, or should it be her vestments? The dog-collar won the day. She was on civic duty, after all. A touch of make-up wouldn't go amiss, and she could wear her hair up for a change.

Decisions were made. Sarah was ready for whatever lay in store in the day ahead.

Henry arrived a few minutes after eleven. He had opted for a blue blazer over a crisp, white open-necked shirt with grey flannels; he topped it off with a straw Panama hat. His black leather shoes shone.

He presented her with a bunch of red roses.

"For the love of my life," he said, kissing her on one cheek. Then, he stood back to avoid crushing the gift and causing consternation among any curtain-twitchers watching.

"Oh, they're wonderful, Henry," said Sarah, "come inside, and I'll get these in water."

The village show opened at noon. Henry and Sarah mingled with the crowds. They visited all the marquees and displays; tried their hand at guessing the weight of a fruitcake and how many marbles there were in a large glass jar.

They threw wooden balls between bales of straw towards nine skittles that dodged everything thrown at them. As the afternoon wore on, the couple received less and less attention from the crowds of village families surrounding them.

"Do you know," whispered Sarah. "I think they're getting used to seeing us as a couple,"

The heavens opened at half-past three. The wind speed increased, and everyone scurried for the relative safety of the marquees. Even the dog-show entrants lined up with their owners in the tent where Henry and Sarah sheltered.

"A typical summer's afternoon," groaned Sarah.

"It doesn't appear to be blowing over," said Henry. "those dark clouds in the distance are heading our way. They look menacing."

"Let's dash to the cake tent and grab a few goodies," giggled Sarah. "We'll have afternoon tea at the vicarage. If there's any left."

They dashed across from the marquee to the cake stall. Two ladies huddled together under a large golf umbrella.

"Ah, vicar, I'm glad you've arrived," cried one lady. "Your gentleman friend's guess for the weight of the cake was the nearest."

"He was within five grams," added her friend, Lilian, looking impressed.

"The winner gets the cake, so here you are," her colleague Edith said.

Edith handed Henry a perfectly baked, creamy fruit cake in its square box. He and Sarah hurried back to the vicarage, leaving the two ladies staring after them.

"They seemed in a rush, Edith,"

"I can't wait to hear the Reverend Sarah's sermon in the morning, Lilian."

"For what I'm about to receive, may the Lord make me truly thankful,"

"Lucky girl. Oh well, let's clear away these soggy paper plates and doilies. Nobody will want these fancies we've got left. I'll make us a nice cup of tea at my place."

"You're on, Edith. A Viennese whirl is all I've got to look forward to, with my husband gone these past five years."

"If that cake tasted as good as it looked, perhaps that military-looking gentleman would stay for a while. I hope so; the vicar has been a breath of fresh air in the village. I'd hate to see her leave."

In the vicarage, the tea things sat on the dining room table. The kettle had boiled several minutes ago. Upstairs in the bedroom, Henry and Sarah stood facing one another.

"Are you wearing the red underwear I discovered by chance at Larcombe beneath your grey uniform," Henry asked as he removed his blue blazer.

"I have a confession, Henry," blushed Sarah as she removed her dog collar. "I hope you're not too shocked. I didn't want any problems to arise that might restrict our progress. Instead, I found it exciting to spend the afternoon with you, wearing nothing under my outer clothing."

Henry was folding his flannel trousers as Sarah undressed. He dropped them in a heap as she stood naked before him at last. She shook her hair loose from the comb that held it.

"Heavens," said Henry.

"One thing at a time, Henry. Just one heaven will suffice for now. Then we can enjoy a large slice of that cake."

Henry joined Sarah on the bed. His hopes for good weather had faded. Conditions certainly took a turn for the worse, for which he would be eternally grateful. Nevertheless, his wishes for their relationship to move to a new level were about to be satisfied.

He thought two out of three wasn't bad; he prayed his secret would remain hidden.

On Saturday evening, while Henry and Sarah tucked into their late afternoon tea at Larcombe Manor, Phoenix and Athena met up for the first time all day.

"There you are, at last," Athena said as Phoenix returned from the orangery.

"Sorry, darling," he replied as he flopped onto the sofa beside her.

"Hope has gone to bed. She tried to stay awake long enough to see Daddy. What kept you so long?"

"I wanted to get started early, so I crept out before seven. Rusty joined me at nine o'clock as we agreed. We worked on our action plans until four this afternoon. Artemis was coming off-shift from the ice-house then."

"I assume you thought there was more tinkering required to your plans. You're never satisfied."

"No, I was happy to sign off on what Rusty and I completed. I'm looking forward to having my new logistics chap here in a few weeks. Standing back to look at the bigger picture will do me good. If I hadn't been so blinkered, I might have spotted the Irregulars opportunity Ambrosia unearthed."

"Hugh Fraser hasn't agreed to take up the post we've offered yet, darling," Athena cautioned. "You may have to soldier on alone."

"He'll come," said Phoenix, "he'd be a mug not to seize the chance of working with me,"

Athena spotted the grin her husband did his best to conceal.

"For a second, I thought you were serious," she said.

"The past two hours I've spent catching up with the reports Minos and Alastor prepare for us. I'm always watching the pile of their data growing in my in-tray."

"It has the habit of growing when you only spend a few minutes each day close to your desk," said Athena, shaking her head. "So, what was it that caught your eye this time?"

"Rusty and I worked on our response to the anti-Muslim attacks, and I wonder whether the government's focus on extremism might have contributed to the problem. Recent policy has centred on counter-terrorism measures and the prevention of violent extremism. Over the past decade, most young Muslim men engaged with the police due to 'stop and search'. That was one of the core pillars of the Terrorism Act. Minos reported that over half a million stop and searches had occurred, but none had resulted in a terrorism-related conviction."

"You're suggesting the procedures alienate and place a stamp on youths of Muslim appearance and help to reinforce the justification of those with white supremacist views?"

"If only it were that simple. It's not the whole story. White youths from the working-class areas in the North of England where these latest attacks centred suffer in education and employment. They feel abandoned and without hope; they target those of different ethnic and religious backgrounds seeking to find someone to blame for their situation."

Athena sighed.

"Since Olympus formed, we have seen an increase in extremism in whichever part of the spectrum it lies. Everything seems to move so much faster too."

"The basic messages remain the same," said Phoenix. "But the exponential growth of the internet and social media means the language of hate can increase at the click of a button. It's in an app, compared to when a pamphlet took weeks or months to permeate to an organisation's followers."

"The world has shrunk," said Athena. "Two hundred years ago, many people didn't travel further than a few miles from where they were born. Regardless of what the activists of the day promoted. A message of love, or hate, took years to take hold within these shores. The outside world was unaware of what was happening here, and vice versa."

"When we follow that idea to its natural conclusion," said Phoenix, taking hold of Athena's hand, "our greatest fear is that a charismatic extremist emerges whose message spreads like wildfire. Then, instead of fighting a local threat, we could face a global conflict."

"What sort of world have we brought little Hope into?" sighed Athena.

"The cynic might say it's one with little hope," said Phoenix, with a wry smile, "but while people still fight against evil, our daughter will have a future. What she makes of it will be up to her."

"Will you be working again tomorrow?" Athena asked.

"Not if I can help it," replied Phoenix. "We deserve to spend the day with our daughter. The weather may not be great, but I fancy a trip to the coast."

"We'd better get to bed then if we intend to make an early start in the morning."

Phoenix did as instructed.

Chapter Seven

Monday, 14th July 2014

Athena and Phoenix arrived early for the first meeting of the week. They had enjoyed an afternoon of dodging the showers while in the resort of Bournemouth. Little Hope didn't appear to care; she enjoyed having her parents to herself for a change.

As the storm clouds blew away and a watery sun offered a brighter end to the day, they made their way home to Larcombe via Lymington.

Phoenix never missed an opportunity to visit Elizabeth, the yacht that had belonged to Erebus. He told Athena that being on board, even for an hour or two, helped him reconnect with the old gentleman.

"While this beautiful craft is at our disposal, his memory will never fade and die. I'm not one for visiting a family vault. I find no connection or consolation there. Onboard Elizabeth, among the equipment, books, and charts he equipped her with, I can sense him watching over me as I consider problems we face."

"Has he helped you come up with the right answers," asked Athena.

"I haven't heard a 'tut' if I'm wavering over a decision yet, if that's what you mean. Although, the ship's bell did emit a single ring once when I had finalised a planned mission. There was no one else on board, and the breeze was non-existent. That was spooky."

Phoenix spotted the ice-house party through the windows as they crossed the lawns.

"Here they come," he said. "Henry got home in one piece, by the looks of it,"

"I hope he and Sarah had a great weekend," said Athena, "we can't ask for details, of course. I'll ring Sarah tonight and squeeze the juicy gossip out of her."

"Won't she claim the rights of the confessional apply to matters of the bedchamber?"

"That's the other lot, Phoenix," said Athena. "Your religious knowledge needs a refresher course."

"I'll give it a miss," said Phoenix.

Minos and Alastor were next to arrive.

Giles, Artemis, and a cherubic Henry Case entered soon after.

"I know you worked part of this past weekend," Athena began, "but I trust you are ready for another busy week?"

Henry stifled a yawn.

In the background, he heard Athena running through the morning agenda and updating everyone on missions from other areas forwarded to her by Zeus. Henry had crept in under cover of darkness and reached his quarters in the stable block at eleven o'clock last night.

After the events of late Saturday afternoon, he and Sarah spent the evening cuddled up on her settee. However, there was no question of him staying the night. Sarah was reluctant to let him go. But when it was time for the barman to call time up the road at the pub, Sarah said that was the perfect time for him to leave.

"I need people leaving the pub to see you are driving away from here, Henry," she said. "I hope you will attend the morning service at St Mary's to listen to my sermon at eleven o'clock?"

"I look forward to it," said Henry.

After the service was over the following morning, the couple visited the pub for a lunchtime drink. Sarah had promised to cook dinner later. With the exertions of Saturday, Henry was hungry. The smells from the pub's kitchen only made matters worse.

"Let's drink up and get home," said Sarah.

"Are you still hungry, Henry?" she had asked him three hours later.

"Not in the slightest, darling," sighed Henry as he lay beside her.

"I meant for food, you goose," giggled Sarah, "let's shower and get dressed. We can still get something to eat at the pub."

"Alone, or together? The shower, I mean," Henry had asked.

"Alone," said Sarah, "we'll not make it out of the house otherwise,"

It had been half-past eight when he dropped Sarah back at the vicarage.

"Safe trip home, Henry," she had said as they kissed goodbye. "Call me, and write when you get a chance, won't you? It will seem months rather than weeks until Hope's christening. I can't wait for us to be together again."

"Is that okay, Henry?" asked Athena.

"I can't wait," replied Henry, startled by the intrusion on his reverie.

"I'm sure Kelly Dexter is eager to work with you, too," said Phoenix.

Henry realised he must have missed something important.

"We'll leave you two to assess the suitability of candidates from the lists Giles and Artemis compile," Athena continued, "while Hayden Vincent continues with the training schedule."

"Will do," said Henry, hoping Kelly Dexter knew what was happening. He needed to catch up with what he had missed while daydreaming.

"We need your report for the fourth of August when Ambrosia returns to Larcombe," added Phoenix.

"I shall give it my undivided attention," said Henry.

"What progress did you make, Giles?"

Giles told Athena and the others of the methods they were using in the ice-house to identify where the homeless ex-servicemen and women lived. Over the weekend, he and Artemis had traced eight hundred veterans.

"I don't wish to start the week with bad news," said Artemis, "but our initial research suggests we won't get the high positive return Ambrosia hoped. She might wish to believe the system has failed these seven thousand homeless souls. Somehow, they fell through the safety net and are entirely blameless for the state they find themselves in. That's not the case, I'm afraid."

"I feared as much," said Rusty. "When I was a serving soldier, some men liked to drink more than was good for them. Several combined that with using recreational drugs. So, it's not hard to imagine those parts of their life taking hold when they left the forces. Once the security blanket and camaraderie they enjoyed were removed, they undoubtedly struggled to come to terms with life in civvy street. Many may find it impossible to cope."

"In a depressingly large number of the cases we've looked at so far, their service records highlight problems well before they got discharged," said Giles.

"They had disciplinary issues," said Artemis, "and when they left their quarters, the conditions they left behind were a disgrace. The term 'shit tip' was often used to describe the state they lived in when off duty."

"So, when they found housing in the public or private sector," added Giles, "they were likely evicted by a housing association or a landlord. Either for rent arrears or not keeping their place clean and tidy."

"Thank you, Giles," said Athena, "it's not what we hoped to learn, but keep plugging away at the rest of the names on your list. If we can trace the entire seven thousand over the next three weeks, we will have a firmer grip on the potential number of Irregulars the operation will unearth."

"When can we start work on the balance of the eight hundred that survive Henry and Kelly's analysis?" asked Minos. "Finding suitable accommodation for them will take time."

"When I've discussed the matter with Kelly Dexter, we'll set up a system which releases details to you and Alastor every twenty-four hours," said Henry. "If that's acceptable?"

"That sounds perfect, Henry," said Alastor. "We'll compile lists of potential addresses in each region, then match your candidates with the nearest suitable accommodation."

Athena was anxious the meeting didn't get embroiled in too much detail.

"Minos," she said, "can I leave you to get this running smoothly?"

The former High Court judge nodded.

"We'll summarise where we stand ready for the fourth of next month, Athena," he confirmed.

"Do you want to tell the others what you're up to later in the week, Phoenix," Athena asked.

Artemis looked at Rusty. He hadn't spoken of what he and Phoenix had discussed in the orangery meetings over the past few days. Her partner didn't look up from the notes on the table in front of him.

"Rusty and I will head to the North East on Wednesday," Phoenix replied. "To carry out two planned missions against those responsible for the anti-Muslim attacks in Bradford and Newcastle. We expect to be home on Friday."

"Neither mission is related to organised crime or the Grid, then?" asked Artemis.

Phoenix paused for a while.

"We succeeded with our selective strikes against the Grid across the country. At first, I believed we could continue to cherry-pick soft targets as often as we wished. The objective was to draw Hanigan and the other gang bosses into the open. To expose them to the possibility of either being taken out by us or arrested by the authorities."

Phoenix stood and walked to the fireplace. He felt the presence of Erebus at the other end of the mantel.

"The further you delve into the characteristics of our UK crime groups, the more you realise how fluid they have become. They adapt rapidly. In the few months we've been on their case, several of their numbers shifted towards lucrative markets where detection is more difficult. These markets are less risky and less violent; therefore, our method of direct action might not be appropriate."

"The severity of the crime doesn't warrant their deaths, you mean?" asked Henry. "That's a shame."

It was the first bit of good news for Henry this morning. The prospect of violent criminals visiting the ice-house for his attention over the summer was fading. The last thing he needed was a full house of prisoners to handle when Sarah was at Larcombe. He realised that Artemis was speaking.

"Traditional crimes are still thriving," she said, "drugs and human trafficking show no signs of a downturn."

"True, yet fraud, counterfeiting, and vehicle crime are showing rapid growth. Bank robberies and jewellery heists occur now and then. But you're more likely to find these criminal gangs operating in the financial sector, in renewable energy, waste, and recycling. So to show you why the Grid's activities are getting harder to detect, perhaps Giles can explain."

"Try to keep it simple, Giles," said Rusty, "we're not all computer geeks."

"The modern criminal uses apps and encrypted messaging to evade the police," said Giles, "as a result, their online deals are less easy to trace. The Regulations of Investigatory Powers Act came into force fifteen years ago. As you will remember, there has been fierce debate around its use. The latest amendments are six months away. Telephone software has moved significantly in fifteen years, and gangs now possess sophisticated security levels. How the police secure communications data in the future will require firmer legislation and a change in their methodology."

"How do these changes affect Larcombe, and how do the ice-house teams capture data?" asked Alastor. "Are we in danger of missing vital information?"

Giles smiled.

"We don't face the problems the authorities do," he said, "we don't have to play by the rules. If Athena wants a wiretap, we don't need to apply for a warrant from the Home Secretary."

Phoenix returned to his seat alongside Athena.

"You can get an idea of the problems we face," he said. "We believe our intelligence-gathering systems are robust enough to keep us abreast of the competition. Stand still, though; we will see them disappear over the horizon. Athena and I will do everything we can to avoid that situation."

"Zeus and the others are aware a significant proportion of our budget must go on security," said Athena. "Of necessity, it will receive higher priority over the number of agents in the field. Without up-to-the-minute intelligence, those agents would chase shadows."

Athena sensed a sombre mood in the room.

"We must stay positive," she urged, "the enemy may constantly be changing, but it remains the enemy. Whether we target drug dealers, human traffickers, or those criminals conning the public out of their hard-earned savings in cyberspace, we're still upholding the core Olympus principles."

"Every crime has victims," said Phoenix, "I would remind you what Erebus told me the day after I arrived here: the police and the judiciary have weakened due to political correctness. Support from successive governments has been spineless. The days of handling crime with a firm hand and meaningful sentences are history. The results are clear. Organised crime now operates the length and breadth of this once great nation. The authorities will object to the suggestion these gangs act unchallenged. They will point to their success in removing criminals from the streets. Yet our experience tells us these are few and far between."

"Not only are they as rare as hen's teeth," added Minos, "but the punishment never fits the crime. I despair of the proliferation of suspended sentences. If we don't have enough prisons, then build more."

"Don't get Phoenix started," cautioned Rusty. "You know he believes the only suspended sentence should be at a rope's end."

"I was catching up on my reading over the weekend," said Phoenix. "It's OK, Minos and Alastor. Nothing you do is ever wasted. I apologise for falling behind. If and when Hugh Fraser takes up our offer, I'll be free to keep pace with the frequency of your reports. I was fascinated by your item on the Scottish criminal scene. Imagine how much simpler life would be if capital punishment still existed."

Minos nodded.

"Phoenix is right. A killer in a high-security Scottish prison went to jail for a minimum of eighteen years in 2003. He bludgeoned his victim to death. Then, a year ago, Police Scotland's Organised Crime and Counter-Terrorism Unit began to disrupt and eventually dismantle a drug empire. The convicted killer has been running a heroin ring from his prison cell, using a secret stash of ten mobile phones to arrange drug deals across Scotland. A family recycling firm was a front to help flood the country with heroin. When the police finally piece together the evidence, and the case gets to court, seven men will get charged with supplying heroin. The police caught those men after seizing a million pounds worth of heroin and amphetamine."

"Six months ago, police saw a family member with one of his couriers," continued Alastor, "but he palmed them off with a tale that the man was discussing the sale of a motor vehicle. He also said a visit to the home of another known villain was to buy a wide-screen television. They observed him hiding a drugs consignment under the bonnet of his car. According to the brother, none of the family had visited his brother in prison for years."

"It beggars belief it takes so long to tie down these cases," said Phoenix. "You can bet it will be another twelve months before they get this to court. The average time for prisoners on remand is hovering around ten weeks. High-profile cases such as this take longer because they're scared shitless they've not got every detail one-hundred per cent validated. Otherwise, the defence will seize on any miniscule infraction, and another bunch of criminals will escape justice."

"Is it that simple to get hold of mobile phones in prison?" asked Athena.

"I heard rumours while I was at Avonmouth," said Artemis, "that there wasn't much you couldn't get in many prisons across the country. Drugs are rife and have been for years. Violence is always bubbling under the surface. The staff are as vulnerable as the inmates."

"Let's remember what happened eleven years ago," said Phoenix, "a killer was imprisoned for eighteen years. I could excuse the system if that represented a life sentence, but my preference would be the return of the death penalty. The empire he constructed would not exist. The drugs he peddled, spreading misery across Scotland, might never have reached the streets. We're reaping the wind for an ill-judged decision fifty years ago."

Artemis broke the short silence that followed.

"My old boss, Phil Hounsell, who we know as Orion,"

she said, "used to tell me we had to work with the system as it was, not how we wished it would be. I believe he's amended his view since he quit the police service. His tasks for Olympus have often resulted in villains receiving far more than a slap on the wrist, yet he has been supportive of the action taken."

"We haven't had many cases to pass his way this year, have we?" asked Athena.

"Out of sight, out of mind, perhaps?" asked Alastor.

"Hayden Vincent speaks highly of his qualities," said Minos. "How do you think he might react to an offer?"

"To work here, at Larcombe Manor, do you mean?" asked Artemis.

"Would it be a problem?" asked Athena.

"Not for us two," said Rusty.

Artemis smiled at him. If only it were that simple. Not only had she and Phil had a one-night stand, but Phoenix had been a constant thorn in his side. There were twenty deaths DS Phil Hounsell knew were committed by Colin Bailey before he 'drowned' in Pulteney Weir four years ago. So how would her old boss react to meeting Phoenix and discovering his nemesis was still alive?

The cosmetic surgery might mask his identity from the man in the street, but could it fool a policeman who had been 'old school'; in other words, he knew his job inside-out.

"Orion's married, with children, and lives three miles away," said Artemis, stepping into the minefield, trying to think her way through to safety on the other side. "So, he wouldn't need to live on the premises. He could operate as a daily visitor to Larcombe. It might be possible if he reported to Hayden Vincent in the stable block and kept out of the main building and the ice-house."

Phoenix and Athena saw this avenue was fraught with dangers.

"Are we convinced we have a role for him?" asked Athena.

"With the change of emphasis in organised crime gangs I outlined earlier, there will be an increasing role for operators like Orion," said Phoenix. "As the years go by, it's Rusty, Henry and me who will become less active. We'll become dinosaurs."

"We're agreed then?" asked Athena. "I'll ask Hayden to approach Orion, to see whether he's interested in a permanent role with Olympus. If Orion says no, we will continue using his services at arm's length. If he agrees, then I suggest we thrash out how to handle accommodating him. I'm keener than anyone sat around this table to protect our secrets."

Different people had differing views on what they had heard when the meeting ended.

Henry returned to the ice-house with Giles in silence. His colleague was already planning the afternoon hunt for homeless veterans. Henry was thankful for the lack of interrogations he might expect to carry out this summer but disappointed that his role at Larcombe might shrink in the long term. What if it disappeared altogether? Was he ready to retire? Would Sarah be prepared to throw her lot in with a retiree? Gosh, things were never easy, were they?

Artemis and Rusty headed for their apartments. She wondered how the prospect of Orion being on-site up to five days a week would affect their relationship. She loved Rusty; and hoped they might marry and have children one day. Phoenix and Athena had shown they could succeed; despite their dangerous work.

Rusty knew the risks involved in bringing Orion into the fold.

He wouldn't allow anything or anyone to come between him and Artemis, but perhaps the most significant threat was to Phoenix. If his identity emerged, the Olympus Project's security would be breached, and Larcombe Manor's disguise as a charitable organisation would be exposed as a fraud. Everything Erebus and the others had worked for was in danger of being lost. That could not happen.

Phoenix and Athena had reached their apartment. Maria-Elena was playing with Hope.

"Thanks, Maria-Elena; you can go to lunch now," Athena said, "we'll see you at two."

The Spanish nanny had waved bye-bye to Hope and left the family alone.

"Hello, you," said Phoenix, picking up the little bundle that was so important to them.

"I'll make us lunch, darling," said Athena.

"After we've eaten, we need to talk," said Phoenix.

Hope used the pincer grab to get chunks of banana and mini rice cakes into her mouth. They thought she wasn't listening to their conversation. Little did they know what an interest their daughter took in Olympus affairs.

Her parents were discussing a man called Orion, who was very talented. He was a valuable agent for Mummy's Olympus Project, but Daddy called him a rude name. Hope didn't know what it meant yet, but Mummy told Daddy off for using it in front of her, let alone when their daughter was in the room. So, it must have been naughty.

"How the heck can we invite Orion here, day in and day out, without him seeing Artemis or me at some point?" Phoenix asked.

"The fact Artemis *is* working here could offer the solution," replied Athena.

"How on earth do you come to that conclusion?" he asked.

"Calm down and think it through," she said. "Artemis left the police force after a chance meeting with Rusty during the attempted terrorist attack on the Royal Family in Bristol. Her old boss didn't know where she was planning to work. If he had any reason to look her up, he would have searched for Zara Wheeler and found a dead end. Giles made certain of that. Once she joined us here, her old persona disappeared. It would be simple enough to explain her presence. Her investigative skills made her a target for Olympus. We headhunted her, and she's been working in our intelligence section. The sensitive material she handles means contact with her old life is restricted. So, to the outside world, she needed to be anonymous. Should Orion dig deeper, Rusty can provide any additional protective shield she requires."

"So, it's only me we need to disguise? Where do I buy a fake beard and glasses?"

"I think the sooner you and Rusty head north, the better," said Athena. "This racist mission has got you agitated."

"When I was a young teenager, I suffered at the hands of two gangs of bullies. One gang was white, and one was black. They made my life miserable in equal measure; I took revenge on both in time. I've always been a fan of multiculturism. Good people are good people, regardless of colour or creed. I object to villains, and the names on my list for later this week have few redeeming features. I don't see this as a racist mission; we're merely ridding the world of vile, objectionable creatures. Now, back to Orion and how we manage this situation."

"Timing will be our best way forward," said Athena, "we get him on-site at nine in the morning. If you're at home, you'll be in the meeting room; if you're on a mission or at an Olympus meeting, his presence isn't an issue. Hayden will need to find an office that doesn't overlook the lawns. That will free you up to visit the ice-house or the pool during the day. He can leave between five and six o'clock, depending on his workload. It would be best if you were in your office or with us having our evening meal whenever you're at Larcombe. Do you see a problem with that?"

It works for me, thought Hope.

"It sounds simple when you lay it out like that," said Phoenix. "I'll need to be wary when I'm in the orangery, the pool, or the fitness room. Can Hayden keep him tied to desk duties, though? The last thing I need is him wandering around when we're playing in the gardens with Hope."

"Tasks we've given his firm so far have involved a mix of office and fieldwork. Hayden will need to ensure he keeps the two quite separate. If there are places he needs to visit, he doesn't come to Larcombe on those days."

"He has an office in Bath, doesn't he, and staff? What will happen to them?"

"He has one permanent member of staff and two temporary security personnel. Our offer will have to exclude anyone other than Orion himself. We will make the financial reward attractive enough to ease the pain of no longer running his firm. If we need to sweeten the pot further and provide a redundancy package for the others, I'm sure Zeus will approve."

"If you want the best, you pay the price," said Phoenix.

"Hayden thinks it's a price worth paying," said Athena.

"He was a good copper. I'll give him that," said Phoenix. "Nobody else has ever come close to catching me. OK, make him an offer. I'll cancel the false beard and glasses."

At last, thought Hope. Can I get out of this chair for a cuddle before my afternoon nap?

Chapter Eight

Wednesday, 16th July 2014

"It wasn't the same, was it?" said Rusty as he emerged from the lift.

"No, but get used to it," sighed Phoenix. "Trips to the armoury for a few minutes of idle banter with Bazza and Thommo are finished. Since they came back above ground to join the training teams, Dad's Army has moved in. It's efficient if slower these days."

"Where did these two guys come from?"

"Somewhere in Africa. A former colony where the existing government is only clinging onto power by using excessive force. Our two agents were too old to keep an effective lid on things in the hot sun. Two younger agents selected from the London teams have replaced them."

"Nice work if you can get it,"

"I recall your training sessions mentioning posts in exotic locations four years ago," said Phoenix, tuning the radio to his favourite station. "Yet, here I am heading for

Bradford. Apart from the Irish mission, I haven't made it out of the country."

"Your fault, not mine," Rusty replied, turning the volume down on the radio to give his ears a break. "First, you made yourself irreplaceable while Erebus was in charge, then you married the boss. Even if your halo slips, she won't send you on an overseas posting. Leave that volume alone; we've got four hours before we hit Bradford."

Phoenix concentrated on the road ahead. Negotiating the junction between the M4 and M5 was always a nightmare. The journey across the country to the M1 would get them there by one o'clock if they didn't make a stop.

"Did you have a good breakfast?" he asked.

"Only managed to grab a slice of toast as I dashed out; I cut it fine."

"I only had a bowl of cereal. Maybe we can stop at around eleven for a bite to eat. Would you check out the nearest service station on our route that fits our schedule?"

Rusty consulted his mobile phone.

"There's one not long after we join the M1," he said.

In the end, they arrived in Bradford at half-past two. The all-day breakfast and a mug of coffee at the service station had set them up for the day.

"Let's use the NCP car park in the town centre," said Phoenix, "it's expensive, dirty, and crowded."

"As good a way of hiding in plain sight as any," replied Rusty, "and these scruffy clothes you told me to wear will help us fit in with our surroundings."

Phoenix and Rusty spent the afternoon sightseeing. They weren't enjoying the local architecture or the parks and gardens; their targets were local pubs and cafes — the afternoon haunts of their targets, the Ferris brothers.

"What's going on over there?" asked Rusty as they passed a construction site.

"This is the hole-in-the-ground development that's been inching forward at a snail's pace for fifteen years," Phoenix replied. "Until January, they had a temporary park here. It will be ready for business in eighteen months, with around seventy-five shops planned."

"I remember it now," said Rusty. "Protesters staged a sit-in a few years back because nothing seemed to get sorted."

"A common theme this far north. They're always complaining about being at the end of the queue. Let's drop into a bar for a while. I need a rest. What's this street called?"

"We're on Cheapside," said Rusty, "it sounds like a place our men might while away an afternoon."

The first bar they visited was chrome and glass, with high stools and prices. They didn't stay long.

"Why don't we move up towards Manningham Lane?" asked Rusty.

"It's a hike back to where we parked the vehicle," groaned Phoenix.

"Fair enough, but the closer it is to hand when the time comes, the better."

They fetched the people carrier from the car park and switched to St Thomas Street.

"This is near the mosque," said Rusty. "Are these guys brazen enough to keep drinking in this district after what they did?"

"Yeah, the Ferris brothers have enough neck to return to the crime scene," said Phoenix as they strolled up the pavement in the late afternoon sunshine. "They don't believe they did anything wrong."

"The graffiti has gone, and the glass replaced," said

Rusty, looking around him. "I doubt if the mosque was so easy to get tidy."

"The faithful have a choice of religious buildings close by," said Phoenix, "they'll be alright. The loss of Farhad Kirmani would have hit the community harder than a mere building."

They both spotted the pub on the opposite corner as they approached a road junction.

"Bingo," they echoed.

"This must be Bradford shabby chic," muttered Rusty as he pushed the door open.

"Or Eighties' retro," whispered Phoenix.

The interior was dark and unwelcoming. A door had been propped open at the rear, and the agents could see a small group of smokers gathered in a courtyard. The barman waited thirty seconds before he glanced up from his newspaper.

"What can I get you?" he asked.

"Two pints of lager," Phoenix replied.

"Not from around here, are you?" said the barman.

"Does it make a difference to the lager you serve us or the price you charge?" asked Rusty, leaning on the counter.

"Only making conversation," the barman shrugged.

Phoenix stared over the barman's shoulder. The smokers had returned to their seats.

The reflection in the mirror behind the bar showed three figures. All scruffily dressed, middle-aged, and loud. It wasn't hard to spot the family resemblance. It would appear that Gary, Terry, and Duncan Ferris spent their leisure time together. The laughter and crude language suggested they had been in this bar, or another one close by, throughout the afternoon.

"Stick the telly on, Shaun," Gary shouted. Shaun, the

barman, found the remote by the till and pointed it at the screen.

The TV showed racing from a nondescript trio of courses across the country, and the first race on the various evening cards was underway. The weather on the screen looked sunny and bright in the parade ring as the runners and riders prepared to do battle.

Inside the bar, it was dark and smelled of stale smoke, cheap spirits, and sweat. Rusty had to admit Phoenix's choice of old, casual clothes had been the right call. They looked unremarkable, the same as their drinking companions — a perfect look to blend in with the crowd.

The Ferris brothers continued to drink while watching the action on the wide-screen television. Several empty spirit glasses and imported lager bottles sat on the table in front of them.

When the horses left the starting stalls, the conversation was hushed. Then, as the race entered the final two furlongs, they became agitated and shouted encouragement. At the winning post, Gary was half out of his seat, punching the air. His brothers thumped the table in frustration.

"Get in," cried Gary, "that's the way to do it. Get us a round of our usual shots, Shaun."

Shaun did as he got told.

Phoenix and Rusty stayed where they were, seemingly ignorant of what went on around them. The pint of lager they were drinking had been a pound cheaper than they would have paid in the south, and they savoured every drop. Their minds needed to be sharp when the time came to act.

Phoenix looked again in the mirror towards Gary Ferris. Good to see he was enjoying his last day on this earth.

Shaun delivered a tray of shots to the table. Phoenix

learned that the Ferris brothers enjoyed a Redheaded Slut. The crude comments that followed five seconds later as the drinks disappeared had nothing to do with the alcohol. These three were vile creatures who didn't deserve to live. Phoenix had to hold himself in check and not turn around and shoot them where they sat.

"Time to drink up," said Phoenix. "We need to get out of here."

Shaun didn't look up when they left. He was studying the newspaper. Another race started, and the brothers had money on it again. As the agents left the bar and emerged into the sunlight, they could hear their braying voices getting louder and louder.

"Gary, Terry, and Duncan," said Rusty. "Any idea which football team their father supported?"

"Daft question," said Phoenix.

"My bet is Leeds United, not Bradford City. Several players called Gary and Terry have worn the white shirt, but there was only one Duncan McKenzie."

"You never cease to amaze me with your knowledge of sporting trivia," said Phoenix, "but that's not important. We need to find a vantage point where we can keep an eye on the front of the bar. We have to see them leave."

"There's a restaurant over on the other side of the road. Let's cross over and check out the view. I'll order food. You grab that table by the window."

"You had better make it a slice of cake or a roll," said Phoenix. "We may need to take it with us if they drink up and make a move."

"They have a dozen more races to watch yet. They won't quit until nine o'clock at the earliest. I'm ordering a hot meal. This Caribbean menu sounds tasty."

Phoenix groaned. He loved the food but killing people after jerk chicken wasn't a great idea.

Their food tasted as good as Rusty predicted. The bar door opened and closed several times during the evening, but the Ferris brothers never appeared. The restaurant closed at ten. Rusty paid the bill at five to ten while Phoenix visited the toilets.

"Keep an eye on the pub door while I pay a visit," he said to Phoenix when he returned.

As soon as Rusty left, the street came alive with people. Men, women, and children emerged from the side-roads, from flats above closed-up shops and restaurants. The Muslim community was on its way to the closest mosque.

The numbers told Phoenix that this was no ordinary occurrence. It was due to the murder of the well-loved imam. The bar door opened, and three drunken louts staggered into the street. It was the Ferris brothers.

The insults spewed from their mouths; they spat at the men and women as they passed. It turned Phoenix's stomach. Rusty appeared on his shoulder.

The restaurant owner joined them by the door.

"They have walked this road every night since last Thursday. Since the mosque fire and the murder of the imam."

"Has this abuse been happening every night?" asked Rusty. "Why weren't the police informed?"

"It has been very peaceful until tonight. Those men hate all foreigners. When they drink too much, they cause trouble. Time for you to go," he said. "I have to lower my steel shutters to protect my windows."

Once they stood on the pavement outside, Gary Ferris spotted them. He recognised them as the strangers in the bar earlier.

"What are you looking at?" he yelled.

"I'll fetch the transport," said Phoenix, "you keep them from killing anyone,"

The crowds had thinned, and only a few stragglers hurried past Rusty. They sensibly stayed on the opposite side of the road from their abusers.

Rusty walked across and joined the brothers.

"We were just heading out," he said, ignoring how the brothers circled him.

Rusty wasn't intimidated. He could see the looks of confusion spread on their faces. Their macho display was usually enough to cause people to back off. It was three to one. What was wrong with this guy?

"Where are you heading?" asked Terry Ferris, standing chest to chest with Rusty.

"Out towards Shipley, that's where you want to go, isn't it?" replied Rusty without taking a backward step. Instead, he stood calmly, with his hands in his jeans pockets.

"How the fuck did you know that?" asked Duncan.

"Well, you wouldn't live in Heaton or any other no-go areas, would you?"

"Not a chance," said Gary. "Immigrants have taken over those streets. Even the school I went to doesn't have an English kid there these days. They get taught by their kind, spreading their message of hate. We're aliens in our city, mate. The country has turned to shit, and it's time we fought back."

It surprised Rusty that Gary Ferris had even been to school. He showed no sign of having learned a thing. A horn beeped a few yards away that told Rusty Phoenix had arrived.

Once inside the people carrier at the car park, Phoenix pressed the button that raised the glass partition. That sealed the rear passenger compartment from the driver and passenger seats. He opened the back passenger door and lowered the nearside window.

"Hop in, lads," he shouted, "we'll save you the taxi fare. Just give us a shout when we get to where you need to get out."

The three brothers looked up and down the deserted Manningham Lane. The Muslim worshippers were praying in a nearby building. No fun would be had without hanging around until they walked home. The taxi fare was dearer if they left it until midnight. This was a free ride. No contest. The three men clambered inside.

Rusty got into the passenger seat. Phoenix locked the rear doors and set off up the Lane.

"The transport section did a nice job," Rusty said.

"The first part worked okay," said Phoenix, "let's see how this bit works."

He pressed another button on the fascia.

As they headed out of the city towards Shipley, snoring came from the back.

"They would have nodded off anyway, with all the booze they've drunk," said Rusty as they slowed to a halt at the rear of the abandoned cinema.

"We won't get a peep out of them for an hour, according to Henry," said Phoenix. "Let's get them secured and then move them indoors."

Fifteen minutes later, the Ferris brothers had been transferred and gagged; they were bound hand and foot and sitting on the balcony floor. There were sections of rusted seats whose fabric cushions had rotted away long ago. The musty smell of the building and the stale beer, cigarette smoke, and sweat provided by the Ferris brothers resulted in a potent mix.

Rusty looked to see if their prisoners were still unconscious. The electricity to the building got disconnected years ago, and the only light came from a lamp on the helmet Phoenix wore.

"The last film to be shown here was over fifty years ago," said Phoenix.

"What did they use the building for after that?" asked Rusty.

"A casino, for a while, and then it was a bingo hall, of course. Entertainment for the masses."

"A sad place to end your days," said Rusty.

"For the bingo players or these three?" asked Phoenix with a wry grin. "I'll be back in a tick."

He left Rusty alone in the dark. He returned, holding a large canvas bag. Phoenix set it on the balcony floor, where it made a loud thud that echoed around the empty auditorium.

"Don't get sentimental. The Ferris's don't deserve any sympathy. Farhad Kirmani's death was neither accidental nor unlucky because the fire brigade was slow to react to the emergency call. They've got it coming to them. I want them to be awake, so they know what's happening and why they will die."

"What have you got planned? Nothing too quick or painless, I hope?" asked Rusty.

"The plan is for them to have time to contemplate the error of their ways," said Phoenix. "Let's leave it at that."

The two agents waited until the three brothers recovered from the effects of the drug one by one. They struggled against their bonds. They tried to hurl threats and abuse at their captors, but the gags prevented any from reaching Phoenix or Rusty.

"Welcome back," said Phoenix when the brothers were

wide awake. "I imagine you're too thick to have worked out why you're here?"

The struggling and muffled words encouraged Phoenix to continue. He hadn't heard any objections. So he asked Rusty to put the brothers in a seated position to look them in the eye, and they could see what lay in store.

Phoenix unzipped the bag.

Rusty watched the reaction on the three faces as Phoenix removed the staple gun.

"Time to test it out," he said.

Phoenix walked across to where Gary Ferris sat and kicked his legs apart. He pointed the gun towards Gary's crotch, seeing the raw terror in the man's eyes. A slight adjustment sent the nail deep into the wooden floor, two inches from any flesh. Gary screamed, anyway.

"Not so much fun when you're on the receiving end, is it, Gary?" he asked.

The three brothers squirmed on the floor, wondering what was coming next.

"Your father was a racist. He poisoned your minds. Ever since your teens, you have been in and out of trouble with the law. Violence is your stock in trade. A good man hopes that when he dies, he leaves behind a legacy — something worthwhile he did while on this earth. Gary, your son, has been poisoned by you and your brothers. What you will leave behind is a brown stain. We will try to correct the path your son, Jack, is following, so he can still do something good with his life. I only pray we're not too late."

Phoenix checked the staple gun was fully loaded. This was only for show. He knew it would need only two or three shots each to achieve his desired result.

"I won't lie," he said, "this will hurt like hell. In the medical books I've read, the blood loss from your injuries will be fatal. But where's the fun in that? These nails will damage your liver and major arteries in such a way it will take you twenty to thirty minutes to bleed out. Time for you to think about what you've done. Time to work out what you'll say in your defence when you meet your maker. If indeed you do."

The squirming and muffled yells continued. Phoenix stepped forward; he delivered three well-directed shots into each man's side. After the noise had quietened and the echoes had died, he and Rusty could only hear the whimpering.

Phoenix placed the staple gun back in the canvas bag. They walked to the staircase leading to the ground floor, and as they neared the bottom, Phoenix switched off the helmet lamp.

They emerged from the abandoned cinema onto a moonlit street. The two agents sat in the people carrier until dawn broke. Phoenix went back to the cinema alone.

"That's it done," he said when he returned. "We're patriotic when we take revenge on these criminals."

"Sorry?" asked Rusty.

"The balcony floor was a sea of red. Add the blue and white from Scotland, and there you have it. Now that's done," he said, "our next call is on young Jack Ferris. We'll pick him up when he leaves home, and you can have a chat. By the time we reach the school gates, we need the message to have registered."

"Understood," said Rusty.

Phoenix lowered the glass partition.

"This worked well. I think we'll hang on to it. I might find a use for it on another job."

"Remember to re-stock the drug dispenser, though," said Rusty, "or things might not go as smoothly."

"Time for a nap, and then we'll get off to Shipley," said Phoenix.

Rusty nodded off, with an image of the Union Jack floating in front of him. Phoenix was right. That was what they fought to preserve. The country they had known in their childhood when the flag had meant something. The limp-wristed liberals and the PC brigade had almost demolished that proud nation inside a generation.

Thursday, 17th July 2014

Jack Ferris strolled along the pavement. His mother had been in a strop this morning. Dad hadn't come home last night; that wasn't his fault. She knew he was with his brothers. His mother moaned that they had probably got too drunk to find their way home. If he ended up at another woman's place, then she'd have his guts for garters. Jack had had enough of the aggravation. He didn't notice the vehicle alongside him until a voice called his name.

"Jack? Jack Ferris? Get in. We've got news about your Dad."

Jack didn't recognise the man sitting in the people carrier's dark interior. The door was open, and Jack leaned in to see what this bloke knew about his father. The next thing he knew, a bag covered his head, and he was dragged inside and face down on the floor. The vehicle sped away from the pavement, out of the estate towards the city centre.

"Where are you taking me," yelled Jack.

"To school," said Phoenix, "but first, you've got to pay someone a visit."

"We know what you did," said Rusty, "and you have two

choices. You can apologise to the ladies you offended, respect people from different cultures and creeds, or suffer the consequences like your father."

"What do you mean?" said Jack.

"We've got bad news. It's you and your Mum, Michelle; from now on, your Dad and his brothers are dead," said Rusty. "The police will learn where to find the bodies later."

Jack Ferris went very quiet.

"How long?" Rusty asked Phoenix.

"Two minutes, and we'll be at Nilima Thakur's house," he replied.

"Did you hear that, Jack? Two minutes to decide whether you live or die. Your choice."

Phoenix pulled up on a stretch of waste ground one hundred yards from Nilima's house. He phoned the number Artemis had provided for Parveen Chowdhury.

"Mrs Chowdhury? I believe you heard from a female colleague of mine regarding Jack Ferris. That's correct. He's upset that he caused you so much distress. We're hopeful he will meet with you and your daughter, face to face, to apologise. Could you get to your daughter's house in fifteen minutes? That's terrific. A gentleman from the authority concerned with victim support will drop Jack at the door. Could we impose upon you further to take him to the school gates afterwards? I hope everything goes well. Many thanks. Goodbye."

"It's time to make up your mind," said Phoenix, turning to Jack, "what happened last week can't define you. You have a chance to change the way your life's going. Grab it."

Jack was still coming to terms with the news of his father's death. Uncle Terry and Uncle Duncan too? He didn't want to die. He wanted his Mum. Jack nodded his head as hard as he could.

"Okay, okay, I'll do it," he cried. "I never meant it, not really. I flipped after a lousy day at school. I only said things my Dad said all the time. My grandfather was the same. It wasn't nice, but even though I learned better at school, at home, there was nothing but anger and resentment."

"That's good, Jack," said Rusty, "let everything out that way when you meet Mrs Thakur and Mrs Chowdhury. Remember what I said. We know where you live. One word to the police concerning this morning, or one word out of line towards your Muslim neighbours, and we'll be back. It won't end so pleasantly, I can promise."

Jack Ferris was scared shitless. He would say anything to get out of this vehicle. Jack prayed they wouldn't remove the bag and let him catch even a glimpse of their faces. If he did, he knew they would kill him in a heartbeat. He needed his Mum. She had him to look after her if it was true his Dad had died. He had to grow up quick. He vowed never to get mixed up in any trouble, racial or otherwise if these men let him apologise.

Phoenix watched the Thakur house. An old Nissan Micra spluttered its way into the driveway, and an elderly lady got out. She rang the doorbell, and when it opened, she walked in.

"We're good to go," said Phoenix.

Rusty opened the rear door. He pushed Jack out onto the pavement, holding him by the wrist.

"I'm taking off the hood, Jack," he said, "don't think of looking back, not for one second. The house you want is number one hundred and eighty-six, on the left-hand side. We'll wait until you've gone inside to make your apologies. Then, in three minutes, we'll call to check. If the ladies give you the all-clear, we'll have gone when you come out. Keep your nose clean, and you'll never see us again. Understood?"

Jack Ferris nodded; Rusty removed the hood. Jack hurried away from the people carrier and along the street; he never looked back. He checked the numbers as he walked. It was the one with the net curtains and a Micra parked behind the Volvo.

Jack took a deep breath and rang the bell.

Phoenix and Rusty watched him from a distance. They saw the door open., and the young man entered. Phoenix started the engine.

"Aren't we going to wait?" asked Rusty.

"After the talking-to you gave him, I reckon he'll grow up to be a model citizen. You frightened the life out of me."

Chapter Nine

Thursday, 17th July 2014

"Time to move on to our next appointment," said Phoenix.

He handed Rusty the keys to the people carrier. A phone call to Parveen Chowdhury confirmed Jack Ferris had been the epitome of contrite. They had tea and biscuits with her daughter and grandchild before driving him to the school gates.

"I sat and watched him go in," she told Phoenix. "He even turned and waved to us when he reached the entrance."

"That's good to hear," Phoenix said to Rusty after ending the call. "He'll need all the support he can get in the coming weeks, and his mother will need him to grow up fast."

Phoenix called Giles in the ice-house.

"We're off to Newcastle, Giles. Can you take care of two things for me, please? Send a clean-up crew to the old cinema in Shipley. Remove any evidence that could be traced back to Olympus. Then, can you arrange for an anonymous tip-off to the Bradford police? It would be a shame to cause further damage to the interior of such a classic piece of architecture by leaving trash piled up inside for longer than necessary."

"No problem, Phoenix," said Giles. "Congratulations on a successful mission. One piece of news for you. Athena received confirmation this morning from Hugh Fraser. He's agreed to come south to work with you. Hugh arrives at Larcombe on Monday, the eighteenth of August."

"Terrific," replied Phoenix. "I knew he'd see sense. Scotland was a waste of his talent."

Rusty was in charge of the radio this morning. Phoenix found the bland music and inane conversation helped him grab welcome sleep. It was preferable to being awake and having to suffer.

Rusty chose the A19 for the trip north; time wasn't pressing. It would take him the best part of three hours to travel one hundred miles. Their first task on arrival was to get to the safe house. Another shrewd purchase by Olympus.

The last time it was used was in April when Maurice Kelly and his wife Dierdre had stayed there hiding from Hugo Hanigan and the Grid. The Kellys were now safe in the Irish Republic, enjoying their retirement. If Hugo's gunmen had caught up with them in Jarrow, things would have turned ugly.

"How far will we be from Cowgate?" asked Phoenix.

"Ah, you're awake," said Rusty. "We're five minutes away from the safe house. Perfect timing."

"You turned off the radio," Phoenix replied.

"It was one o'clock. The news can be depressing," said

Rusty, "and, in answer to your question, five miles, so ten minutes if I get my foot down in this thing."

"A week ago, the Mullen twins were picked up as persons of interest in Solomon Hussein's murder."

"How did their brief get them out so fast?" asked Rusty.

"Years of practice," replied Phoenix, "the lads have been in trouble since they reached double figures. They're only nineteen now, and the list of offences they've amassed would fill two sheets of A4. He had a list of family members prepared to swear they were at a family celebration."

"Birthday? Wedding?" asked Rusty.

"Their uncle, Phil Dwyer, came out of jail. He held a big party in a place on Argyle Street. Hundreds of people attended. The venue is only a mile from the kebab shop where Solomon Hussein died. They could have left, taken a cab, or even walked to the kebab shop. We know how scattered and indistinct the CCTV images were. The police were hoping for witnesses to confirm their suspicions or for material evidence to turn up at the scene. Instead, they got a wall of silence and a bullshit alibi for the twins from blood relatives. The police had no choice but to let them loose."

"So, they've gone to ground on the Cowgate estate?" asked Rusty.

Phoenix nodded.

"Why was the uncle in prison?" Rusty asked.

"He battered a Muslim taxi driver back in 2007. Dwyer skipped paying a fare late at night, and the driver tried to stop him from running away. He waved a baseball bat in Dwyer's face. Dwyer wrestled it from him and left him bleeding in the gutter."

"He only served seven years for that?" muttered Rusty. "If we've got time, can't we pay him a visit later?"

"The safe house is just around the corner," said

Phoenix. "Let's get settled in, then discuss our plans for the Mullen twins. Phil Dwyer will keep for another day."

They spent the rest of the afternoon moving their gear indoors, checking the level of provisions, and then driving to the nearest supermarket for essentials.

"I'll order us a pizza for delivery at six," said Phoenix, "then we can have the evening to ourselves."

"Is there anything good on TV?" asked Rusty.

"No idea. I meant we could get stuck into finding the Mullens twins and correcting the fault in the system that let them walk."

"Giles and Artemis are one hundred per cent convinced these two were among the ones responsible?"

"Yes, and to make sure, when we get hold of them, I intend to use that nail gun again to get them to confess."

Later in the evening, after demolishing the pizza, Phoenix contacted Giles at Larcombe Manor.

"Do you have an update on the whereabouts of Terry and Dale Mullen?" he asked.

"After they walked free last week, they returned to the Cowgate estate. They haven't returned to the bright lights since then. Our bet is a family member has warned them to stay low for a while. The Dwyer gang have more than a toehold on organised crime in the region. The word on the street is that the twins got an earful of abuse from Phil and Annie Dwyer for getting involved in the Hussein business."

"Who's Annie Dwyer?" asked Phoenix.

"Phil's younger sister," said Giles. "He's forty-eight, never done an honest day's work. She's recently turned forty and is the brains of the operation."

"That makes sense," said Phoenix, "considering the assault on the taxi driver."

"Phil was in trouble as a juvenile. Not unusual for

teenagers on the Cowgate. Many grow out of it and get the hell out if they can. Phil stayed near his roots and progressed to organised crime. He's been successful in financial terms but not in staying out of jail. Since he turned eighteen, he's split his time fifty-fifty between the inside and the outside."

"And Annie, how has she fared?" asked Phoenix.

"Kept a clean sheet, so far," Giles replied. "I'll forward everything Artemis has gathered on the estate and the Dwyer clan to give you the background to what you're facing. We have the current address for Terry and Dale in the file, although extracting the Mullen twins without a knock-on effect will be tricky. You need to tread with care."

"Don't I always, Giles?" said Phoenix and ended the call.

Rusty had been clearing away the plates, cutlery, and two Heineken cans. Phoenix always kept a tight rein on the drinks when they had work to do. He picked up the laptop from the table.

"You've got mail," he said, "to coin a phrase."

"Find us a route through this estate, Rusty," said Phoenix. "We need to get in, lift the twins, and get out in no time flat. We'll interrogate them here, deal with them, arrange a clean-up of the safe house as a precaution, and then get home before the morning meeting tomorrow."

"Are you serious?" Rusty queried. "You heard Giles. This mob are well-organised and prone to violence."

"We manage this gang the same way as any Grid members. They don't dictate to us. We decide when we'll attack. They must learn that nowhere is safe. Olympus, their unseen enemy, can strike at will. It's all in the execution of the plan; the Mullen twins need to pay for their crime. Justice must be swift. We can't rely on the police or the courts to do the job. The authorities will wait for Terry and Dale Mullen to slip up. It might be a year or two and a dozen offences later, and they will make a big deal of finally getting their man. That's a joke. We sort it out tonight, and none of those crimes will ever get committed."

Rusty opened the files that Giles and Artemis had collated. He found the house number and planned the route they would take. Rusty called his partner at Larcombe. Artemis was now in their apartment; her shift had ended.

"Hi there," said Rusty, "I need help. Can you confirm the twins are at the address you've given? Now, at this moment?"

"Hang on," said Artemis, "let me check. We have agents on the scene. They're running a mobile fish and chip van; they have monitoring equipment in addition to the deep-fat fryers. The images inside the ground-floor flat show one twin in his bedroom and the other watching TV in the main room. They're indoors for the night."

"Thanks for that. I'll see you tomorrow. Goodbye," said Rusty.

"Short and sweet," said Phoenix.

"She is," said Rusty. "But we didn't have time for a chat. Not if you and I want to leave here by five in the morning."

"I suggest we spend until a quarter to nine studying these files," said Phoenix, "then we start our mission."

The background data on the Cowgate made for grim reading. The bright lights, wine bars and restaurants on the banks of the Tyne were three miles away, yet the two areas were worlds apart. Newcastle's past relied on heavy industry and shipbuilding. Thirty years ago, the decline had taken hold with a vengeance. The banks of the river now showed signs of recovery; the art gallery, the Millennium bridge.

Hordes of party-goers flocked to the streets and nightclubs, while poverty and despair were a short drive away.

Teenagers roam the estate at night. Families complain about the number of drug addicts making their lives a misery. Parents can't afford the bus fare to send their kids to school. If you wanted to know where Britain's forgotten people lived, this estate was the answer. Regeneration projects have taken place over the years to improve the physical fabric of the estate. Nevertheless, the three thousand residents continue to live in one of the most deprived areas in the country.

The area has the highest teenage birth rate in the city. Domestic violence is commonplace. Almost half of those eligible for work are unemployed or on incapacity benefits. Reported crime is higher than the city average. A third of kids reaching school leaving age go no further; they fall into the abyss that holds those not in education, employment or training. Terry and Dale Mullen were now nineteen. They had spent over two years scraping an existence living off their wits. They were in the vanguard of the lost generation of feral kids who inhabited Cowgate's lawless streets.

At nine o'clock, the two agents were in the people carrier and heading for Cowgate.

As they drove onto the estate, Rusty noted the properties with gardens full of stinging nettles, fly-tipped washing machines, discarded mattresses and sofas. Yet, here and there were well-tended, well-looked-after houses, and he shook his head.

"This is the Bent Triangle in Manchester again," he said. "A few poor beggars swimming against the tide. If only they could harness that community spirit, they might drag themselves out of the mire."

"Maybe," said Phoenix, "but the damage runs deep.

Little has replaced the manufacturing jobs these people did in the old days. As a result, the kids on this estate can't aspire to the high-tech, computer-based jobs that have sprung up in the new economy. They have many of the same phones, tablets, and TVs as their counterparts in the city's affluent areas, but their parents have had to borrow to pay for them."

"Which is where the Dwyer family come in," said Rusty, "a bunch of bloody loan sharks."

"We'll switch our attention to them later," said Phoenix, "this is where we need to be, isn't it?"

The Olympus agents in the fish and chip van were still selling its produce. Phoenix parked twenty yards up the road and studied the faces in the queue.

"The twins aren't outside fetching their supper," he muttered, "and this group of young kids and senior citizens don't look like the local mafia. We go ahead as planned."

Phoenix drove into a side street opposite the van. At the next junction, he turned left, switched off his headlights, and crept along to the end of the cul-de-sac. He turned the vehicle around, ready for a sharp exit.

Once outside, he and Rusty donned their balaclavas, checked their weapons, and pushed open the back gate. The weeds and nettles stood waist-high. Rusty narrowly avoided kicking a rusty old bicycle abandoned in what had been a lawn when the twins were at junior school. Finally, they reached the back door. Nobody inside had stirred.

Rusty had seen a neighbour at an upstairs window, a man out walking his dog, and a lady putting more rubbish into an overflowing bin. Nobody had uttered a word. It wasn't hard to see why. On the other side of the estate last year, someone broke in and killed a bloke over a debt of a mere forty pounds. Community spirit only travelled so far. It didn't extend to sticking your nose in where it wasn't wanted.

Phoenix stood aside, gun raised. Rusty worked on the door lock. Fifteen seconds later, they were inside the kitchen. Phoenix made a mental note to tell his friend he was losing touch. He could hear sounds from the TV, and he wasn't sure whether it was hip-hop or another brand of American crap. It was annoying; and loud, which suited their purpose. The Mullen twins hadn't been disturbed.

Rusty waited at the closed door to the first bedroom, checking for movement inside. Phoenix paused at the entrance to the living room, nodded to Rusty and then burst through the open door. Terry Mullen lay on a battered, black leather settee staring at the TV screen. Terry tried to move his head to focus on the intruder.

He's stoned, thought Phoenix, not what we needed. We'll get nothing out of him in this state. It took him thirty seconds to secure the young thug and get him ready to transfer to the people carrier.

Rusty had followed his friend's orders. At the nod from Phoenix, he entered Dale Mullen's room, gun at the ready in case the lad had a weapon. Dale was asleep. Empty bottles of Newcastle Brown littered the upturned cardboard box that served as a bedside table.

"Damn," he said, looking at the clothes strewn on the floor, "please don't tell me I have to get you dressed."

Rusty pulled back the duvet. His worst fears were confirmed.

"My apologies, I should have knocked," said Phoenix when he entered the room a minute later.

"Yeah, very funny," said Rusty, adjusting a pair of jeans on Dale's inert figure. "Give me a hand. Dale's as drunk as a skunk. The bedclothes smelled like he was too lazy to get up for a pee. How's his brother?"

"Stoned out of his head," replied Phoenix. "How are we supposed to get a confession out of these two now?"

"We can take them back to Larcombe; let Henry have them for an hour," Rusty suggested.

Phoenix didn't want to deviate from his plan, but he could see no option. He looked at his watch.

"Right, you finish up securing Dale. I'll carry Terry outside and chuck him in the back. Bring Dale when you're ready. Find something to gag them. I don't want to listen to them mouthing off on the way home."

"Are we returning to the safe house first and driving home in the morning?" asked Rusty.

"It seems such a waste," said Phoenix, "we're here now, and the Dwyer gang need our attention. Let's get these two stowed away first, and then we can discuss it over a beer."

"You only let me buy two cans earlier to drink with our pizza," said Rusty, "we're out of supplies."

"The pubs will be open for another hour," said Phoenix, "we'll have a late one for a change."

As Rusty closed the door of the twin's property behind him, he checked the surrounding homes and gardens. There was nothing to see, and nobody was watching them. Terry and Dale Mullen were soon in the back of the people carrier. The interior window was up, and the agents could drive back to the safe house in silence. In the back, both boys were now half-awake and wondering where they were.

"They won't be going anywhere," said Phoenix when they parked at the safe house, "leave them in the back. Let's walk back to that pub we passed on the last roundabout."

At five past ten, the two agents sat in the corner of the bar. Old habits caused them to sit facing the doors, with an unobstructed view of everyone in the place. Not that there were many drinkers tonight.

The barman told them it was always quiet on Thursday evenings.

"It'll be manic tomorrow and Saturday, mind," he added.

"To be honest, I thought we'd see more activity on the streets," Rusty said to Phoenix as he sipped his pint of lager. "Although there were a few groups of youths loitering on the Cowgate. Over here, nearer the Tyne, it's civilised."

"They don't get the urban street gangs up here or the violence associated with them in the south," said Phoenix, "but that's not to say the threat isn't there. It could surface at any time."

Rusty saw Phoenix was nursing the last dregs of his drink. He offered to get another round. Phoenix nodded towards two men who had slipped in from the public bar.

"Don't stand too close or turn your head," he said, "just try to catch what those two are saying."

Rusty carried the empty glasses to the bar; the barman was in the public bar. Rusty leaned on the counter and studied the row of optics; he could overhear snatches of the conversation. The guy with his back to him was a loud talker; his voice carried. Either he didn't notice anyone else in the bar, or he didn't care. The man with him was facing the counter, and Rusty could lip-read most of what he said, despite his voice being much quieter, thanks to the mirrored wall behind the optics.

"Same again?" called the barman as he walked from the other end of the bar.

"Please," replied Rusty.

The two men moved away from the counter and sat on a table next to the door. Rusty paid for the drinks and strolled back to where Phoenix sat. Both sets of men now sat opposite one another.

"Do you know who the guy on the left is?" asked Phoenix.

"The other bloke called him Phil or Will. Can't be sure."

"I'll bet you any money that's Phil Dwyer," muttered Phoenix. "We had an old photo of him on file, one taken before he went to jail for the assault on the taxi driver. He's spent a fair amount of the past seven years getting tattoos, shaving his head, and building muscle in the exercise areas. While you were hanging around at the bar, I was trying to imagine him without the changes, and now I'm convinced it's him."

"He offered the other bloke a job," said Rusty, "he told him they needed to recruit men for doorstep visits to clients who were late making their payments. I don't think he was interested, but they're still in discussions, by the looks of it."

Phoenix thought for a while.

"I want you to take the twins back to Larcombe tonight. Don't drink that lager, or you'll be over the limit. I'll call the ice-house and leave a message for Henry. You should be home by three. Henry can start the day with interrogation at six; he should have the answers we need before the meeting at nine. I'll tell him to pull out the stops."

"What are you going to do?" asked Rusty.

"Go undercover," replied Phoenix.

"On your own? That's dangerous and not in line with Olympus protocol. You should know that. We rewrote the damn thing after we lost the men in Portsmouth."

"There were two of them, with a handler, and they still died," said Phoenix. "We need another significant result against the Grid. I'm on the spot. It's too good an opportunity to miss. If Dwyer needs a man to knock on doors, I'll be that man."

"Be careful, Phoenix," said Rusty, "keep your phone on you at all times. We can use the GPS to keep track of you from Larcombe. When will your first check-in be? I'll warn Giles to expect it. What codeword will you use?"

"I'll be careful," said Phoenix. "I'll message him every morning at eight. Then, if he doesn't receive 'Judas Priest', send the cavalry from our Newcastle team to wherever my phone tells you I am."

"I don't like it," said Rusty.

"Tough," said Phoenix with a grin. "I'm sticking to the band I love. I will not send 'Abba' as a message to appease your middle-of-the-road tastes."

"You never change. Don't expect me to explain this to Athena, mate. She will not be happy."

"No risk, no reward," said Phoenix. "Now, bugger off back to Bath."

Rusty shook his head and left. Phoenix stared across the bar at Dwyer and the reluctant debt collector. The conversation appeared to have died. It was only a matter of time; he sat and waited.

Dwyer stood up and walked to the bar.

"Another pint, Mick, when you're ready," he called. The barman was serving in the public bar again.

Phoenix sensed Phil Dwyer was checking him out in the mirror. His companion had now finished his beer and was leaving. He glanced at Phoenix as he passed him on his way outside to the street.

The last few customers were preparing to do the same. Mick came through to serve Phil Dwyer and then came around the end of the bar to collect empty glasses. It was the fag-end of the night. Everyone was keen to get home.

"Your pal's had enough then?" said Mick, pointing to Rusty's pint.

"Early start in the morning," replied Phoenix, "it won't go to waste. I'll finish it. I've nowhere to be tomorrow."

When Mick moved to clear the next table, Phil Dwyer sat on the chair opposite Phoenix.

"You're not from around here," said Dwyer. "So, what's your game?"

"Game?" asked Phoenix.

"Nobody comes into this part of town by choice. So, you're either a copper or a nonce."

"I'm neither," said Phoenix, "and talk like that is likely to get someone into a heap of pain."

Phil Dwyer stared at the man opposite. He had met every sort in prison and on the city streets. He could usually get a read on them within a few seconds. This bloke was a mystery.

"How long have you been out?" asked Phoenix.

"What do you mean?" asked Dwyer.

"It doesn't take a genius to see you got your latest tats done inside by an amateur. Of course, you're also busting out of that shirt, so you've had plenty of spare time to work out. Stop pissing me off, and let me finish my drink."

"Where's your boyfriend gone? If you're not the law, then maybe you're a poofter?"

"Wrong again. How many more guesses have you got? The guy I was drinking with was a delivery driver. He's taking two packages south in the morning. I've been working as a delivery driver's mate. A zero-hours contract on minimum wage isn't what I wanted out of life. I told him to stick his job up his arse. Is there a job around here that pays better?"

Dwyer took a large sip of his beer. Phoenix could see the

cogs in his pea-sized brain working. Come on. You can do it, he thought. It's not a great leap.

"If you're looking for a job, maybe I can help," said Dwyer.

At last, thought Phoenix.

"Not sure I want to work for a bloke who thinks everyone has a secret to hide," said Phoenix, finishing up his drink and swapping the glass for Rusty's.

"We need people who can handle themselves, door to door, on the estates around Newcastle and Sunderland," said Dwyer. "You look as if you could fit the bill. The money will be better than riding shotgun for Citylink. Cash in hand at the end of every day."

"So, it's a debt collection firm. I'm cool with that," said Phoenix, "where do I need to be, and when?"

"Meet me here at noon tomorrow; I'll set you up with one of our regulars. My guy will show you the ropes. It's more than a debt collection firm; we loan them the money, and they pay it back with interest. You only call around when they forget."

"How heavy do I need to get?" asked Phoenix.

"Watch, listen and learn from the guy you meet tomorrow. I'm not going to spell it out for you. Either you're in after tomorrow, or you're out. It's no skin off my nose."

"Noon tomorrow then," said Phoenix, finishing his drink. He stood up and headed for the door.

Dwyer watched him leave. As the door closed behind him, he, too, drank up. Then Dwyer walked to the door, held it open for a while, and stepped outside. He saw Phoenix fifty yards up the street, passing under a streetlamp.

"Let's see where you're going, pal,"

Phoenix had heard the door. He walked past the entrance to the safe house and headed for the row of shops and offices where he and Rusty had shopped earlier. He thought he remembered a Chinese takeaway. There it was, and it was still open. Phoenix ordered his food and waited. When he came outside with his carrier bag, he searched the street for Dwyer. He was in the doorway of an estate agency across the road. Right, time to have fun. He turned around, returned to the shop and rechecked the menu board. The local taxi firm had an advert at the bottom. He called for a ride home. Three minutes later, he was in the back of a cab, pulling away from the kerb.

"Where to mate," said the Asian cabbie.

"A mystery tour," said Phoenix. "Make it look like you're heading to the centre, then double back. My place is fifty yards up the road back there. I'll make it worth your while. I'm being stalked."

"You're the boss," said the driver.

The cab dropped Phoenix outside the safe house twenty minutes later. There was no sign of Phil Dwyer. He got fed up and walked home. The people carrier had gone too. Rusty was on the road, delivering two individual packages to Henry Case at Larcombe Manor.

Phoenix let himself in, sat in the lounge, and tucked into his supper. He finished every mouthful. His appetite was piqued when meeting Dwyer. Working undercover was something he had done with success over the years. He had missed it.

At midnight, Phoenix went to bed. He had to be up by eight, to send the message to Giles. That was the simple part.

Phoenix had to call Athena, too, to explain why he was taking such a risk. That was a conversation he was dreading.

Chapter Ten

Friday, 18th July 2014

Rusty arrived at the ice-house at four in the morning. Henry waited for him at the entrance, half-awake and grumpy.

"Why on earth did you have to book customers in at such an unearthly hour?" he asked as the lift took them and the Mullen twins to Level Three.

"Don't blame me, Henry," said Rusty, "it was Phoenix's idea. He wanted me out of the picture as soon as possible. These two tearaways need to confess their sins. Then they can receive a just punishment."

Henry swallowed hard. None of this would improve his chances of a happy future with the Reverend Sarah Gough. Two tearaways, they might be, but they were only nineteen years young.

Both were awake and alert now. The gags prevented their anger from being much more than squirming and struggling against the restraints that secured their wrists and ankles.

"Quit wasting your time," shouted Rusty, tired after the five-hour drive. He wanted to get to bed. It wasn't long before he would be up again and into the meeting room with Athena. Another long day stretched before him.

Henry and Rusty shoved the prisoners into separate interrogation rooms, secured them to steel chairs, bolted to the floor, and left them alone. Henry turned the speakers up to maximum and fed them a selection of classical compositions by Wagner.

"That should soften them up," he grunted. "I'll have an early breakfast. Then I'll return to see if they're softened up sufficiently for the next phase of their short stay here."

"Get them to admit to their role in the murder of Solomon Hussain," said Rusty, "and they can move to Hotel California."

"Do you wish to be present?" asked Henry.

Rusty was taken aback. Head Case had never invited anyone to attend an execution. He shrugged.

"If you need someone to hold your hand."

Henry was quiet for a moment.

"Look," he said, "you and Artemis have a good relationship, am I right?"

"Yes," replied Rusty.

"I want the same for Sarah and me, but if she discovered the reality of what I do here, it would be a forlorn hope."

"So, you need someone to do the dirty work for you?" asked Rusty. "Yeah, I can see that's tricky. My suggestion is you talk it over with Athena in private. She knows Sarah. She would be sympathetic, I'm sure. We have enough agents going through training and retraining on-site these days. The newbies don't need blooding. Most will have killed someone in Afghanistan or Iraq."

"I could explain it away as a final test in their training programme," said Henry, finally seeing a way out of his predicament. "If they can't kill a criminal in cold blood, they won't be fit for purpose in the field. So thanks, Rusty, you have given me renewed hope."

Rusty gave his colleague a friendly tap on the shoulder. It was strange to discover Henry was so enamoured of the vicar. They made an odd couple, but who was he to criticise? He and Artemis might appear to be chalk and cheese to many observers.

"See you later, Henry," he said and returned to the surface in the lift.

Rusty slipped into bed alongside Artemis; it was a few minutes before five. She stirred and opened one eye.

"Hello, darling," she whispered, "you're back. How did it go?"

"The Bradford part of the mission went like clockwork. I've returned with the Mullen twins and left them in Henry's tender care. Phoenix has gone undercover in Newcastle."

Artemis was awake now.

"Undercover? When did Athena sanction that? Why did you bring the Mullens here?"

"Phoenix sent me back and decided to infiltrate the Dwyer's loan shark gang without consulting Athena."

"Shit," said Artemis. "Athena won't appreciate that."

"No, you won't like me if I don't get at least two hours of sleep. We'll get up at seven and talk it over then. Phoenix's calling in at eight to let Giles know he's okay, and then he has to spill the beans to Athena."

"The morning meeting will be fun," said Artemis, kissing Rusty on the cheek and turning over. Rusty nodded off and dreamed of Phil Dwyer wielding a baseball bat.

Over breakfast, at a quarter past seven in the morning, Artemis and Rusty chatted over the crimes the Dwyer gang carried out.

"In a tough economic climate, illegal money lending happens," said Artemis, nibbling at her croissant. "The lenders target vulnerable people in the community and generate a spiral of debt; they find it impossible to escape. The deprived estates scattered across Tyne and Wear are fertile hunting grounds for gangs such as the Dwyer's."

"Loan sharks can be a scourge on poor communities," said Rusty. "The bully boy tactics a thug like Phil Dwyer favours forces clients to pay back far more than they borrowed or can afford. Phoenix has gone into a viper's den. Heaven knows what he will have to do while he's undercover. To refuse will put his own life in danger. Going in alone was reckless, but he wouldn't listen to reason."

While Rusty and Artemis were deep in conversation, Henry Case could already confirm every young man involved in the vicious attack on Solomon Hussein last week in Bradford. Terry and Dale Mullen were brash, cocky young thugs who strutted like peacocks on the Cowgate estate. There they had their uncle, Phil Dwyer, to protect them.

On Level Three of the ice-house, there was no protective shield.

In his domain, Henry Case was king. Something he now detested. Henry derived no satisfaction from having broken these two thugs in a few hours. They pleaded for their lives and abandoned the vile threats of what their Uncle Phil would do to him long ago.

"Resistance is futile," Henry had told them. "How long did you travel in the dead of night? In which direction? You are many feet underground, and only three people know you are here — the man who sent you, the man who delivered you, and me. You have admitted your guilt. All that remains is for my superiors to decide when punishment will get carried out. The police will learn the names of your accomplices within the hour."

Henry had now moved both brothers to the room at the far end of the corridor; the infamous Hotel California.

Terry and Dale Mullen were chained, seated back to back, and hooded. He closed the door and walked back to the lift — time to prepare for the morning meeting.

A little earlier, at eight o'clock, Giles had received a message from Phoenix. Rusty had contacted him before he left Newcastle for Bath. Giles was prepared for 'Judas Priest' to arrive from Phoenix's mobile phone. The GPS coordinates put him in the safe house. Everything was okay so far.

Giles left to head to the main building a few minutes before nine. He saw Henry striding out in front of him. Artemis and Rusty would arrive together. She didn't start her shift in the ice-house until two this afternoon.

Athena sat in their apartment, thinking over the conversation she had just had with her husband. Hope was being bathed and dressed by Maria Elena. The happy sounds of their daughter splashing in the bath carried through to the sitting room. Hope didn't have a care in the world. Athena had the concerns of the world on her shoulders.

What was Phoenix thinking? Going undercover in a dangerous gang with scant protection and forward planning was madness. It was so unlike the man she knew. He was always so meticulous at every stage of a mission. It was no good. She had to steel herself to face the others.

The other senior agents were waiting for her to arrive in the meeting room.

"Apologies for being late," she began, "and for Phoenix's absence."

"Did he not return with Rusty?" asked Minos.

Athena realised that Minos and Alastor were the only ones not in the loop. She filled in the gaps and then moved on to the published agenda. Her heart wasn't in it. She rushed through matters more swiftly than usual and asked if anyone had anything urgent.

Henry Case cleared his throat.

"I have a proposal," he said, "about the Mullen twins. Would it be possible to discuss it with you after the meeting?"

"It will need to be brief, Henry," said Athena. "I want to ensure Giles and his team can keep a constant watch on Phoenix."

"I'll keep it as brief as possible," said Henry.

"If there's nothing further, then we'll stop now," said Athena. "Giles, can I visit you in the ice-house in ten minutes?"

"Of course, Athena," he replied.

"I know my shift isn't due to begin for three hours," said Artemis, "but I'll come with you, if I may?"

Athena nodded. Rusty and Artemis went to their apartment.

Giles headed underground. Minos and Alastor returned to the administration offices.

"Right, Henry. What was it you wanted to raise?"

"My relationship with your friend Sarah has reached a stage where I can no longer fulfil my role here at Larcombe."

"Henry, surely you don't want to leave us?" exclaimed Athena.

"Oh no, that's not what I meant," said Henry. "I worry that she will realise my security position utilises far darker skills than those I described to her when we met. Every day since I've dreaded her finding out. Could you assign an agent to help me with the Mullen twins this morning? From now on, could we use our new and retrained agents in matters where the crime merits capital punishment?"

"Ever since you arrived, you have carried out those duties without complaint. Erebus was always concerned about the stresses of such an occupation would play on your mind in time. Yet, although you never showed you enjoyed that part of the job, you never asked for help. So, of course we will find someone to assist you."

"Rusty and I discussed it earlier this morning," said Henry. "He suggested that any man unable to carry out the task was a doubt for active duty in the field. He who hesitates is lost, and all that."

"There's your solution, Henry," said Athena. "Every man must be eligible while in training here if active duty is their target. We'll make the selection by drawing a name out of a hat. Anyone who refuses will get opportunities in non-combative roles only."

"Thank you, Athena. I can't tell you how relieved I am."

"Well, I'm due in the ice-house, so carry on, get Rusty to help you with the draw. You can supervise the disposal of the bodies, I trust?"

"Of course, Athena," said Henry, and he scuttled off to find Rusty.

Athena followed him, hoping to catch Artemis leaving her apartment. Perhaps they could walk over together. She was concerned about Phoenix. She didn't want to be alone.

In their office, Minos and Alastor were resuming their daily work. Alastor was compiling folders containing lists of possible accommodation sites for the Irregulars. Each establishment would offer a roof over their head and a range of facilities, but nothing fancy. Alastor likened it to almost all mod cons.

Minos had completed an appraisal of the first retraining intake. Only a third were suitable for active duty. After Phoenix and Athena had cleared his report, it would pass to Zeus. He would allocate the agents to where they provided the best fit.

"This appraisal is ready to go," he said, "the trouble is I don't want to upset Athena by asking her to read it through and add her signature."

"Of course," said Alastor. "It needs Phoenix to see it too. I don't suppose she knows when he's returning home."

"If ever," said Minos, "he's in bandit country. We can only pray he gets out and returns to us safe and sound.

"I echo that sentiment," said Alastor. "Illegal loan sharks are chasing some of the most vulnerable families in Britain. In Tyne and Wear, the Dwyer gang offer short-term cash loans from a hundred to a thousand pounds. They target the big estates and unearth those struggling to make ends meet. The doorstep lenders live cheek-by-jowl with their customers. Dwyer recruits his staff from the estates. They stand beside them in the pubs they drink in and watch them going in and out of the betting shop. It doesn't take long for them to spot a likely candidate for a house call."

"Can Phoenix blend in with that scene, I wonder?" said Minos.

"If he can't," said Alastor, "they'll spot him a mile off, and the rules about who signs off appraisals will need to be updated."

Phoenix was eating breakfast when he heard a noise from the front door. It was half-past eight. He had checked in with Giles Burke at eight and asked for a favour. Then he had called Athena. That had been tense, but it was what it was. He was here to do a job. One he believed was worth a little discomfort.

Breakfast over, he wandered into the hallway. A jiffy bag lay on the doormat. He carried it to the lounge window. Outside in the driveway sat a seven-year-old saloon car. A quick check proved the fob key in the bag belonged to his new set of wheels.

"Not as good as I'm used to," he said, "but in line with a man in my supposed income bracket."

The nearest Olympus team had dropped it off quicker than he had imagined when he talked with Giles. It was good to know they were close by; he felt less vulnerable.

Phoenix hoped he wouldn't need to call in the cavalry. Things would be better if he could work undercover and become an integral part of the gang. He decided to walk to the shops. The last thing he needed was a morning paper, but it gave him a chance to check for anyone watching. He thwarted Phil Dwyer's interest last night. That didn't mean he wouldn't send someone up to the area to get a fix on where he was living.

The stroll to the shops and back took fifteen minutes. The paper went straight to the bin. Traffic was busy on the roads, and the pavements were full of morning shoppers. Nobody stood out as a lookout. Nobody paid him the slightest attention.

A few minutes before noon, he left the safe house and walked to the pub. Inside the bar, there was no sign of Dwyer. Mick, the barman, acknowledged his arrival with a nod and pointed to the door behind him. A weasel of a man had just crept in.

"Are you the bloke I'm looking for?" he asked.

"If you're showing me the ropes on the collections today, then yes, I am," replied Phoenix.

"I'm Benny,"

"Call me Frankie," said Phoenix. "If we're working together."

It was lost on Benny. The chain of two hundred and fifty restaurants probably targeted a younger market.

"Do you have a car?" asked Benny.

Phoenix nodded; Benny headed for the bar door. He explained the facts of life as they walked.

"We'll take my car today. Phil doesn't care if your car is taxed or insured, nor whether they took your licence away. Most cars on the Cowgate are in the same boat. You're on your own if you do something stupid to attract the cops. There's no paperwork connecting you to Phil, so he'll drop you and move on to the next guy who's desperate for work."

"Understood," said Phoenix.

Benny's car was a BMW with a personalised number plate, BEN 10 GGS. The interior was immaculate. Phoenix tried to reconcile the rat-faced human being sitting beside him with the car he drove. He failed.

Benny drove like a typical Sunday afternoon driver. Everything moved at a sedate pace. Fellow road users got frustrated, but Benny didn't seem to care. Phoenix noticed they were now on the Cowgate. He wondered why Benny used his car on a job like this. There were so many villains on the estate.

There had to be a risk it would get nicked while he was on a doorstep, or he'd return to find his wheels gone and his pride and joy standing on a pile of bricks. The temptation to run a knife blade or a set of keys along the paintwork would be enormous.

"This is my first call," said Benny. He parked the car,

and the two men got out. As they approached the door of the terraced house, Benny said: -

"Keep your mouth shut. Stand a yard behind me, on my left-hand side. Mrs Archer lives here, a single mum with four kids under the age of nine."

Benny rapped the door with his knuckles. The bell had broken, with its wires hanging out of the wall. The door opened, and a large woman in her late twenties appeared.

"Hello, Mr Giggs."

"I see your Wayne's trousers have fallen out with his shoes, Bethany. Just as well that he's still got that pair of bright red socks, or his little legs would get cold. He's a growing boy. I'm sure you want to see him smartly dressed when he trots off to school?"

"Yeah, well, I can't get any more money from the social, and my credit rating's shit, so what am I supposed to do?"

"I'll tell you what," said Benny, "why don't I lend you a hundred quid? I'll pop round weekly, and you can pay me back."

"How much do I have to pay?" asked Bethany Archer.

"You give me fifteen quid next Friday, and we'll see how we go," said Benny, counting off five twenty-pound notes from a wad he produced from his jacket pocket. Bethany Archer's eyes lit up.

"Make sure you spend it on clothes for those lovely kids, mind Bethany," said Benny. "I don't want to come by next week and find half a dozen empty bottles of Prosecco in your recycling bin."

"Yes, Mr Giggs."

Benny turned to walk to the car. Phoenix followed and waited until they pulled away from the kerb before asking: -

"How long was the loan term? I didn't hear you say."

"If they ask, I tell them for three months. Twelve weeks

at fifteen quid means Mrs Archer would pay one-eighty. Every week she fails to pay up, I add another two weeks to the length of the loan. Mrs Archer won't be able to keep up with the payments. In a couple of months, she'll want another wad of cash. It'll be for Halloween or Christmas. Once they're on the hook, I keep calling around and collecting."

"What if they don't ask, like Mrs Archer?" asked Phoenix.

"I keep collecting fifteen quid until she asks why it's taking so long to clear the debt. Then I scratch my head, look at my notebook, and tell her she's got three more payments. If I see her, Wayne, or one of the younger kids needing shoes, or a winter coat, I'll mention it. You'll catch on if you stick around. You need to keep your eyes open to see who's in need. That's most of them on this estate. It's easy money."

"Where do you live, Benny?" asked Phoenix.

"Two doors down from Mrs Archer. The end terrace house with the bigger garden. Nice spot. I can see everything I need to from my place."

The next house they visited was a flat on the opposite side of the road. Benny could have told Phoenix what pattern wallpaper they had in every room from his front window.

"This one will be different," said Benny, as he stepped over broken glass on the pavement and eased past plastic bags of rubbish on the path leading to the door.

"Why?" asked Phoenix, following Benny's route.

"They're not keen on paying. It's good you're here. If the lady's alone, she tends to ask if there's another way we can settle the amounts they owe. When he's home, he can be a mouthy devil."

Benny rang the bell.

"Stand on the doorstep and get right in their faces," said Benny, "if he kicks off, then chin him. It's time they saw sense and paid what's owing."

Benny rang again.

A bleached-blonde woman in her forties threw open the door. Tattoos covered the whole of her right arm. Her left shoulder carried the message 'Jake is my life'. She recognised Benny straight away, but her eyes fixed on Phoenix.

"What's a threesome worth, Mr Giggs? This one's tasty. We don't have the forty quid. So, you can whistle for it."

"I'm sorry to hear that, Mrs Fouracre. My boss won't be pleased. This gentleman might call around with his friends when Jake's at home. Neither of you will whistle after that. Most likely, you'll be taking your food through a straw."

Amy Fouracre was scared, there was no question, but she put on a brave face. Phoenix stepped back from the doorstep.

"What can you offer us today, Mrs Fouracre, in the way of cash?" he asked.

"I could manage twenty, maybe?" she replied, fetching her purse from the kitchen table.

"What's your game?" asked Benny quietly, poking Phoenix in the chest.

"Twenty is better than nothing, and I don't hit women," said Phoenix.

"Here, take this," said Amy, who was back at the door, "we'll try to have the money for you next week, Mr Giggs, honest."

She closed the door. Benny stuffed the twenty-pound note in his notebook and returned to the car. He was steaming.

"This isn't a charity," he told Phoenix when they sat in the BMW, "I thought Phil explained things to you."

"Not really," replied Phoenix. "I needed a job, and he said I could come out with you to learn the ropes. I thought after that; I'd get to collect from different addresses across the region, not act as your muscle. You know these people, Benny. They're your neighbours. You know their history. I could never do your job as well as you."

Benny was placated. He misread Phoenix's contempt for the misery which Benny piled on the poor sods who scratched a living on the Cowgate as a compliment.

"Well, yeah, I suppose it is a talent," said Benny. "I didn't always do this, you know. I was in insurance for forty years. I've spent a lifetime knocking on doors and picking up bits and pieces."

"Have you ever taken Amy up on her offer?" asked Phoenix.

"Not with my back," said Benny, shaking his head, "and you ain't set eyes on Jake yet. That's why I said you might be back mob-handed. You would need three or four big blokes to take him."

"How much did they borrow?" asked Phoenix.

"Five hundred," said Benny. "Bloody stupid mistake I made there, Amy batted her eyelids at me, and I gave her the money rather than risk her dragging me inside."

The rest of the afternoon gave Phoenix further examples of the sad, hand-to-mouth existence that defined life on the estate. It was depressing. At last, it was over.

"I'll drop you back home if you want," said Benny as they drove off the estate.

"No thanks," said Phoenix, not keen to let Benny give his address to Phil Dwyer, "drop me at the pub. I'll have a beer before I pick up a takeaway. Thanks for today. It was an eye-opener."

When they stopped in the pub car park, Benny said: -

"I might see you again if Phil wants someone given a frightener. If you hang around until six o'clock, he'll be there. They stop off for a drink before they head home."

"They?" asked Phoenix.

"Him and his sister, Annie," replied Benny. "She's the brains of the operation. Phil's the brawn. I guess you worked that out already?"

Phoenix let that go. He wouldn't say a bad word against Phil Dwyer or his family. But, according to the reports he'd read, it wasn't beneficial for your health. So he waved Benny goodbye and went inside. Mick wasn't working this evening, but the young girl behind the bar poured a decent pint, and Phoenix sat in the same seat as last night to await the Dwyers.

As he sipped his drink, he remembered the clients he and Benny had visited. Bethany Archer, the single mum; Amy Fouracre, the nymphomaniac. The gambling addict two roads further on from Benny's house who took out short-term loans every three or four months and whose debts were mounting to dangerous levels. Dangerous to his health.

The deeper they travelled into the estate, the more the threats and intimidation grew. Benny piled on the pressure. When he had talked about Bethany Archer, he said a missed week meant two more added to the term. With the real no-hopers and the term extensions, the interest rate also rocketed.

Phoenix went through the details as he could remember them. Benny's existing loans and the fresh ones he had added this afternoon totalled eight thousand. Even if everybody paid on time for a minimum of three months, Benny collected thirty thousand. The doorstep lender never revealed his cut, but the Dwyers were making an obscene profit. When you took a close look at what they did, it boiled down to demanding money with menaces.

The door from the public bar opened.

"He's in here," said Phil Dwyer as he walked through, carrying a whole pint.

Behind him came his sister Annie, carrying a large glass of white wine.

Phil Dwyer was a thug, pure and simple, from his shaved head and body tattoos to his steel-capped working boots. Annie was eight years younger. She was different gravy. They were the same height, but there was no comparison after that. Her dark hair hung in curls on her naked shoulders. Hooped golden earrings framed her face. Annie's figure was full and shapely. No way would she blow over in a breeze. She was solid. Her legs, shown off to good effect by the shortness of her skirt, suggested she exercised often.

Annie Dwyer was stunning. Phoenix had to keep reminding himself she was behind an operation that meant misery for hundreds if not thousands of people in Tyne and Wear.

"You'll know me again," Annie said, sitting opposite Phoenix. She crossed her legs slowly, guaranteeing he saw the white panties beneath the black skirt.

"How did it go with Giggsy?" asked Phil Dwyer.

He was used to blokes drooling over his sister; this one was playing it cool. Phil still couldn't make him out. He might need to warn him to keep his hands off her.

"Educational," said Phoenix.

"I didn't get your name last night," said Phil.

"I didn't give it," replied Phoenix, "but you can call me Frankie."

"Are you interested?" asked Annie, sipping her Chardonnay.

Phoenix allowed himself a brief grin.

"She means do you want to start work Monday?" said Phil.

"I know what she meant," said Phoenix, "yeah, I'm ready to start work. I told you last night. I need the money. I haven't got anywhere else to be."

Annie studied Phoenix for a while.

"OK, Phil, get Frankie started next week. We'll see how he goes. I'll leave you boys to sort out the financial details."

With that, she stood up and walked out. Phoenix took another drink from his pint. It was thirsty work watching a black panther from this close as she glided across the room towards the door.

"I'll only tell you once, Frankie," said Dwyer. "Collect the money, hand every penny over to Annie or me, and you keep breathing. Got it? As for my sister, she's off-limits to hired help."

"Got it," said Phoenix.

"I'll get us another beer, and then I'll tell you where you'll be working and your daily rake-off."

Phoenix watched Phil at the bar, chatting up the barmaid while she served him their drinks. He wondered whether Annie Dwyer would stick to her brother's rules.

She didn't look the type. She was dangerous.

Phoenix knew he might need to play a dangerous game if he remained undercover and believable.

Chapter Eleven

Monday, 21st July 2014

In London, Michael Terrence Quinn was starting a new week. He had been a leading East End gangster for decades. When the Mighty Quinn spoke, people listened or suffered the consequences.

Quinn enjoyed the trappings of success his criminal enterprises provided. The large, detached property he shared with his wife, Cassandra, twenty-five years his junior, was full of high-quality furniture, state-of-the-art electronics, and several attack dogs. Children had never been a requirement, just a luxury.

Quinn owned villas on the islands of Majorca and Tenerife. The garages at home and abroad contained cars with eye-watering price tags. Life was good.

Quinn didn't have a working week as such. So, Monday mornings were no different from any other day of the week. Rise late, swim in the indoor heated pool, take a leisurely breakfast, and read the morning papers.

Before he knew it, it was time to drive around the borough that Quinn as good as owned. He would drop into a bar here, a club there, to chat briefly with his people. By mid-afternoon, he was ready to get to his office in Hackney.

Miriam Rowlands, his assistant, had been with Quinn for twenty years. Miriam knew every one of Quinn's secrets. Her husband had always worked for the gangster, which meant those secrets would go with her to the grave. A plump, unattractive woman in her mid-fifties, Miriam was approved of by Cassandra Quinn. She was good at her job and posed no threat to the lifestyle the younger woman had become accustomed to.

"Morning, Miriam," muttered Quinn as he passed her desk and entered his office.

"Coffee?" asked Miriam, already up and shuffling towards the percolator.

"Perfect," replied Quinn and sat in his captain's chair, surveying the view from his office window.

"Lovely out, isn't it?" said Miriam when she placed Quinn's coffee cup on his desk.

"Looks can deceive, Miriam," growled Quinn. "Something is going on, and I can't work out what."

"That's not you, Mr Quinn," said Miriam, "what have we got to sort out today, then?"

"Nothing urgent. Why don't you take off for the rest of the afternoon? I need to sit here and think awhile. Switch off the office phone so I don't get disturbed; there's a good girl."

Miriam looked back at her boss as she left the office. She'd never known him to worry about anything in the years she'd known him. Quinn was a hard man, typical of men born and bred in the East End after the war. They had to be tough in those days to survive.

Mick Quinn had done more than survive. He'd risen to the top of an organised crime gang, earning millions each year. Quinn had clawed his way out of the gutter with his fists. At sixty-three, he was still a force to be reckoned with; yet, something or someone was eating away at the kingdom he could see from his window.

Miriam switched off the phone and collected her handbag and car keys. As she left, she clicked the latch on the door so the Mighty Quinn could be alone with his thoughts. Then, as she drove her Mini out from the underground car park, she decided to take advantage of the sudden change in her routine.

Miriam headed for the West End shops and retail therapy. As she passed King's Cross, she told herself that everything would be back in its proper place in the morning.

Colleen O'Riordan sat in her penthouse suite. She had been busy in the two weeks since Tommy's funeral. The feet of the people working for her had hardly touched the ground. Hugo Hanigan had huffed and puffed to identify the killer or killers of his security team. All to no avail.

Her assassin had appeared and disappeared like a will-of-the-wisp.

While her sworn enemy Hanigan floundered, Colleen had increased her control over Tommy's old gang and made inroads into areas controlled by her neighbours. Colleen finished her cup of Earl Grey tea, stood up, and walked to the window.

It was four o'clock in the afternoon. The sun shone bright, winning the battle against scattered clouds. The temperature was in the mid-twenties centigrade outside. In her apartment, the air-conditioning kept Colleen as cool as a cucumber.

"Not long now, Hugo," she called.

Hugo couldn't hear Colleen, of course, or see her. She had taken care not to reveal her new address to anyone connected to the Grid. With everything else Hanigan had on his mind at present, Colleen doubted he would waste time finding out. Hugo Hanigan was an arrogant swine. He always had been as a young boy. He thought himself better than the rest of them.

After tonight, Hugo Hanigan and the Grid would have another problem to solve. Colleen would be ready to make her final move in a few days. Everything was in place. Nothing could stop her now.

Meanwhile, in the far north of the country, Phoenix drove door to door, collecting small amounts of cash. The client list comprised the elderly, the disabled, and the unemployed. The only thing guaranteed was there would be someone home when he knocked on their door.

The most frequent question they asked was, "Where's Alan?"

Phil Dwyer hadn't told him who Alan was or why he wasn't around any longer. Phoenix knew better than to ask. Whoever Alan was, he must have been a nasty piece of work because every house Phoenix called on seemed pleased to see a new face on their doorstep.

Phoenix kept notes in the same style as Benny for Dwyer to confirm he handed over the right amount. Not everybody paid in full, but he explained the consequences to them. His message was politer than they were used to, and by the end of his list, only one couple had been unable to offer anything. Phoenix stuck the eight pounds needed into his money bag from his pocket.

The husband lost his job two months ago, and the

couple's benefit had been cut, despite their belief that the reduction was an error. His wife still looked after their youngest two kids full-time, but the eldest boy had gone to his grandparents in Sunderland.

"We couldn't afford to keep him," said the wife, bursting into tears.

"We went over on the bus to visit him the weekend before last," the father explained, "he doesn't understand. He thinks we don't love him."

"On the estate where my parents live," the wife continued, "collectors take pension and child allowance books away. Then, they return on allowance day, give the books to the householder and take the money as soon as they've collected it."

"The cuts in the younger people's dole money have caused crime rates to soar," said her husband. "There's been a spate of burglaries around here in recent months.

"The older people are scared burglars will come in even while they're home," said the wife, "they're that desperate."

Phoenix sat outside the house in his car for several minutes after that visit.

Phil Dwyer and others like him needed to be removed from the game.

Phoenix counted the money, four hundred and eighty-six pounds. Time to head back to the pub and another uncomfortable meeting. He parked the car at the safe house and walked to the pub.

The quiet bar was empty. Mick was back behind the bar.

"The same as last time, mate?" he asked. Phoenix nodded. As he exchanged the pint glass for cash, he added: -

"Phil won't be in tonight. He's gone to watch the match. His sister will be along soon."

Terrific, thought Phoenix. If the other night were typical, I'd be fighting her off. He didn't have long to wait. He had hardly sat down with his back to the window when the pub door opened.

Annie Dwyer stepped in off the street. She wore her hair up, her shoulders bare. Her breasts threatened to spill over the top of her flimsy blouse with every stride. Phoenix immediately spotted one thing she had left at home: a bra.

"Get me a drink, Frankie," she said.

Phoenix did as he ordered. A please would have been nice, but Annie was a no-nonsense woman, used to getting her way. He would go along with it for now.

Mick waited with the large Chardonnay when Phoenix reached the counter.

"Hope she's not in one of her drinking moods," he whispered, "or you won't have much of your commission left when you leave here."

Phoenix took the white wine to the table; he sensed that Annie's eyes hadn't left him. She hadn't taken the chair opposite him this time. She sat next to him on the cushioned bench.

"How did your first day go?" she asked.

"Four eighty-six," he replied.

"It should have been five twenty," she said, "what, are you going soft already?"

"That's not a complaint I've ever had," said Phoenix.

Phoenix had timed it to perfection. Annie had taken a large sip of her drink, and his deliberate double entendre caught her mid-swallow, causing her to cough and splutter.

"Bastard," she said as she recovered.

"Only when someone provokes me," said Phoenix.

"Slip the money bag onto the seat between us, Frankie," she whispered, "I'll give you your cut later. Ten per cent is the going rate. It's worth much more. You don't have to fret over tax and national insurance."

Phoenix placed down the bag. There were still no other customers, and Mick paid no attention.

"What game has Phil gone to watch?" Phoenix asked.

"A pre-season friendly at St James's Park," replied Annie.

"Cricket?" asked Phoenix, in all innocence, remembering his local park with men in whites when he was a young boy.

"No, football, of course. Newcastle United, the Toon Army. What planet are you from, mate? Fifty thousand fans will turn up at the Park to watch the grass grow. They're fanatical."

"Right," said Phoenix, "sport's never been my thing, I'm afraid."

"Phil says you're an odd one to fathom. He'll be even more confused when I tell him this."

"Phil warned me off, you know," said Phoenix. "Do you think it's wise to tell him you met me without a chaperone?"

Annie squeezed his knee and left her hand resting on his thigh.

"I'm my own woman, Frankie," she said. "I see who I choose, whether Phil approves or not."

Phoenix wondered whether his approval mattered, or maybe Annie was used to taking what she wanted, regardless.

"I'm ready for another," said Annie, draining her wine glass. She picked up the money and her handbag and headed towards the toilets.

Phoenix looked at his unfinished pint. It was decision time. He walked to the bar, caught Mick's attention, and ordered a fresh glass of Chardonnay. Mick smiled.

"One for yourself?" he asked.

"No thanks, Mick. I'm off soon. If the lady wants to stay the whole evening, that's up to her; I need my beauty sleep. I've got another day on the road tomorrow."

"Annie won't be happy," warned Mick.

The lady in question made her way back to the table as Phoenix turned away from the bar. When he sat beside her, Annie placed fifty pounds on the seat.

"No point messing around with change," she said, "are you not drinking?"

"Can't stay long," said Phoenix. "I've got another early start in the morning."

"Don't let anyone con you with their sob story tomorrow," she said, "we're not a charity. You should bring six hundred for Phil tomorrow night."

The atmosphere was more relaxed now. Phoenix had drawn a line, and Annie had sensed it. Her hand stayed well away from his thigh. Phoenix downed the rest of his drink.

"You're off already?" Annie asked.

"No, I'll keep you company until you finish that glass or someone else comes in. I hate to see women drinking alone. It might be old-fashioned, but that's my way."

"There's plenty I don't understand about you yet," said Annie. "Where are you from, what brought you up here, and where are you living?"

"I'm the hired help," shrugged Phoenix. "The less we know about one another, the better, considering the business we're operating. That's what Phil said the other night."

"If you let me finish this wine, I'll give you a lift to your place," she offered, "you do have coffee, I take it? So we can get to know one another better."

Phoenix realised he wouldn't brush her off without offending her. A woman scorned can be dangerous in normal circumstances. A woman from a crime family known for her violent tendencies was someone he needed to avoid annoying, if possible. His health depended on it.

"I'm only a five-minute walk from here," said Phoenix, "across the road from the shops. The place is a tip just now. I'll tidy up before having company. Maybe we can walk from here together another night and forget the coffee."

Annie's eyes lit up. She had him on the hook. She leaned forward, ensuring he got an eyeful of her naked breasts. As her lips brushed against his cheek, she whispered: -

"You won't regret it. I'll dream of you tonight. I know I will."

"Sweet dreams," said Phoenix. He stood up and walked to the door. Outside on the pavement, he breathed a huge sigh of relief.

Phoenix waited on the corner to see if Annie followed, but the pub door remained closed. A visit to the pizza parlour filled another ten minutes, and when he reached the shop door with his takeaway, he saw Annie's car speed past. She was heading into the city centre.

It was safe to walk home. Once inside the safe house, he called Athena.

"Hello darling," he said, "is Hope still awake?"

"Hello to you too," Athena replied, "and yes, she's sat on my lap. Do you want to talk to her?"

Phoenix and Hope shared a one-sided conversation. She was excited to hear her father's voice, and Phoenix enjoyed her squeals and gurgles. He missed his daughter so much. When Hope finally lost interest in the phone, Athena resumed her catch-up with her husband.

"Is it safe to talk?" she asked.

"I'm alone in the safe house. I've just ended my first day

working for the Dwyers. I was collecting door-to-door on one of the council estates. It's grim up here; you have no idea. The Dwyers are making a fortune out of these people. So far, I haven't seen any physical violence, only intimidation and threatening behaviour up to your armpits."

"Are you taking every precaution to avoid danger?" asked Athena.

"My biggest threat is Dwyer's sister. She's a man-eater. I pray she's not feeling hungry whenever she looks at me."

"I trust you to do the right thing if she takes a bite out of you," said Athena. "You must get out of there alive. We need you back here; we have other battles to fight. You must do whatever's necessary to eliminate the Dwyer gang; the quicker, the better."

Phoenix understood. Athena would let what happened undercover stay undercover if Olympus achieved the desired result. He hoped he could conclude matters before Annie made her move on him. He was thankful he had escaped the clutches of the Geordie Amazon for now, even if it was only temporary.

The pizza didn't taste as good as the other night; his appetite had deserted him. So Phoenix went to bed early. Sleep brought no dreams nor nightmares, only a solid eight hours of rest.

The outer door creaked. Mick Quinn stirred from a fitful sleep. He had to think for a second about where he was. Quinn was in his office, in his captain's chair. The scotch he drank while thinking through the things that troubled him must have made him tired. He looked at the clock on the wall — ten o'clock.

Mick thought he should get moving, lock up, and drive

home to Cassandra. She'd wonder where he was; as the fog cleared, he remembered the creaking door.

"Good evening, Mr Quinn."

Mick spun around in his chair. A young man stood on the other side of his desk. He knew the face, but a name wouldn't surface.

"How did you get in? Miriam locked the door behind her when she left."

"I have my methods," his visitor said, "I needed to see you urgently. There will be changes in London. The old rubbish is getting chucked out."

"You want to watch your mouth, sonny," snarled the Mighty Quinn, "I don't take kindly to threats."

The old gangster was halfway up from his chair when the visitor struck the two fatal blows. Quinn slumped back in his chair. His assassin turned the chair to face the window once more.

"I hear you enjoyed the view of this part of the city, Mr Quinn. It doesn't belong to you any longer," he said and left the office as quietly as he had come.

Tuesday, 22nd July 2014

Miriam Rowlands arrived for work at five minutes to nine. Mr Quinn's car was still in the garage where he'd left it yesterday afternoon. It wasn't like him to be in so early. As she climbed the stairs to the office, she thought maybe he had got a taxi home. Perhaps that bottle of malt he had hidden in his bottom drawer had helped.

As soon as she stepped inside, she sensed something amiss. There was a smell she didn't like, although what caused it was beyond her. She dropped her bag and keys on her desk.

"I'll sort this phone out, and then I'll open a window, get the fresh air in here."

Miriam switched on the office phone.

There were three messages, all from Cassandra Quinn.

Miriam ran to Mick's door and threw it open. Her boss was staring out the window, just as she had left him. He flopped sideways in his captain's chair as she touched his shoulder. Miriam screamed.

Michael Terrence Quinn had died eleven hours earlier from two stabs of a stiletto delivered to his brain through his eyes.

Across the city, Colleen O'Riordan caught the buzz of a message arriving on her mobile phone. She waited until she had finished her breakfast before she glanced at it.

"I've put the rubbish out."

She smiled. No time like the present. She would get ready, call for her most trusted hard men, and then visit the hangouts Mick Quinn had once frequented. The news of the Godfather's death would spread quickly. Colleen was determined to claim the areas he had controlled before a young upstart decided to step into his shoes. Parts of his kingdom had fallen into her hands already, and Quinn had never lived long enough to work out who was responsible. The King was dead. Long live the Queen.

Her grip on London's criminal network moved forward at a relentless pace. She would control everything in a matter of weeks, if not days.

Only one man stood between her and her goal; that worm, Hugo Hanigan.

Phoenix arrived at Westgate to start another day's collecting; he referred to his book. Annie Dwyer was right. If he got every penny on this list, he would carry six hundred pounds to the pub tonight. Fingers crossed, Phil Dwyer would be there alone, and he could grab his sixty pounds and get off home.

A new day, but there was a familiar pattern. The sight of a new collector brought questions. Where was Alan? Phoenix noted the door opened quicker than when he'd been riding shotgun for Benny Giggs. Little things, but they added up.

As the morning wore on, he asked questions of his own — a gentle probe here, an innocent follow-up question there. Most of the men and women on the Westgate were frightened to answer. They were keen to pay up and close the door, even if the man who had replaced Alan seemed a decent sort.

"I keep getting asked about Alan," he said to an elderly couple. The wife had joined her husband at the door when she heard him asking why he saw a new face.

"He was a nasty man," she said, pushing her thin cardigan up her arm. Phoenix had wondered why she wore one on such a warm summer's day. Her right arm was purple, yellow and black from wrist to elbow, adding more colours to the Olympus palette.

"Did Alan do that, Mrs Hatch?" he asked.

"Mary wanted to go to the coast on a day trip. We haven't been away for years. The money was due, and we couldn't afford that and our weekly loan payment. Alan twisted her arm behind her back. He told me he'd snap it like a twig if I didn't hand over the cash."

"Jim paid him," said Mary Hatch. "Alan warned us not to breathe a word, or he'd come back and finish us,"

"Well, he's not around now, so would you make a statement to the police if they were to hear about it? If someone tipped them off, for argument's sake?"

"Oh, I don't know," Jim Hatch said, "if word got back to Annie Dwyer we talked out of turn, she'd burn us out of our home. She can be evil if she doesn't get her way. We've lived here thirty-eight years, man."

"So, it's not just blokes like Alan and Phil Dwyer that get nasty then?" asked Phoenix.

"No way, they're all tarred with the same brush," said Jim Hatch. "Annie Dwyer, the Mullens, the other blokes they use; they're thugs, every one of them."

"You don't fit in with the people we've seen or been told stories about," added Mary Hatch, "are you sure you're in the right job, love?"

"You're a nice couple," said Phoenix. "How did you get involved with these loan sharks in the first place?"

"Have you ever tried to live on a state pension?" asked Jim with a dry laugh.

"The kids help out when they can," said Mary, "but they've got their troubles. We needed a new boiler to keep us warm in the winter. We've been paying the loan off for three years so far."

Phoenix told the old couple he'd be in touch and credited their account with ten pounds in his book. He used a note from yesterday's commission.

"Bless you," said Mary Hatch, on the verge of tears.

"It's the least I can do," said Phoenix.

At five in the afternoon, he had six hundred pounds. He received slammed doors, and no comment replies to his questions, but he gathered snippets of information from addresses across the estate that encouraged him. He would have enough damning data to pass to the authorities in time. Then, the Dwyer gang's grip on the poverty-stricken inhabitants of the North East would end.

Phoenix drove across the city to the pub.

"Usual?" asked Mick. He poured a pint of lager and pushed it across the counter.

"Thanks, it's been a warm one today. This will hit the spot."

"How's it going?" asked Mick.

"Early days," replied Phoenix, unsure whether the barman knew how Dwyer earned his money. He may be on the payroll too, so least said, soonest mended.

"Take my advice," said Mick, checking nobody was listening, "get out of this business, and quick."

"It's only temporary," shrugged Phoenix. "As soon as I get enough cash together, I'll be heading south again."

Customers arrived at both ends of the bar. Mick left him to serve the public bar first; Phoenix went to his seat. He wondered how long before Phil Dwyer arrived.

The voices at the bar grew louder. Mick was at the other end, serving.

"Hurry, we're dying of thirst here," shouted one man. His two colleagues were laughing, encouraging him. Phoenix could tell they spelt trouble.

Mick wandered to serve them. He didn't appear bothered by their attitude.

"Three bottles of Newky Brown, pal," said the mouthy one, "and get a bloody move on."

Mick placed the drinks on the bar and told him the price.

"Sod that, I'll run up a tab. I'll settle up later."

Mick shrugged and pointed at a sign behind the bar that read No Credit and made to move the bottles back towards the till.

The man grabbed Mick's arm.

"Touch my drink, and I'll slash your throat from ear to ear," he yelled.

The door opened from the public bar. Phil and Annie Dwyer walked in, drinks in hand. They were the customers Mick had served first.

"What's got under your skin today, Alan?" asked Phil.

"This twat wants us to pay up front. I'm good for the money. This barman needs to show us respect."

"Pay the man, Alan. There's a good lad," said Annie, her voice hardly above a whisper, but the menace it held was clear to the three men at the bar.

Mick took the cash offered, thanked Alan, and disappeared to the public bar after putting the money in the till.

So, this was the 'nasty man' Mary Hatch and others had described, thought Phoenix. He knew the type. He couldn't wait to punish him for the damage he'd done to the frail old lady and the intimidation he handed out around the estates.

Annie spotted Phoenix and headed over to sit beside him. Phil Dwyer noticed him, too and scowled in his direction as he saw his sister's choice of seat.

"Alan, I want you and your boys to meet Frankie," he said. "He started working for us yesterday."

"He's got his feet under the table, I see," said Alan, staring at Phoenix. He swaggered across to the table and pulled his chair closer to Annie before sitting. She moved nearer to Phoenix when Alan's knee touched hers.

Phil sat opposite Phoenix.

"Enjoy the match last night, Phil?"

"Terrific, Frankie. This could be our season," Phil replied.

Phoenix ignored the other three men. He placed his

money bag onto the seat. Annie picked it up and slipped it into her handbag.

"All there, Annie," he said quietly.

"Good to hear," muttered Phil.

Phoenix waited to see whether Alan handed over his cash. The other two goons didn't look like they provided much more than window-dressing. Alan headed any collection run they operated.

"Whereabouts in the city do you collect now, Alan?" he asked. "I seem to have taken over your old books."

"Missing me, are they," sneered Alan, and his goons nearly wet themselves with laughter.

"Not really," said Phoenix. "I got the full six hundred and never needed to hurt anyone."

Alan pushed back his chair and got to his feet. He shook a fist towards Phoenix.

"You need to watch your mouth,"

"Telfer, will you act your age? Sit down and behave yourself."

Alan Telfer glared at Annie Dwyer; nobody had used his surname since he worked for the Dwyer gang. Phil preferred nicknames or first names to keep people's private lives private. You never knew who was listening. Bloody Annie Dwyer had been in the same class as him at school. She had thought herself too good for him back then, and now she was all over this new bloke like a rash.

"Give Annie your takings, Alan," said Phil, "let's settle up commissions, finish our drinks, and get out of here. We're attracting too much attention.

Five minutes later, the commissions got paid, and drinks finished, with little conversation. Alan Telfer and his goons gave Phoenix the stare. He ignored them and watched

Mick, the barman, drying glasses at the counter. He wondered how long he had been back at this end of the bar.

"We're off," said Phil, "come on, sis, let's get home."

Annie looked crestfallen. She squeezed Phoenix's hand. A gesture that Phil missed as he turned towards the door, but Telfer saw it as he and his men trotted after their boss.

"Later," she whispered and left Phoenix on his own in the quiet bar.

He walked to the bar. Mick was drying glasses.

"I would have stepped in if Telfer had taken a swing at you, Mick," Phoenix said.

"Thanks, now you understand why I warned you earlier," said Mick. "I don't know your game, but you must stay away tomorrow night. I don't want to see you get caught up in the fallout,"

"You're undercover, aren't you?" asked Phoenix, the penny finally dropping. "Is there going to be a raid tomorrow?"

Mick stopped drying the glass. He thought for a moment.

"I've decided to trust you. I don't think you're mixing with these low-life scum for fun. I don't know who you work for, but we have enough for an arrest. We've been tracking the Dwyers' for eighteen months."

"I've got a few extra pieces of evidence and possible witnesses to add into the mix," said Phoenix. "I'll pass them on to your HQ before I leave here."

Mick and Phoenix shook hands.

The net was closing on the Dwyer gang.

Chapter Twelve

Phoenix drove back to the safe house and parked the car. Once inside, he tidied up. He knew he must complete one more day's collecting tomorrow. He couldn't give Phil Dwyer any clue that everything wasn't one hundred per cent normal.

Mick had fooled him for days. Phoenix hadn't reckoned him as a policeman working undercover. The pub was the ideal spot to gather intelligence, but the man had the guts to put his head into the lion's mouth. Almost as much as he did working for them. It would be over in twenty-four hours, and then he could get home to Athena and Hope.

The place looked immaculate when he finished cleaning. The takeaway containers were in the bin, and he'd done the washing-up. His Olympus gear and spare clothes were in his bag. Phoenix looked around him. He was confident the safe house seemed as good as he would wish it to be if he was next to use it.

Phoenix rang Athena and relayed the good news.

He called Giles to arrange help for Jim and Mary Hatch. They deserved a holiday.

Phoenix checked the address for the couple who sent one of their kids to her parents because they couldn't afford to keep them together as a family. Giles would sort that out in the morning.

Phoenix looked in the fridge. One can of lager left. You might as well drink it. It might be out of date before anyone else stops here. There was an unopened bottle of wine there too, but he didn't feel in the mood.

"I'll see what films we have in that pile of DVDs, and then it's an early night."

Ten minutes into 'Man of Steel', the doorbell rang, and Phoenix's heart sank.

Later meant later tonight then, he thought.

Phoenix opened the door. Annie stood there in a tight red dress and black high-heeled shoes. Her hair hung down, and her makeup accentuated those fiery eyes. Annie looked hot.

"I realised which was your car in the car park earlier," she said, "so I checked the driveways opposite the row of shops to find you."

"You're persistent; I'll give you that,"

Annie didn't wait for him to ask. She pushed past Phoenix and walked into the main room.

"My, you have tidied the place," she said, "it doesn't look as if anyone lives here,"

They won't after tomorrow, sweetheart, Phoenix thought.

"Can I get you a drink?" he asked, "there's a bottle in the fridge."

"I'm driving," she replied, "I know it doesn't usually stop me, but there's something I want more."

Annie kicked off her shoes and closed the distance between them. She wrapped her arms around him, and her teeth pulled on his lower lip. Annie lifted her hair from her neck, inviting him to unzip the red sheath dress. It dropped to her feet, and she faced him in only a white thong. Phoenix had to admit; she was something else.

"Take me upstairs, Frankie," she said.

There was no escape; Phoenix carried her upstairs and tossed her onto the bed. There would be no foreplay, no conversation, no afterglow. He wanted to screw this woman until she couldn't take any more. He knew he must remain detached and cold. He must maintain the Frankie persona he'd adopted. It was the only way he could cope with having sex with another woman.

Phoenix lowered his hand to his zip, but she pushed it away. His erection was evident, and Annie wanted to feel him, taste him. She eased his trousers and pants over his hips. When his member sprung free, she gasped.

"Holy cow," Annie cried. "I've won the lottery."

Phoenix couldn't let her have her way. He flipped her onto her back and moved up her body, planting feathery kisses on her thighs and stomach. He kissed Annie hard, holding her hands above her head.

His hand moved to a breast, squeezing the nipple hard. Phoenix ripped the thong with his strong fingers. Annie moaned as he settled between her thighs; he pumped his fingers into her wet folds, hard and deep. He steadied his breathing. Phoenix knew he was in danger of enjoying this far too much. He hated himself for having to act out this charade.

Phoenix rescued a condom from the bedside table drawer. He had prepared for the possibility he couldn't keep her at arm's length, thank goodness. She begged him to be inside her. Her hands gripped his buttocks, clamping him on top of her again, his hardness pressing against her welcoming body.

He ground into her with an urgency that shocked him. His strokes were hard and powerful. Their bodies thrashed together on the bed. Phoenix watched Annie's breasts as they shuddered on her chest, her sturdy legs locked around his waist.

Phoenix closed his eyes and kept thrusting until Annie cried out with the intensity of her orgasm.

"Oh, Frankie," she cried, "you are amazing."

Phoenix was ready to explode. As he heard Annie cry out Frankie's name, he found his release. He wasn't there; it was his body, but she didn't have his heart or soul. That belonged to Athena. Annie clung to him, ready to go again. Phoenix rolled away from her.

"Another long day tomorrow," he sighed, "let's have that glass of wine, and then we can finish watching that film I started before you arrived."

"What were you watching," she said, curling up on the bed.

"Man of Steel," he said, slipping on his clothes.

"I think I saw him just now," Annie said. She had no clothes upstairs, not with her ripped thong on the floor, so she walked downstairs naked and slipped into her dress. When Phoenix returned from the kitchen with two glasses of white wine, she lay on the sofa.

"Will you zip me up, or should I stay ready for more?"

Phoenix zipped her up, picked up the remote and started the film. Annie rested her head on his shoulder, and they watched in silence. Phoenix hoped she wasn't planning to burn the place down because he'd knocked her back.

"I'll be in the pub tomorrow," Annie said as the credits

rolled, "I'll bring spare underwear and a nightie. Tonight's appetiser has given me a taste. I want to spend the night with you tomorrow."

"Time for you to leave," he said, kissing her hard, "tomorrow it is. I'm not going anywhere." It seemed Annie was satisfied for now, at least. She found her shoes, put them on and walked to the door.

"Phil was in a funny mood tonight," she said, changing the subject, "he can't find his nephews. They're always in trouble. The cops picked them up a week or so back, but we found too many witnesses placing them somewhere else, so they let them go."

"Did they do it?" asked Phoenix.

"I expect so," laughed Annie, "but nobody's seen them for a day or two."

"Youngsters, are they? They're on a bender or shacked up with girls."

"Out of their heads on smack, more like it," said Annie, "a mug's game, that is. I hope Phil finds them tomorrow, though. He's doing my head in, with his moaning."

"See you tomorrow night," said Phoenix. He stood by the door until Annie drove away.

Good luck finding the Mullen twins, he thought as he returned upstairs to change the bedclothes. As he loaded the dirty washing into the machine, he wondered where Henry found a spare patch of ground in the pet cemetery. It was getting mighty crowded.

Phoenix headed upstairs to bed; he knew his conscience wasn't entirely clear. He had been right; Annie Dwyer was something else, but tomorrow was another day, and the Dwyer gang were in for a big surprise.

Wednesday, 23rd July 2014

Phoenix knew it would be a long day; He woke early and made his usual eight o'clock check-in to Giles. His list took him to Byker this morning. In the east of the city, Byker suffered social problems common to other inner-city urban housing areas, including juvenile crime and vandalism. Turnover of tenancies was high. Families in employment moved out. Shops stood empty and abandoned. One in three of the estate's adult inhabitants was unemployed.

The only good thing about today's route was it took him to the opposite side of the city, away from the chief haunts of the Dwyer gang. Phoenix aimed to avoid contact with anyone except the people he needed to visit.

Things started well. Although Byker had more signs of poverty than yesterday's route, the people were cheery enough. They appeared to have accepted their lot, shrugged their shoulders and got on with life as best they could. The payments were small, and the money rolled in. By lunchtime, Phoenix had almost two hundred of the four hundred and fifty pounds due.

Phoenix couldn't dismiss his thoughts of Annie Dwyer or what lay in store this evening. He rationalised what he did last night. It was for the greater good; Olympus would get the desired result. Dwyer's gang would be under arrest, the loan-sharking operation dismantled, and many lives the better for it. Intimidation, threats, and violence would stop.

Time stood still as the afternoon dragged. He reached his final doorstep at four fifteen. Phoenix needed to collect eleven pounds from a reluctant middle-aged biker. His accent was as broad as the River Tyne, and Phoenix weathered a volley of abuse before the cash got thrown at him. As the door slammed in his face, Phoenix offered a prayer of thanks. No more houses to visit.

Phoenix walked to the car, double-checked the money against the book, and confirmed the figure. The cash and the collection book, with its lists of names and addresses, would add to the other intelligence he gathered. Phoenix planned to travel south by train after delivering the package to a police station en route.

It was too risky to return to the safe house until the police operation concluded. Mick hadn't given specific times, but Phoenix knew the Dwyers arrived at the pub by six. If they were due to deliver their takings, collectors like Benny Giggs and Alan Telfer stayed in the bar until they received their commission.

Phoenix calculated he could drive back under cover of darkness. He headed out of Byker and made for South Shields. He read somewhere Ocean Beach had a lot to offer. All he needed was a restaurant and a place to sit and watch the sunset.

The sun had disappeared by ten to nine. The last few sips of his glass of wine followed seconds later. A leisurely drive back to the safe house took Phoenix forty minutes. As he got near the pub, he noticed lights on, but the car park lay empty, and the place looked deserted. As he passed, he saw the pub door shut, and it now wore a 'Police-Do Not Cross' sticker.

It was always wise to be careful. Phoenix slowed as he approached the driveway to the safe house; it was empty. He appeared to be in the clear, yet he made a detour to check for anyone following him. When satisfied that there wasn't, he made his way back. After donning latex gloves, he gathered the items for the police and wiped everything clean.

It was after ten, and if he wanted to be away early in the

morning, he needed to get to bed. So he sent one last phone message to the local Olympus team leader. He told him he was returning to Bath to collect the saloon car from the railway station.

Phoenix woke up at one o'clock; someone had activated the alarm. The flashing light told him that. There were no bells or sirens; the agents didn't want the intruder to know they were aware of their arrival.

Phoenix pulled on his trousers and grabbed his Sig-Sauer P226 with its carbon fibre suppressor. Then he hurried downstairs, slid the weapon under a multi-coloured cushion on the sofa and sat facing the kitchen.

Whoever was outside didn't count on the house belonging to Olympus. They had three problems. First, the silent alarm was also triggered in the home of the local team leader, which meant that four agents were already on their way. Arrival time, ten minutes. Second, even with a weighty battering ram, it would take too long to keep the element of surprise. Third, Phoenix was armed and cheesed off at having his beauty sleep disturbed.

The door gave way at last, and a figure emerged from the kitchen doorway. He wielded a baseball bat. Phoenix called out, "Lights." His would-be assailant blinked in the sudden brightness.

"Voice command, Alan," he said, "clever, isn't it?"

"I turned up twenty minutes late tonight," Telfer snarled, "and your lot had raided the pub. I managed to get clear. When I called my mates, they never answered. I drove to their place, and the cops had just taken them away. I should have known you'd be a copper. Sniffing around Annie, conning her into thinking you were something special."

"I'm no copper," said Phoenix, lying back on the sofa

with his hands spread across the back, "and Annie came on to me, not the other way around."

"I sat outside last night when she was in here," Telfer continued, "I told you she was my woman. It's time you got taught a lesson."

Telfer moved towards Phoenix with the baseball bat raised.

His eyes opened wide as he saw the gun. Phoenix whipped it out from under the cushion.

"Wrong again, Telfer," said Phoenix and shot him in the heart.

The thug dropped to his knees and pitched forward. His head landed by Phoenix's feet.

"Revenge comes in many colours," said Phoenix, patting the cushion.

The front doorbell rang three minutes later.

"You made good time," Phoenix said.

"Less traffic than in the daytime," said the team leader.

"One body to go, and you can have the carpet cleaned at your leisure. The back door might need replacing. Our friend here hacked at it for ages."

"No problem. We'll secure the door, dispose of the body, and collect the car in the morning. Anything else?"

"I don't think so," said Phoenix. "Was the pub raid a success?"

"The police lifted Phil and Annie Dwyer, plus five others at the pub. The co-ordinated raids across Tyne and Wear recovered a massive amount of cash, and the police made eight further arrests."

"Terrific news," said Phoenix. He would shed no tears for Annie Dwyer or her brother. Olympus had to hope they got their just desserts when the case came to trial.

"We'll let you get back to bed then, Phoenix," said the team leader ten minutes later, "goodnight."

Thursday, 24th July 2014

"I dropped everything I gathered into the Central Police Station," Phoenix said, "for the attention of Mick, the barman, and his superiors. That should find its way to the right people."

"I'm so pleased, darling," said Athena, "what time will you be home?"

"Can someone collect me from the station at around half-past two? I bought a supersaver off-peak ticket to reduce costs."

"You're incorrigible," sighed his wife. "See you later. I must dash. The morning meeting is due to start."

Phoenix rang off and looked up and down the platform. There were crowds of people, but he spotted no familiar or threatening faces. The train pulled in, and he got on board. He stowed his kit bag in plain sight. He wanted no one to wander off with it. Phoenix settled in for the five-hour journey.

At nine o'clock every weekday morning, Hugo Hanigan had been used to talking with his senior gang leader. Hugo liked to feel he kept his finger on the pulse. Tommy O'Riordan told him what he needed to know, even if he sometimes kept back a few misdemeanours his men committed. Those chats filled in the time nicely until Hugo went across to the

Grid's private bank. That was where he carried out his real business.

This morning, he was alone. He hadn't seen Seamus McConnell for weeks now. No loss, as the lummox was only good for telling him the basics of what happened on the ground. Colleen O'Riordan had sent him packing and assumed control of her late husband's men.

Hugo found her brother, Sean Walsh, simpler to manipulate. He was not as bright as Tommy, but he always appeared loyal to the cause. Until the last few occasions, he had been in his penthouse. Hugo had been taken aback by Sean suggesting that a new outfit might be responsible for the Grid's losses in May. It wasn't until Tommy died that Hugo wondered over Sean and his conniving sister.

Sean hinted at an outfit unconnected to the Grid, maybe not even connected to the criminal fraternity. Hugo had laughed at that suggestion until his security guys got blown to bits. Perhaps Sean had been involved in the suspicious deaths from the beginning?

Colleen sent Sean and his family abroad after Tommy's death. That didn't feel right to Hugo. Sean would have wanted to attend his brother-in-law's funeral. Why was he living on the other side of the world?

Hugo needed someone he could trust. Things were still progressing well for the Grid's finances, but these bewildering deaths kept wounding them. Two mornings ago, news reached him at the bank that the Mighty Quinn was dead. Hugo didn't have any time for Quinn. He had been 'old school', a criminal who followed in the footsteps of the Kray and Richardson families.

Times had changed. These days, men like him ran things —brilliant, sophisticated men who dealt in billions on global markets. The local villain who lived by his wits and knuckle-dustered fists was history. So only one thing bothered Hugo about Quinn's murder. Was it related to the Grid's other losses, or was it a changing of the guard gangs often experience? Had a younger man decided Quinn was past it and removed him? Or was Sean Walsh exercising his influence from afar?

If Tommy was still alive, he could have discussed it with him over a Jameson's. Hugo slammed his fist on the arm of the chair. No, it had started to unravel when Tommy murdered Michael Devlin. True, the man was a grass, but O'Riordan should have ordered a hit and let one of his lesser goons earn a big payday.

It had been downhill from there. The more Hugo wondered about Sean Walsh, the more sense it made that he tied into the conspiracy. It seemed lunacy when he put forward McConnell's name to become his second in command. In hindsight, it could have been a calculated move. McConnell would never be acceptable to him as a leader once Sean had left the country. The other gang members thought it ludicrous, but when Sean's sister Colleen told them she was taking control, they fell in line like a well-drilled platoon of soldiers.

There it was, the sticking point, the thing that antagonised Hugo. Colleen O'Riordan had taken control of her late husband's gang like a natural. She had them working harder and more efficiently for the Grid, and her ruthless elimination of Conor Key in her first few days in charge had quashed any thoughts of resistance.

Hugo knew he should call Colleen and invite her over. He had her number but was still trying to learn where she had moved after selling Tommy's house. She was moving far too fast for Hugo's liking. Did she and her brother have designs on Quinn's borough? Might they both have been behind his killing? These were questions he had no answer to, and if he invited Colleen to his apartment, she wouldn't help him. She was a sly one; always had been since he first bumped into her on the streets of Dublin, aged five.

Hugo grasped the nettle. He called her.

"Colleen, how are you?" he asked, more cheerily than he felt.

"Oh, I'm fine, Hugo," replied Colleen, "this is a surprise."

"I think it's time we buried the hatchet, don't you? I wanted to congratulate you on the sterling job you've done since taking control. Can you come up and see me?"

Colleen thought for a second or two. She needed to get the image of a hatchet buried in Hugo's skull from her mind before she answered.

"I could drop in one morning next week, Hugo, say Friday, if that suits you. What time is convenient?"

"We'll say ten o'clock, shall we?" said Hugo. "I need to be at the Glencairn by noon."

"I won't delay you, Hugo, don't fret," said Colleen, "until next Friday then."

Hugo stared at the huge picture window. That went better than he expected, even if she pushed the meeting back as far as she dared. What was she planning?

In her penthouse, Colleen thought how unusual it was for the fly to approach the spider. Her web lay ready, and Hugo would be trapped in it before he realised.

"Time for a glass of champagne to celebrate," she said.

"Whatever you say, boss," replied her young assassin. He fetched the bottle from the ice bucket, skilfully removed the cork, and delivered it to the table with two champagne flutes.

"Death to our enemies," said Colleen.

"Just say the word," replied her young assassin.

Phoenix arrived at Bath Spa station at a quarter to three. The Olympus transport waited to take him back to Larcombe. He threw his kit bag in the boot.

"Welcome back, Phoenix," said the driver, "successful trip?"

Phoenix nodded and climbed into the back of the car. He wasn't in the mood for friendly banter. Things couldn't have gone much better during his time in the North East on the outcome of the missions. But he still had to decide how much to disclose about what happened.

Rusty and the others wouldn't ask for details. Athena had told him to do what was necessary, but women often said things like that. The time would come when she would ask pointed questions.

He was no closer to a decision when the car turned into the grounds of the Manor.

The driver dropped him at the front door.

Phoenix retrieved his bag and went inside. Rusty and Artemis walked down the stairs.

"Thank goodness you're back safe," said Artemis, "Athena has been so worried."

"You got them then, Phoenix?" asked Rusty.

"Yes," said Phoenix, surprised at the tone of the question.

"You had an early morning visitor, according to Giles. How did he learn the address of the safe house?"

"One thug, Alan Telfer, evaded capture on the night of the police raid. The fact he visited me suggests I was lax in covering my tracks. He must have followed me home, and I didn't spot him."

Rusty wasn't convinced. He taught Phoenix well when he arrived four years ago.

"Why did he come after you?" asked Artemis.

"Because I wasn't in the pub when the cops arrived, he thought I must be the undercover cop. He never suspected Mick, the barman who worked there for months. I was a newcomer, so it had to be me."

"I'd better get going," said Artemis, "I'm due in the ice-house."

Rusty carried a sports bag over his shoulder. He brought it forward to show Phoenix.

"I'm off for a swim. A few of the trainees are coming over later. They're up for another challenge. Will you join us?"

"No thanks," said Phoenix, "I'll find Athena, report in, and rest up before whatever tomorrow brings."

"See you at nine in the morning then," said Rusty. He and Artemis left the main building, arm in arm, and walked across the lawns.

Phoenix watched them go. Life was simple for those two.

He headed for the apartment; time to face the music.

Chapter Thirteen

Friday, 24th July 2014

When Phoenix was reunited with his family yesterday afternoon, much was left unsaid. When he dropped his gear in their apartment, Athena had been in the administration offices with Minos and Alastor. He went to find her.

"Ah, you're back," she said, welcoming him with a warm embrace and a kiss on the cheek.

"Glad to see you made it back in one piece, Phoenix," said Minos. "You took an awful risk going undercover without the usual support system."

"It was a calculated risk, Minos," shrugged Phoenix, "which paid off. The Dwyer gang will be out of business, thanks to the police. My role was only to eliminate one of their enforcers, Telfer. A nasty specimen who enjoyed beating up old ladies."

Phoenix sensed Athena watching him. At this stage, least said, soonest mended.

Alastor gave Phoenix a brief update on progress regarding the billeting of the Irregulars.

"Slow but steady," Minos added. "We can expect little more, I'm afraid. PTSD and mental health problems among our veterans are far greater than anyone imagined."

"I'll leave you two to it," said Phoenix, "we'll see you in the morning."

When they reached the privacy of their apartment, Athena welcomed Phoenix back. Then, as they stood, wrapped in one another's arms, she asked the question Phoenix dreaded.

"Did anything I need to know about happen between you and Annie Dwyer?"

Phoenix felt relieved at the phrasing of the question.

"No," he replied, "things never got personal in any way, as it turned out."

Athena continued to cling to him. Phoenix was happy he hadn't had to tell her an outright lie. Annie and Frankie had sex; Phoenix had only been there in body. With the subject closed, he could move on. The Dwyer gang was now consigned to history, just like the criminals on every other Olympus mission. They weren't worth talking about in life. They figured even less in the Project's dealings now.

The last morning meeting of the week proved to be an odd mixture. Giles Burke reported the aftermath of the police raid and the clean-up teams' actions across Tyne and Wear. Giles and Artemis would do everything possible to hide Phoenix and his alter ego Frankie, from Mick, the undercover policeman and his superiors.

Henry Case was quiet and reserved. Athena understood her security chief wrestled with his conscience. The Mullen twins now lay buried in the pet cemetery. There were no new guests on Level Three to occupy Henry's time. His thoughts were full of the killings he had carried out in the past and the woman he loved. Henry received a new letter from Sarah Gough this week. Henry's heart filled with joy when she wrote of their passionate weekend and how much she longed to be with him again. In three weeks, she was coming to Larcombe Manor for the christening.

Rusty and Artemis discussed Phoenix and the undercover mission late last night when she ended her shift in the ice-house. Rusty guessed there was more to the story than Phoenix admitted. Artemis had reservations, too but gave Phoenix the benefit of the doubt. They sat opposite one another in the meeting and followed matters closely, searching for hints that would confirm their opinions. Neither was any the wiser as the session ended.

"Before we go our separate ways," said Athena, "I have dates for your diary. On the first Monday in August, Minos will chair this meeting. Phoenix and I are entertaining Ambrosia. We will update her on our progress with the Irregulars. On the eighteenth, Hugh Fraser will join us as our Logistics chief. He will attend our morning meetings whenever Phoenix is absent. I need not remind you of the following Monday as that's the date for Hope's christening in the Manor's church."

"We are entering what used to be termed the silly season," muttered Phoenix, "when the press printed frivolous news stories in high summer because nothing seemed to happen. Let's hope the Grid's members take a break for the rest of the summer, or the mountain we have left to climb will have grown higher."

The Olympus senior team left the room. While the weekend and then the following week unfolded, they remembered Phoenix's words.

He was right; everything hung, suspended in time,

waiting for an event that kick-started the mayhem. They weren't the only people holding their breath, wondering what came next.

Friday, 31st July 2014

At ten o'clock sharp, Colleen O'Riordan entered the lion's den. That was how Hugo Hanigan liked to imagine the situation as he watched her exit the lift.

"Colleen, welcome," he said, "it's been too long."

Colleen ignored his hands, spread wide, hoping for a show of affection. There would be no hugs today.

"So, you believe it's time we played catch-up, Hugo," said Colleen, one hundred per cent focused on business.

"How's Sean, Maeve, and those lovely children?" he asked. Hugo moved over to the coffee machine and poured cups for them both.

"Will you have coffee with me? You take it white, without sugar, if I recall."

Colleen didn't wait for the invitation to sit. Instead, she made herself comfortable in one of the leather chairs near the picture window.

"I thought we had got past the need for small talk, Hugo," she said, "but if you insist. Sean's fine in the villa near La Romana. The dust has settled on the fallout from Tommy's prison break and his murder. My brother and his family will return home soon. After that, Sean can get back to doing what he does best. I need him to assume responsibility for areas acquired in the recent past. As for my coffee, show the milk the cup. I prefer it hot and strong."

Hugo paused before bringing over the coffee. Acquisitions? He had heard rumours about the Mighty Quinn's parish, but nobody told him Colleen had already acted. He must be off the pace, and he didn't like it.

"You appear to have done well since you replaced Seamus McConnell as leader of your late husband's people," said Hugo, who remained standing. He looked out of the window and across the city.

"McConnell was never in charge," sneered Colleen.

"Ah," thought Hugo, "I was right. Walsh only appointed him as a ploy to deceive me. Even though he's thousands of miles away, he still holds the reins."

They drank their coffee in silence.

"I hope these acquisitions are for the right reasons, Colleen," said Hugo. "The Grid should be the sole focus of every gang leader in our network. Together we are stronger. We can't sanction the actions of a loose cannon, seeking to disrupt the benefits we collectively enjoy to satisfy their ambitions."

"It's taken you a long time to work out that we're expanding, Hugo," said Colleen, rising from her seat and joining him by the window. "Perhaps, you haven't got your finger on the pulse any longer? I've improved every operation within Tommy's old patch, for which the Grid coffers should be grateful. I see no borders between our neighbours and us. Quinn was an anachronism. Sean will keep that area under control as soon as he gets home. Other areas will follow. I mean to control the whole of the capital, Hugo. One leader at the head of the major player within the nationwide network. It makes far more sense than a dozen yes-men from different nationalities. You should welcome it, but perhaps you can't congratulate me on my progress because I'm a woman?"

Hugo was tongue-tied. He never expected this. Colleen

and Sean intended to take the rug out from under him. His power base would be in the hands of two Dublin children that ridiculed him on the seven streets where they played. He must act decisively and with the utmost speed.

"What do you see when you gaze out of this window, Hugo?" asked Colleen.

"I look down on the City and the Glencairn Bank. I'm in one of the world's great capitals and know that the Grid controls every criminal activity as far as my eye can see. It was me who made that happen; Ardal James Hanlon, the boy from Dublin who became Hugo Hanigan, a world-class entrepreneur."

"Do you know what I see, Hugo, from my eagle's nest over there," said Colleen, pointing up towards the new tower block where she now lived, "my future."

Hugo shivered. The woman was delusional, quite mad. He had been right; he needed to act.

Colleen made for the lift.

"Must dash, Hugo," she said, "you need to be at the Bank. I, too, have important business that demands my attention."

The lift doors closed. Hugo picked up the phone.

"McConnell," he said, "get over here. I know. You didn't think you'd ever hear from me again. I have a job for you. Oh, before you leave home, check your passport is valid,"

Hugo had made up his mind. Sean Walsh was a danger. He didn't have all the answers, but Colleen had shown her hand. Sean was returning to a position of power, and his sister regularly mentioned 'we' when talking about their future. He had been right to suspect Sean of being involved since the start.

Seamus McConnell left the penthouse an hour later

with his orders. His loyalty to Sean Walsh had been bought for ten thousand pounds in cash and the promise of a further handsome sum of money for completing his given task.

Monday, 4th August 2014

It was the morning of the second meeting of Athena, Phoenix, and Ambrosia.

Piya Adani drove onto the Larcombe Manor estate at eight forty-five. Her hay fever was better if not finished for another summer. Piya was eager to meet up with Athena and Phoenix once more. Time was of the essence. Ambrosia wanted the sweet smell of success to follow her to the next Olympus meeting. Her ambition knew no bounds. Anything that pressed her claims for a more senior role in the organisation needed exploiting to the full.

Athena met Ambrosia by the front door.

"Good morning," she said, "and welcome back. Please come with me to our apartment. We'll not be disturbed there."

"Phoenix is there already?" asked Ambrosia.

"He's playing with Hope before Maria Elena takes her away from us for the morning. Of course, you wouldn't appreciate a little one crawling around your feet."

Ambrosia wasn't sure how to take that remark. She had never married, but nobody measured up to her father. He had been a dominant figure in her life, and every prospective husband introduced to her paled by comparison. But, unfortunately, it was too late now; she was forty years old, and although a child of her own would be fantastic, time was running out.

Ambrosia heard Hope's laughter as they reached the door. There was a lump in her throat as Athena paused with her hand on the door handle.

"Isn't that a beautiful sound?"

Ambrosia could only nod and attempt a smile. She couldn't trust herself to speak.

"Come on, Phoenix," said Athena as she entered the room, "time to start work."

Hope looked up from the floor. Mummy and that Indian lady had arrived. Daddy would be off-limits today again. She missed him when he went away the other week. As her eyes flicked from one grown-up to another, in walked her nanny.

"Hello," she said, "I'm ready to take Hope for a walk. Would you enjoy a swim later, Hope?"

Hope clapped her hands. This morning might not be so bad after all.

As the door closed on Maria Elena and their daughter, Athena broke the news to Ambrosia that the report from Minos and Alastor was less favourable than they had hoped.

"There is a far higher percentage of damaged goods than we expected," said Phoenix.

"We might get a thousand good agents from the homeless community," explained Athena. "If there's one good thing to come out of this, Minos has identified sufficient places to house them."

The news was a crushing blow to Ambrosia. Hopes of legions of new agents on the ground had slipped through her fingers like grains of sand.

"I sense your disappointment, Ambrosia," said Phoenix, "and we share it. It was a great idea, and it still is. If we get a thousand good men, that will be terrific news to those agents in the field stretched thin now in certain areas."

"In a fortnight, we will have a new logistics chief to assist Phoenix," continued Athena. "He comes to us highly recommended and with Phoenix's full support. He will allocate these agents to areas where they can have the greatest impact. Hugh Fraser will be our Holmes to the Irregulars."

Ambrosia was happier now. Progress was being made. Not as much as she hoped for, but she had a name on which to focus. She must learn everything she could of this, Hugh Fraser. If Phoenix recommends him, he must be a select type of man. He would live at Larcombe, and she was a welcome guest. Hugh Fraser would find Ambrosia a frequent visitor. Her vision of the Irregulars was only a few weeks away, and with Hugh Fraser's cooperation, she could propel herself up the Olympus ladder.

"Shall we visit Minos and Alastor? You can inspect the details of the veterans cleared by Henry Case, and the medical team, as being fit for duty. They can also show you the accommodation sites they have gathered where they could live. They are still matching people to regions, but this will remain fluid until Hugh Fraser arrives. He will decide who goes where once he sees the bigger picture. Then, he and Phoenix will make the final decision."

"I can't wait to read what Minos and Alastor have achieved so far," said Ambrosia. "I'm impressed at the volume of work you've done in such a short time."

"It's what we do," shrugged Phoenix, "we can't be idle. Evil doesn't sit on its hands for a second. So we must do more, to a higher standard, every day with less. That's the Olympus mantra for departments like those Minos and Alastor operate. Those men are two of our greatest assets."

Athena smiled as she led Ambrosia and Phoenix to the

administration offices. If only Ambrosia heard what Phoenix called these two at times. In the early days, she believed he thought little of their abilities. Now, she knew how proud he was to work alongside them.

Over the next few hours, the Two Amigos took Ambrosia through the Irregulars' files. After that, they broke for lunch and completed the task mid-afternoon. Ambrosia was confident her thousand agents would be an asset.

"I can't wait for Zeus to learn of the progress you have made," she said, "may I return in a few weeks?"

"Of course," said Athena, "we will be happy to see you."

Ambrosia said her goodbyes, drove towards the M4, then onto the M5, and north to Leeds. As every mile disappeared under the tyres of her car, she ticked off the hours in her head until she would meet this Hugh Fraser. She needed to form a strong alliance with this man. A bond Athena and Phoenix were not party to and could not break. Together, they could make the Irregulars her vital asset, her instrument of change. They could be her express-way to the summit of Olympus.

On the other side of the Atlantic, Sean Walsh spent another day in the rain with his family.

Since arriving in the Dominican Republic in June, the sole communication he received from Colleen had been to confirm a quarter of a million pounds had been transferred into a bank account in his name in the Cayman Islands.

It was enough to keep them going for ages if they were sensible. Of course, they had the upkeep of the villa to consider, but the building was theirs for as long as they needed it, and the cost of living was a third cheaper than back home.

Sean knew he could find a job if money got tight. But since they flew out of London seven weeks ago, it had always been his plan to wait until the dust settled on his brother-in-law's death and get the all-clear to return.

Relations had been strained between the four of them when they first arrived. However, Maeve soon forgave him for the slap he gave her when the stress of the prison break-out got too much. He had reduced his drinking also.

Saiorse and her younger brother Kevin thought missing the start of the new school term at the beginning of September was a hoot. It had become something for them to brag about to friends back in London. The longer they stayed here, the better.

Maeve looked at the possibility of finding places in the local schools for their kids, but Sean kept telling her their stay was only temporary. Maeve remained unconvinced, and there were the grown-up children to consider too: -

"I miss Sean Junior and Michael," she said. "I know they're married, and we hardly saw them while we were back home, but there could be grandchildren soon. Can't we at least find out how long this will last? I can't stand much more of this weather."

Sean shrugged. They were halfway through the wet season. It was sweltering and humid, as well as producing a lot of rain. For weeks, conditions had become uncomfortable outside. Only the air-conditioning made it bearable. There were another five weeks of this before the situation improved.

"Think yourself lucky we've only had the rain and the heat," he said. "It's hurricane season, and until we get to the end of September, the island of Hispaniola is a high risk for a major storm."

"How often do they hit," asked Maeve.

"Every ten years, roughly," replied Sean. "La Romana was devastated back in nineteen ninety-eight. Category three storm George cost hundreds of lives and thousands of homes. Flooding and landslides were widespread. This villa will withstand that type of storm, but there would be a major disruption if the area got hit again."

"I wish we lived back in London," said Maeve. "I used to moan at the weather there, but it was never as dangerous as this sounds."

"Don't worry, Maeve, we're safe indoors here, whatever nature throws at us. Anyway, there's still a good amount of sunshine during the wet season. It's not prolonged periods of rain. It's a sudden downpour."

"You're right, as usual," sighed Maeve, looking at her tan. "I've spent many days on the beach with the kids, lying by the pool, and then watched it bucket with rain in the evening."

"There you go," said Sean, "we've got nothing to worry about, have we? I'll call Colleen at the weekend to see how things are progressing. I don't want to be stuck out here until Christmas either."

That placated Maeve while she and the kids watched a cable TV show from the States. It was one that everyone fawned over, another celebrity family with more bling than class. That never interested Sean Walsh. He walked outside to the verandah and sat alone with his thoughts.

Sean knew what he was; a gangster, pure and simple. He didn't look forward to working for a living. He wanted nothing more than to be back in his old haunts among the people he knew and understood. Why hadn't Colleen been in touch? What game was she playing? Sean couldn't make head or tail of it, no matter how long he sat in the sticky heat listening to the rain.

At La Romana International, Seamus McConnell made his way through customs and left the terminal. The heat was oppressive in the cab as it ferried him to the budget hotel, where Hugo reserved him a room. The rain fell steadily, and the old taxi's wipers fought a losing battle.

Seamus was confused. His role in the organisation that Tommy O'Riordan ran for years had been simple. Whenever they wanted muscle on a job, they gave him a call. He often only needed to stand by while Tommy or Sean discussed things with someone who stepped out of line. The threat of violence was usually enough.

If it was a bank raid or a jewellery robbery, he did the heavy work, drilling, wielding a sledgehammer, and overpowering the security guards. He had never needed to do much thinking.

The money offered for this job meant he could quit that life and return to Portmarnock. He could find a house near his family and spend the rest of his days in comfort. That was the simple part. The hard part was doing what Hugo had paid him to do. He wanted Sean Walsh dead.

The taxi arrived at the hotel. The driver left with a smile that told Seamus he should get used to this foreign money fast. He must have paid him twice what he asked. Inside the hotel, when he reached his room, he learned what budget meant over here. He'd slept in worse places, but the Ritz it was not.

Seamus opened his suitcase. He had brought several changes of clothes, despite only being here twenty-four hours. The separate elements of the 3D-printed weapon were concealed between his clothes and in his wash bag. He assembled the gun, loaded it, and checked the instruction leaflet Hugo provided. It was fine.

Sean Walsh had never done Seamus any harm. He chose him as his lieutenant when Tommy went to prison. Hugo never agreed with the decision and cast Seamus adrift as soon as he could once Sean flew out. Yet, he was chosen as Sean's killer.

It was late. Seamus began to feel the effects of the long flight. He slept.

Tuesday, 5th August 2014

In the morning, the rain clouds had dispersed. A watery sun climbed in the sky. Sean could tell they were in for another hot, sweltering day. The best place for a pale-skinned Irishman was indoors or on the shady verandah.

His kids were as boisterous as ever. They needed the open spaces to get rid of that extra energy they possessed. He looked across the breakfast table at Maeve. We had the strength to spare at that age, he thought. In our twenties, it was as much as we could do to get out of bed; we had so much energy.

"Do you want to take a trip, kids," he asked, "drive out into the countryside, go to the beach?"

The shake of the head told Sean that a trip with their parents was not required. That was not cool.

"We're going into town later, Dad," said Saiorse. "Then I want to swim in the pool this afternoon when it's hot."

"I have a hair appointment," said Maeve, "can you run me into town for eleven o'clock?"

"Sure," said Sean. "I'll take you in, drop you off, and you can find your way back."

"Aw, Dad," said Kevin, "the buses are always so crowded, and taxis are expensive."

"Your Dad was only kidding, Kevin," said his mother, "I'll ring him when I leave the hairdressers. You meet me there, and Dad will collect us, won't you, Sean?"

"Yeah," replied Sean, "or you can take the car; that would be simpler. I don't need anything in town."

"Whatever," Maeve said.

In La Romana, Seamus McConnell made his way to breakfast. He was a simple man who liked to start the day with traditional Irish fare. However, the budget hotel favoured introducing international travellers to native cuisine. Seamus looked at his plate of plantains, salami, fried eggs and cheese. The sooner he got on a plane home, the better.

Seamus returned to his room and collected the gun. He had brought a light, linen suit to wear a shoulder holster. When Seamus was satisfied it didn't make the jacket look too bulky, he checked his map and found the quickest route to the villa. Seamus was roasting when he hopped onto a bus that took him to within fifty yards of the Walsh family home.

He watched the bus disappear into the distance and waited until the passengers that got off with him went their different ways with their shopping. Even in Portmarnock, he couldn't recall women taking live chickens home, tucked under their arms. He walked past the lane to the villa. There was nobody on the road. No sign of a car by the villa. Was the Walsh family even at home? He turned back and crept closer to the building. It was tranquil. No sounds of the children playing or Sean's wife giving him earache.

Sean Walsh sat on the verandah overlooking the swimming pool. A Panama hat on top of his head at a jaunty angle shielded his face from the sun. Seamus stood and watched for a moment. The time had come for his day of reckoning.

When he heard Seamus give a deep sigh, Sean turned towards him.

"Seamus," he cried, jumping out of his seat, "at last, what news have you got from Colleen? I haven't heard a whisper from anyone since we got here."

Seamus approached the verandah.

"Are Maeve and the kids alright?"

"Yes, they're in town this morning; they'll be back by lunchtime. I don't know why you had to hand-deliver Colleen's message. We've got the phone and email out here. It's not that backward."

Seamus's breakfast was repeating on him. He might have argued the point with Sean if he hadn't had his orders from Hugo.

"Come on, Seamus, when can I get home? What did Colleen say?"

Seamus drew the gun from inside his jacket.

"I didn't bring a message from Colleen, Sean."

Seamus fired twice.

"Sorry. That message was from Hugo Hanigan."

Seamus looked at the dead body of his colleague. The look of confusion on Sean's face would stay with him forever. He needed to get back to the hotel, confirm his flight details, and leave this hot, sticky country as soon as possible. But, whatever Hanigan was paying him, it wasn't enough.

No passengers waited at the bus stop, so Seamus walked back towards town, keeping off the main road wherever possible. He didn't want people to recall a huge white man standing near the villa. If Maeve and the kids returned earlier than Sean said, they might recognise him.

Seamus heard the bus chugging behind him as he neared the next village. He waved an arm. The driver stopped. He got to town and trotted up the hotel steps before noon. He stripped off, jumped in the shower, and tried to cool off. It was pointless. The only thing he saw when he closed his eyes was Sean's face, fixed forever with a look that asked. 'what the hell?'

While Seamus confirmed his flight time and decided whether to risk lunch in the restaurant, Maeve Walsh turned the car into the narrow lane that led to the villa.

"Ha, ha," said Kevin, looking through the windscreen, "Dad's asleep on the verandah."

Saoirse was first out of the car. She ran up the steps. She screamed and fainted when she saw the bullet holes in her father's chest. Maeve had remained in the vehicle. Thousands of miles from home, the thing she always feared had happened, given her husband's chosen profession. It had to be a gangland hit. Why Sean? Why now?

Maeve knew she must be brave for the kids. She had things to attend to here in La Romana. The one person she needed to talk with before they flew home with Sean's body was Colleen O'Riordan.

Colleen might know who was responsible. But, if she did, Maeve was certain her sister-in-law knew what to do about it.

Chapter Fourteen

Thursday, 7th August 2014

"The job's finished, and I'm home," said Seamus McConnell.

"Come around later today, and I'll pay the balance," said Hugo Hanigan, punching the air.

"You'll have to transfer the money into my bank account," said Seamus, "I'm in Portmarnock. I'm never returning to London. That was the dirtiest job I've ever had to do,"

"The man had become a liability," said Hugo, losing patience with the slow-witted giant, "he and his sister were in league together, working against the interests of the Grid."

"Maybe, maybe not," said Seamus.

"Well, it's done now. You'll have your money tomorrow. So keep your head down and your mouth shut, McConnell. Do you hear me?"

"Loud and clear, Mr Hanigan, as always."

In the Dominican Republic, Maeve Walsh's world had turned upside down. Ever since she returned from town on Tuesday, she knew nothing would be the same again. When she finally got out of the car, she called the tourist police, the politur. It was what Sean had told her would need to be done if something happened.

Kevin and Saiorse were in bits. Maeve comforted them as best she could while being desperate to go to Sean. A police car arrived an hour later. The politur checked the body and called the coroner. It was three in the afternoon before he turned up to give the official certification her husband was dead.

When he solemnly told her the facts she already knew about how he died, he also told her the police would now arrest her.

"Why?" she asked.

"Normal procedure with sudden death in the marital home," he replied.

"I drove into town with the kids for a hair appointment at eleven. Tell the police to ring this number. They'll confirm I was nowhere near here when he died. His death was no domestic dispute. This was a hit."

The threat of arrest disappeared as soon as it came. A car from the funeral home for all ex-pats collected Sean's body and took it for the autopsy required by international law.

Dusk had fallen before Maeve, and the kids were alone. She called Colleen and broke the news to her sister. The silence on the other end of the phone unnerved her.

"It will be forty-eight hours before I can register the death at the Embassy," she told Colleen, hoping she was listening, "once the official death certificate is issued, we can fly him home."

"I'll get Tyrone to fly out," said Colleen, "he can help you with the arrangements. You need a man out there to get things moving. I'll also talk to the priest and get a date for the funeral."

"Thanks, Colleen. Who could have done this?"

"Not the time to be thinking about that, Maeve," said Colleen, "when's the earliest you think you will be home?"

"Next Tuesday, or Wednesday, I think."

"Hug those kids for their Auntie Colleen. Tyrone will be with you in a day or two."

The painful call had ended, and Maeve returned to cry with her children.

Colleen was in her penthouse, instructing Tyrone.

"Pack your bags. Take a dark suit and a black tie. Do everything you can to make things as easy as possible for Maeve and the little ones. When you're at the villa, look for clues. If the police took anything away, bribe someone to discover what they have. Check the local hotels, and see if anyone stayed there that we know. Take enough cash to grease the palms of the staff at the hotel and the airport. Find out if a familiar name appeared on a passenger list flying to the UK on Tuesday or Wednesday."

"Got it, Mum," said Tyrone, "leave it to me."

Tuesday, 12th August 2014

Sean Walsh returned to London in the afternoon. His coffin was carried from the rear of the plane and taken to his home. Tyrone, suited and booted, accompanied his aunt and cousins in the dark limousine Colleen had sent to collect them.

Colleen waited outside the Walsh residence when they arrived. She had let the funeral director indoors herself, so Sean's body could go to the games room. It could stay there until the funeral on Monday.

Tyrone took the children indoors while Maeve ran to her sister-in-law. The two women hugged briefly.

"Our priest has arranged the funeral for noon Monday, " Colleen said. "I've contacted as many people as I thought you would want to attend. The list is in the kitchen by the kettle. So you have a day or two to get your head together if you need to call anyone else."

"Thanks, Colleen. I don't know how we would have gotten through this without your help. Tyrone was marvellous."

"He's his father's son," smiled Colleen. "Tyrone has hidden depths."

While Maeve went to the games room to be with her late husband, the children settled back into their old surroundings. They were quiet, but they had British TV, mobile phones to be reactivated, and cases to empty.

Tyrone was alone with his mother.

"What did you learn?" she asked.

"Seamus McConnell," he replied.

"Hanigan sent him," said Colleen. "Right, as soon as the funeral has ended and the wake gets underway, you know what to do."

"Death to all our enemies," said Tyrone.

Colleen's smile reached her eyes, a rare event. Her son

was proving to be a priceless asset. His talents would be put to further use when the time came.

Monday, 18th August 2014

At noon, the funeral service for Sean Walsh began at St Mary's church. The Walsh family attended in numbers. Colleen stood beside them with her son and daughter; Rosie had flown in from Marbella on Saturday.

The priest glanced in Colleen's direction as he passed. A mere six weeks had passed since Tommy's funeral. Now her brother-in-law was dead. Too many of his parishioners got caught up in this madness. Too many lives ended prematurely. Would they never learn?

Although members of families who had arrived in the UK from the seven streets of Dublin filled the congregation, there was no sign of Hugo Hanigan. The service travelled its painful course, and Sean's body went for cremation at one o'clock. Maeve and her four children followed the hearse, as did Colleen, Tyrone, and Rosie.

They held the wake at the same social club Tommy and Sean had drunk in together for years. Those mourners who wished to pay their respects went there after the church service. Maeve, Colleen, and their children joined them by two o'clock.

The club was filled with people who were drinking, chatting, and reminiscing.

Colleen nodded to Tyrone. He made to leave.

"Where are you going?" asked Rosie.

"Mum needs a matter dealt with," replied Tyrone.

Hugh Fraser arrived at Larcombe Manor at lunchtime to take up his post as Logistics Chief. A steward met him in the car park as soon as he drew outside the main building. He learned his billet was in the stable block, and the steward escorted him to his door.

Hugh dropped his kit in his room and searched out Henry Case.

"Welcome, Hugh," said Henry, "we've heard good things about you. Phoenix has needed a helping hand for ages."

"I'll do my utmost to live up to the high standards you expect from your agents here, Henry," said Hugh.

"Phoenix told me this morning; you should get settled in, read the files he left you, and knock on my door at six this evening. I'll give you a guided tour of the areas for which you have clearance. I'll issue your passkeys later."

Henry left Hugh at the door. The newbie spent the afternoon unpacking, getting stowed away, and reading files on half a dozen future operations. He found a thick file on something called 'The Irregulars', which was too much to take on in the time available.

Hugh felt hungry. He wondered whether anyone in the neighbouring rooms could help with directions. Then, as he stood outside the door, he heard the unmistakable sounds of a couple doing what came naturally. Hugh retreated to his room. It was almost six. Henry could tell him where everything was in a few minutes.

The phone rang. Hugh answered, thinking it must be Phoenix or Henry.

"Hello, is that Hugh Fraser? I'm Ambrosia, one of the senior Olympians working with Athena and Phoenix. I wanted to wish you every success in your new role. I look forward to meeting you in person and hope we will work closely together on the Irregular project to make it the absolute best it can be."

"Thank you," said Hugh, "you're very kind."

Henry rapped at the door.

"Are you ready, old chap?"

"I must dash, I'm afraid," Hugh said to Ambrosia. "I'm off on the guided tour. Until we meet then, face to face,"

"Until then," said Ambrosia. She put the phone down. What a confident-sounding man this Fraser sounded. She allowed herself to dream.

Hugh joined Henry in the corridor. The head of Security stood with a younger couple. Henry introduced them: -

"Hugh, these are our senior Training Officers, Kelly Dexter and Hayden Vincent. You're sure to bump into them. They're your next-door neighbours.

Hugh Fraser blushed. Kelly and Hayden picked up on it immediately.

They looked at one another and burst out laughing.

"Sorry," said Kelly, "but we're trying for a baby, and the time was right."

"You've lost me," said a puzzled Henry, "we'll get on with the tour, Hugh, shall we?"

The two men left, and Kelly and Hayden returned indoors. The coast was clear.

Saturday, 22nd August 2014

Phoenix and Athena awaited the arrival of her parents. Geoffrey Fox called last evening to say they would travel down by train to spend the Bank Holiday weekend at Larcombe. Athena's mother had been under the weather recently. Her latest check-up in Harley Street had produced more headshakes than nods of approval.

"You must try to lose weight, Mrs Fox," Dr Ramanayake, her consultant cardiologist, had told her, "and stop running around as if you are still a young woman. You are in danger of undoing the good the past two years have seen."

"Hope dotes on her grandmother," said Athena, "I hope Daddy can persuade her to slow down and take it easy. It would be awful to lose her."

"We can ensure she puts her feet up while with us," said Phoenix. "Geoffrey will have to stand up to her if things are to improve. What time does the train arrive?"

"A car is picking them up at a quarter past twelve. Sarah Gough is coming by train, too, since her VW camper went to the dealership in the sky. I suggested Daddy travel to Waterloo with Mummy to meet her. They can have a chat on the way to Bath. Daddy usually gets a taxi to Paddington, but there's little in it, and the company will help Sarah."

"I'm surprised Henry didn't offer to drive the car into Bath," said Phoenix.

"Oh, he is," said Athena. "I offered him the chance after yesterday morning's meeting. He was over the moon."

"How many of us will there be in the church?" asked Phoenix.

"Fifteen, including Hope," replied Athena.

"Almost a full house, then," said Phoenix.

"We're privileged to live on an ancient estate like this, with its own church," said Athena.

"I suppose so, but we hardly use it. We get far more use out of the orangery, stable block, and the ice-house."

Athena gave him a look.

"I wonder when the last christening took place?

Perhaps, we should have a re-think when our second child is born. It will give us a reason to hang onto the church for a while longer before you bulldoze it to make way for accommodation to house the Irregulars destined for the west."

"Come on," said Phoenix, "let's check that the rest of the house is ready for the arrivals this afternoon.

After lunch, Henry Case drove into the city to collect the Reverend Sarah Gough and Athena's parents from Bath Spa station. Geoffrey spotted the affection between the younger couple and nudged his wife gently as the couple left them to meet their daughter after arriving back at Larcombe.

"That relationship has moved on somewhat since the wedding, dear,"

"Who will officiate at their wedding, I wonder," said Grace.

Geoffrey smiled.

"What did I say?" asked Grace, confused.

"Nothing, darling," he replied. "I just thought you could guarantee they would get married for definite. I imagine a vicar living in sin would set hearts aflutter at the head of the Anglican Church."

"Geoffrey, you're incorrigible," said Grace as Athena came down the stairs to greet them. Phoenix walked a few steps behind her, carrying an excited Hope.

They exchanged greetings, and Hope stood on the floor, holding her grandmother's hand so that she could totter along. The weekend had begun.

In the stable block, Sarah and Henry had already climbed into bed.

"We won't be disturbed, darling," said Henry. "Nobody hangs around here on a Saturday afternoon if they can help it."

"I wish I didn't have to sleep in the main building, Henry," said Sarah, "but we must keep up appearances. Now stop talking and remind me what I've been missing since the weekend of the flower show."

Two doors along, Hugh Fraser ploughed through the Irregulars file. He had lots of catching up to do. He'd realised that from the minute he'd arrived. Phoenix had taken him to the orangery for the first time yesterday. No wonder he used that place as a sanctuary. It was so quiet and peaceful. They got far more work done there. He wondered if it would be okay to move there this afternoon. That thudding noise against a wall somewhere close by was very distracting.

On the other side of the city, Phil Hounsell explained to his wife Erica why he was calling a halt to Hounsell Security Services.

"I thought you enjoyed working with Wayne and the others," she said as they sat watching the children playing in the garden.

"After I left the police, I needed to do something. The pension was enough to keep us going, and your thirty hours a week at the building society meant we were far better off than many families. But, unfortunately, work has been thinner on the ground these past three months. Jake Legg and Dusty Miller needed more regular contracts, so I had to let them go. They're working in Weston now and earning a decent wage at a place that's only an hour's drive from home. Travelling around the country mothering pop stars took its toll, and the hours were ridiculous."

"Have you talked to Wayne? He'll be gutted. Anyway,

what will you do? I can't see you becoming a house-husband."

"I've been offered a post with the Olympus Project charity out at Larcombe Manor. Because of the nature of the work, it's not practical for Wayne to accompany me, nor do I think I can retain the HSS office for only one staff member. If I accept their offer, I need to tell Wayne, and we'll wrap up our outstanding jobs, pass on those we can't complete to local companies in the same field, and close the office. Larcombe wants me on-site in a month. I would start work on Monday, the twenty-third of September."

"Call Wayne now," said Erica. "Invite him over for lunch tomorrow. Get it over with."

"You're right," Phil sighed. "I shall miss the big lump, he's an odd character, but it's been fun. Wayne will find another gig with a uniform. He usually does."

Monday, 25th August 2014

You can never depend on the weather in England, especially if it's a Bank Holiday. The weekend had been warm, with passing clouds. The day of the christening promised to be warm, with frequent and heavy showers.

Phoenix and Athena had decided weeks before that 'options' needed to be a top priority when they planned the day's schedule. So, the outdoor BBQ became an indoor brunch without a hitch. They abandoned the walk across the lawns to the little church on the edge of the estate. The transport section provided three vehicles; one carried Phoenix, Athena, and Hope, plus her grandparents.

Rusty and Artemis accompanied Giles and Maria Elena, Hope's nanny.

Minos, Alastor, Kelly, and Hayden were the first to arrive. They had travelled over with Henry Case and Sarah Gough.

Hope wore a new white dress for the occasion.

The Reverend Sarah Gough welcomed the congregation to the church. The service followed its traditional path to baptism, the signing of the cross, and welcoming Hope into the Church. Rusty and Artemis promised to fulfil their roles as her godparents.

Kelly and Hayden wondered how long it might be before they could ask to use this church again to be married and then return to baptise their own child.

Artemis wondered whether she and Rusty would ever marry and have children.

Henry watched Sarah with pride. She was so suited to this role.

Henry loved her with all his heart. He was determined never to let anyone or anything come between them.

The rain had relented when they left the church. The transport was ready, and they were soon inside the Manor house. The party began.

Hope was in her element. Lots of grown-ups fussing over her, lots to eat and drink. She would dance with her Daddy soon after he had finished cuddling Mummy. If only things could always be this nice, she thought. The bad things they face appear to have gone away.

She remembered what Grandma had said last night to Grandpa when the clouds got dark and the birds stopped singing: -

"The lull before the storm,"

While the folk in the West Country celebrated a joyous occasion, something quite different took place in the centre of London.

Hugo Hanigan rested. It was late in the afternoon. He had spent the weekend in the country and had only returned at three o'clock. So his schedule was empty until tomorrow at noon when he was due at the Glencairn Bank.

The intercom buzzed; someone wanted to come up. It had to be a stranger. Anyone he had agreed to meet in his apartment knew the entry code. Hugo walked to the lift and studied the face on the CCTV.

"The ghost of Tommy O'Riordan has come to call on me," he cried. "The last time I set eyes on Tyrone, he was ten years old."

He pressed the buzzer. Tyrone entered the lift.

Hugo poured himself a large Jameson's and stood with the bottle hovering over an empty glass.

"Will you have a glass with me, Tyrone? You gave me a turn just now. You're the spitting image of your father. He and I often shared a glass."

Tyrone nodded. Hugo poured until Tyrone lifted a hand to stop.

"What can I do for you, Tyrone?" asked Hugo. "Is it something your mother couldn't face doing herself? She had to send her lackey?"

"There's plenty you don't know about me, Hugo," said Tyrone, sitting in the same chair his mother had occupied the other day. "My father did everything he could to give Rosie and me an education. He wanted us to take up a profession that would earn us enough money, so we would never be tempted to follow in his footsteps. I became an accountant. My parents didn't travel to Spain often, so I had time on my hands.

Marbella is teeming with ex-pats; many have fled to the sun to avoid arrest. I was Tommy's son, so those old boys treated me like one of their own when I reached eighteen. I learned the things my Dad didn't want me to learn. I'm good at what I do. My so-called friends laughed behind my back when Dad went to prison. They're not laughing now. My mother asked me to come home to help her after Dad got killed. I told her I was ready to be better than Dad had ever been."

Hugo was edgy. He kept wiping sweat from his brow.

"We never did discover who was responsible," he said.

"Now, only weeks later, Uncle Sean has been slaughtered. Two of your most senior men dead within two months. Some might say you were careless. Others might see a pattern."

"I had nothing to do with either of those killings, Tyrone," Hugo whined, "you must believe me."

"Seamus McConnell didn't agree," said Tyrone, "when we had a brief chat yesterday."

Hugo was up and out of his chair now, his glass empty. He was shaking.

"You've lost control of everything, Hugo, including your bladder by the looks of it. Who do you think executed Fergus Mallon and his team? Who erased Michael Quinn? McConnell, your hired assassin, won't spend a penny of the blood money you paid him."

Tyrone got out of his chair, removed the stiletto from his coat pocket, and flicked out the blade. He closed the gap between him and the shivering jelly of a man that had been Hugo Hanigan, master entrepreneur and leader of the Grid.

Hugo watched in slow motion as the blade pierced his chest twice. The third, fourth and fifth times never registered. He was on the wooden floor, swimming in his blood.

"Death to all our enemies," said Tyrone.

He called his mother while watching the deranged banker draw his last breath.

"I've avenged my father's and Uncle Sean's deaths," he said.

"Good," said Colleen. "Come home. That merits a celebration. The Grid is ours for the taking now. You will assume control of the Glencairn Bank in the morning. I shall inform the Grid's associates that if they wish to continue laundering their money, it will cost them an extra five per cent, with immediate effect."

"What about Hanigan?" asked Tyrone.

"Don't leave any trace of yourself in the apartment. Then, remove the body and take it to Smuggler's Way. Wrap it from head to foot in those orange waste bags they use. Dump Hanigan on one of those large barges that take rubbish to landfills further along the Thames, out in the Marshes. He doesn't deserve any better."

Tyrone followed his mother's orders. If the police didn't get here in the next twenty-four hours, it would do until they could get the clean-up done professionally. As he looked around, he thought this place suited a young banker making a name for himself in the City.

Moving a dead body around London isn't a simple task, even in the dead of night. It took Tyrone O'Riordan until dawn as he dodged and weaved his way to the riverside. Hanigan was in the boot of his car, something else that needed a deep clean — even wrapped in dozens of orange bags. Then, he saw his chance; a heavily laden barge was at the dockside. He checked nobody was watching. Tyrone opened the boot and bundled the body onto the barge. Later this morning, it would be on its way. He drove away from the quay and parked further along the riverbank.

Two hours later, a string of barges moved past where he stood, waiting.

There, he recognised the barge with the blue tyres instead of the usual fenders at the bow — Chelsea supporter.

Everything on that barge was orange. Tyrone was satisfied. He could go home and sleep. It didn't matter what colour it was; revenge was sweet.

Epilogue

Tuesday, 26th August 2014

It was back to work after yesterday's celebrations for the senior staff at Larcombe. As the morning meeting ended, the news broke that the Rotherham Inquiry report had concluded that fourteen hundred local children had suffered sexual abuse over fifteen years.

"Children as young as eleven, brutalised, and their lives damaged forever," said Athena.

"An inquiry, a report, the hand-wringing that follows, are far too late," said Phoenix, "they can never regain their innocence. What rankles with me is that Olympus' actions in Swindon showed the template against which the rest might follow. Yet the number of towns and cities that display systematic cases of abuse continues to escalate."

"It's heartbreaking," agreed Athena, "we should consider taking direct action."

Olympus was unaware of the events of last night and this morning. The landscape has altered. The Grid was always a force for evil, but Hugo Hanigan has now gone. Instead, Colleen O'Riordan and her son Tyrone have taken command. With them at the helm, things are soon to get much worse.

Next in The Phoenix series

vinci-books.com/three-weeks-september

A nation in turmoil. A shadow organization. 21 days to save the UK.

As the UK teeters on the edge of anarchy, the secretive Olympus rises to battle organised crime and religious extremism. Amid the country's rising lawlessness and new leadership, Olympus operatives must navigate a labyrinth of passion, treachery, and sorrow, all compressed in a three-week period.

Turn the page for a free preview…

Three Weeks in September: Chapter One

Monday, 1st September 2014

Sandy Moloney stared through the glazed front window of the Docklands Light Railway EMU. The Electrical Multiple Units have become a familiar sight above and below ground over the past two decades.

He glanced at the increasing cloud cover drifting across the sky. It aimed to obscure the sun. Nevertheless, rain showers would not be far away —a great way to celebrate the first day of his final working week.

The annual medical did for him. Retirement was possible between sixty and sixty-five, and several colleagues had already taken advantage of that. They badgered him to quit when he met them between trips abroad or after golfing days near London.

Sandy was sixty-four and divorced. Although he saw his daughter on high days and holidays, they weren't as close as thirty-five years ago when he bounced her on his knee.

Cora, his wife, took a fourteen-year-old Amy with her when she walked out.

Living in London wasn't everything people made it out to be, not if you lived alone. So, thoughts of retirement went on hold. Sandy knew of others in their seventies still putting in a shift on the railways. You could continue to drive a train or fulfil the role of a train attendant on the DLR if you kept passing the medical. With the prospect of four walls to stare at every day, Sandy determined to keep working as long as possible.

Then, he attended that medical. The doctor sighed as he looked at the paperwork before him. Sandy steeled himself for the news.

"How long have I got?" he asked.

"If you reduce the drinking, give up the cigarettes, take regular exercise and switch to a healthy diet, you might have another fifteen to twenty years, Mr Moloney."

"Oh," Sandy said, "I thought I was a goner when you sighed."

"Something showed up on your scans we can control with medication. We can delay the condition from radically influencing your everyday life for a while. Those things I suggested you do will be essential in supporting that treatment. However, I couldn't pass you fit to drive either a car or a train. Nor can I let you be responsible for the lives of hundreds of passengers on those driverless units you run on the DLR."

"It's not cancer then, doctor?"

"Do you remember the initial cognitive and psychomotor skills tests you took before you came for the scans?"

"Oh, those," said Sandy, "I remember. What of them?"

"Your results showed a marked difference from earlier

tests. That's why we carried out the scans; to discover what might have caused it. Deterioration in those skills is a natural result of ageing, but it can be an early indicator of dementia or Alzheimer's. The comments from your line manager suggest you live alone. Do you have family members living close by? Do you have an active social life?"

Sandy Moloney shrugged; he had little to offer in reply. The doctor nodded.

"Another factor affecting performance on these tests is depression. We'll get you on a more even keel, Mr Moloney, and check any changes as we progress. If the more serious conditions I mentioned manifest themselves, we'll manage those issues as and when they happen,"

Sandy had collected his prescription, driven home, and poured himself a large glass of red wine. Of course, he was depressed. Who wouldn't be? The wrong side of sixty, with no wife or partner. A daughter with no kids living out in the suburbs. He had a handful of friends across London in his social circle, with wives, children, and grandkids, but with each year, the company newsletters informed him of another death, and that handful of friends grew less and less.

What of his immediate future? The doctor recommended he give up his car and advised that his only safe choice was to take the retirement package. He could no longer captain passengers on the DLR.

One by one, the things he held precious had been taken from him. He dragged his eyes away from the last few bright moments of sunshine ahead and considered his fellow travellers. They looked a disparate bunch — nothing new there. London was a cosmopolitan city when he moved from Southampton as a young man. The bustling port on the south coast had suited him. There was terrific nightlife for a teenager, plenty of job opportunities, and living at home had never been a problem.

His grandparents arrived in Southampton from the southwest coast of Ireland towards the end of the nineteenth century. Many relatives emigrated to the United States, and when he reached twenty-one, Sandy Moloney considered searching for long-lost cousins in Boston and New York. The bright lights of London in the mid-Seventies won him over. The train that carried him from Southampton to Waterloo pitched him into a colourful, noisy mass of humanity that never hushed or stopped.

Working for London Transport, above and below ground on various jobs, kept Sandy next to the throbbing heart of the metropolis. It had been intoxicating, with everything and everyone always on the move. However, nothing stayed the same for long. The skyline altered with new buildings shooting skywards, jarring with the centuries-old structures the millions of tourists visited.

Sandy watched it as he worked on the overground and underground trains that crisscrossed the capital's network. He met Cora Flynn on a late-night tube as she returned home to Dagenham from a gig. Fashions in clothes and music altered too, and he cringed when he thought of their wedding photographs, now consigned to a suitcase at the bottom of a wardrobe.

The attraction between them had been immediate. Cora always said she knew the second she spotted Sandy walking through the compartment that he was Irish and the one for her. For Sandy, her wild, curly hair and dark brown eyes captivated him. The punk clothes, with slashed jeans, safety pins and chains, didn't deter him.

He grabbed the closest hanging strap and stood, swaying to the train's rhythm next to her. He knew his uniform and her outfit signalled an odd couple to the rest of those late-night travellers. But they melted away, so Cora and Sandy became the only two people in the world.

"Do you want to see my ticket?" she had asked.

"I want your phone number," he replied.

"Is this a new London Transport policy?"

"I prefer to think of it as an initiative. Do you think it will work?"

Their wedding at St Peter's Roman Catholic Church occurred nine months later. Sandy's uniform and Cora's slashed jeans were replaced by a modern suit and wedding dress for the occasion. The 70s fashions dated faster than any decade before or since. The following year, even the photos at the christening of their daughter, Amy, disappeared before the decade ended. Then, by 1990 both the women in his life left him.

The sights and sounds still flashed and crashed around Sandy as he threw himself into work to ease the pain. He nodded his assent whenever a colleague asked him to pick up an overtime shift. The money was little compensation. He had nobody on whom to spend it. Before he knew it, Sandy allowed twenty years to drift by, and when the doctor gave him the ultimatum, it suddenly made him realise that life had all but passed.

He had spent every day since arriving on that train from Southampton serving the public. He doubted any people travelling with him this late morning even cared. During his last week at work, he would move from Bank to Lewisham and back again. Colleagues told him there were regulars if you took the trouble to look at their faces. Sandy had to admit he stopped noticing. The different shapes and sizes, colours and creeds, men, women and children had become wallpaper.

Had he seen that elderly couple before, two rows back? Could he remember where they boarded? What of the students? What did they study? There were surely tourists; you could spot them, even without the cameras. He gazed at another elderly lady for a while. He remembered her getting on at Greenwich. She had been out of breath when she took her seat. The same as Sandy, she carried more weight than good for her.

It was no good; he couldn't recognise anyone. Nobody nodded or uttered a kind word. That was common when he began working in London many years ago. Millions travelled on the Tube, crushed together, hurtling from station to station in artificial light or, occasionally, total darkness. Even in the days before wi-fi, a conversation was out of the question. The deterioration speeded up the day Sony Walkman arrived. It was much easier to stick headphones in their ears and shut out the world.

The EMU slowed. They were pulling into Crossharbour on the Isle of Dogs; Sandy kept an eye on the passengers. People got ready to leave the train. Others shifted in their seats and watched people waiting on the platform. They were interested enough to look but not talk when they found a spare seat next to them. The doors closed. Another stop was successfully negotiated. Nobody tripped when making their way to the door or had to dash back for a forgotten item. More got on than left, so there were more straphangers.

Could he remember having seen any of the new arrivals? He saw nothing extraordinary about any of them, old or young. Several carried umbrellas or wore light rain jackets. Sandy checked the glazed window ahead. The sun had disappeared, and a smattering of showery rain now dappled the glass.

South Quay came next, and then Heron's Quay. Sandy walked towards the front of the cab. He wished he could get back in the driver's cab, but progress had almost eliminated that job. The captain operated the train manually in an emergency, but the occasion never arose since the DLR started.

Sandy and his driver colleagues weren't the only ones to find their posts being eliminated or transformed. The automated light metro system used minimal staffing on both train and major interchange stations. They staffed the underground stations on the DLR to comply with Fire and Safety requirements, but there was little to spare.

Young Moloney had arrived in London when the IRA wreaked havoc. He spent many nights underground wondering whether a bomb sat waiting around the next corner. Different brands of terror drifted in and out of London over the decades. Attacks on London Transport personnel had followed a steady upward trend. Everyone had to be vigilant. Many wanted to harm their fellow man for one cause or another. The Dockland bombings in 1996 had been the final atrocity from the Provisionals. Al Qaeda soon became a significant threat, and the events of July 2005 were shocking and brutal.

Sandy had been working nights that week. When Amy called, he was getting home and climbing into bed after an uneventful shift. She wanted to check he was safe. It took something dramatic to stir her interest in her father. The next call came in late December.

The minimal staffing levels concerned Sandy. How could you stop someone walking onto a station platform carrying a bomb if nobody was watching? A determined soul could wait until the coast was clear and then plant a device on the forum. Who would challenge them? Simple enough to buy a hi-viz jacket these days. What if they wandered up the tracks a hundred yards between trains and buried an IED? Who thought it worth checking they were supposed to be there?

They had arrived at South Quay.

Sandy scanned the platform for bombers or hi-viz jackets but saw none. Only suited and booted office-workers and business types from Canary Wharf. A group of middle-aged women, who Sandy imagined were ladies who lunch, followed the men onto the train. So many things have altered over the years.

The doors closed. The next stop was Heron's Quay.

The medication prescribed for him was working. It soon became routine to take it every day. The doctor said he needed to get more stable. He now suffered fewer bouts of depression. Sandy felt he had mellowed. He stayed alert the entire time the train stopped at the station. Although he hadn't admitted it to the doctor at their meetings, his concentration drifted over the past five years, especially on a warm afternoon.

It was time to move to the rear of the train. There were checks to carry out before they reached Canary Wharf, and finding a new vantage point for a change of scenery eased the boredom.

He took one last look at the front glazed window.

The rain had stopped. Sandy Moloney turned and headed up the aisle.

As he passed the elderly couple, something made sense that barely registered at first. There had been a dark shape across the track two hundred yards ahead. The EMU was travelling at 40mph. Sandy Moloney's ten seconds were up before he could react.

The IED detonated from a remote location in an apartment in Canary Wharf. The glazed front window of the EMU disintegrated. The sudden jolt caught every passenger unawares. Glasses flew off faces, and phones were knocked out of hands. Shouts and screams of alarm followed as the derailment nightmare unfolded. Everything shook as the train rapidly decelerated. People's belongings flew everywhere.

Sandy was hurled back into the standing passengers he passed. Seated passengers were tossed around like rag dolls as the cab twisted and turned. The elderly couple now lay under the seats opposite where they had been sitting. The lady's right leg suffered a break. Her husband had suffered a significant head wound.

The screams Sandy heard as he drifted in and out of consciousness came from the middle-aged ladies who got on at South Quay. The older woman, on her own and who joined at Greenwich, slumped in her seat. Apart from a massive swelling above her right eye, she looked calm. She was the last person Sandy saw.

As it ground to a halt, the stresses and strains on the three-car EMU played out against a cacophony of tortured metal and human suffering.

For a few seconds, there was silence.

The front car was a mangled wreck. The second and third cars had tilted precariously for endless seconds, then toppled onto their side, their bodywork remarkably intact. Those passengers, still mobile, attempted to escape through the rear of the third car. Heads appeared from the windows and doors of the rear cars. Help was arriving from members of the public who had been at the station. They summoned rescue services, but access was restricted. Those inside the EMU requiring urgent medical help lost valuable minutes from their golden hour.

The automated system controls were triggered, and traffic halted on the Lewisham-Bank DLR network. The bomb squad was alerted. The first explosion witnesses reported inside and outside Heron's Quay had to be confirmed. Then the search would begin for additional devices. The DLR would stop for a considerable time.

The terrorists in the apartment surveyed the scene from a safe distance — no words were necessary. The two men turned from the devastation they caused and removed every trace of their presence in the room. Thirty minutes later, they walked to the lift in the corridor, descended the twelve floors to the street, and went their separate ways. Busy pavements swallowed them in seconds.

Conversations they overheard as they passed by concerned their handiwork. The sense of panic they picked up in the voices was music to their ears. They both smiled on the inside; this was only the beginning.

Half a mile away, the streets next to Heron's Quay were filled with ambulances, police vehicles, and fire appliances. Police erected barriers and cleared the immediate area. The capital's media swarmed across every inch of ground, as near the action as possible. Overhead, helicopters circled. The police, security services, and Air Medical Services (HEMS) out of Whitechapel performed an unchoreographed dance routine.

Officers ran into every side street, shouting at every human being they spotted to move as far away from the blast site as possible. General traffic was at a standstill. Every parked car was scrutinised in case it posed a threat.

On the rail track, the bomb squad personnel edged their way forwards, checking for evidence that more explosions were imminent. Colleagues swept the platforms and approach roads, allowing ambulance crews to move forward.

Twenty-seven minutes after the explosion, the first paramedics reached the first car. The scene was one of overwhelming devastation.

Behind them, members of the public who had risked life and limb to scramble along the track helped the walking-wounded thread their way through emergency services personnel. Those fortunate enough to walk unaided were reaching the platform.

There were still passengers trapped inside the rear, two cars crying out for help. Everyone near the stricken EMU knew the poor devils in the first car had suffered the most. Those crying out as the paramedics dashed past were still breathing, their airways clear. They were not their priority, as harsh as that might sound.

The quiet ones demanded their urgent attention.

The paramedics entered the rear of the first car. Ahead of them, a shapeless mound of people. The blast and sudden deceleration of the train threw dozens of passengers helplessly forwards. People lay trapped by bodies and debris. Here and there, voices were shouting to get out. Elsewhere they made only moans and groans. The paramedics made rapid assessments as they drew closer. An older woman they passed was beyond help. A man pinned to his seat by a metal bar was unconscious but breathing. On the floor, trapped under the seats, lay an elderly couple. The woman had a badly broken leg and suffered a collapsed lung. A man, perhaps her husband, lay next to her. He wasn't breathing. It was going to be a long day.

Minute by minute, the situation moved from chaotic to controlled. The critical and seriously injured were extricated with help from the fire services where necessary and transferred to waiting ambulances. Local accident and emergency departments had already received dozens of casualties needing various degrees of treatment. Doctors were primed for worse injuries to arrive later, knowing that life-saving operations would be necessary and scheduled routine operations needed deferring again.

Hours passed. The only passengers who remained on the EMU were beyond help. Paramedics continued to work on their standard procedures after the bombing. The scene should be as undisturbed as possible. They must preserve the casualties' dressings, clothing, and belongings for forensic evidence. They had to keep pieces of shrapnel from the device inside the first car for examination.

The authorities had learned many lessons over the past twenty years. Every scrap they encountered could be the key to determining responsibility. Knowledge added to the vast data security services had amassed increased the odds of preventing the next attack.

They removed the bodies of the eighteen people who perished on the EMU to the nearest morgue. The first bodies arrived a few minutes before four o'clock. A final body arrived at half-past five. Six hours had elapsed since Sandy Moloney started what turned out to be his final journey. There was a certain irony that the EMU's captain was the last to leave.

News bulletins on TV and radio had carried reports of the original incident. As the drama unfolded throughout the afternoon, the scale of the attack became more evident. Derailments are not an uncommon event; often, they don't result in any injuries. It was a while before the explosion witnesses reported hearing was confirmed as an IED. Everyone soon forgot about the minor disruption to the network and the passengers involved. The tone of the bulletins grew more sombre as the afternoon progressed.

Across the capital, in many households, family members waited for news. The DLR carried one hundred million passenger journeys each year.

Many Londoners rode the EMUs daily to and from work, school, or college. The cars ferried people to business meetings, shopping trips, and social outings. But, until they heard from their loved ones, nobody could be sure they hadn't been on the Lewisham-Bank train that left the terminus before noon.

In Vincent Gardens, Belgravia, Geoffrey Fox awaited the return of his wife, Grace.

Geoffrey had been in their small rear garden after lunch. Grace travelled by bus and train to meet a school friend in Greenwich. This visit was a regular occurrence on a Monday. The mode of transport might have changed in recent months, but Grace kept in contact with as many old friends as possible. There were fewer and fewer each year. Time was short and precious.

He pottered in the flower borders and trimmed a few overhanging bushes. He was careful not to do too much damage. Then he planned to sit on the seat they often shared and study his efforts. The late morning showers had scudded through, and now a warm sun peeped through the clouds. Their sheltered spot was a sun-trap. Geoffrey rested his eyes and fell asleep.

Three o'clock had come and gone when he awoke. He rechecked his watch. Grace should have been home by now. He returned indoors and called upstairs in case she had just come indoors. There was no reply. He stood at the bottom of the stairs. Perhaps, he should call Daphne? To check whether they chatted longer than usual and whether Grace had caught a later train.

When he replaced the phone, Geoffrey was worried. Daphne had told him she dropped Grace at the DLR station in Greenwich at the same time as always. She begged Geoffrey to ring back with news.

It was rare for Athena's parents to watch TV during the day. Geoffrey couldn't stand the nonsense between the music on the radio, so he was happy to do without entertainment, apart from his Times newspaper. That kept him abreast of everything he needed to know. It often occupied several hours of his day as he went through one thoughtful article after another. Finally, he switched on the television.

Geoffrey Fox perched on the arm of a leather settee as he watched the rolling news report from Heron's Quay. Grace would have been on that train. She could be injured or even worse. It was time to call their daughter, Annabelle Grace Fox-Bailey. He hoped she was at Larcombe Manor with her husband, Phoenix. Whatever needed doing, those two would want to be involved. He returned to the hallway, picked up the phone, and dialled.

"Daddy?" asked Athena, surprised to hear from her father.

"I'm afraid your mother travelled on that train today, darling," said Geoffrey. "I haven't heard from her."

"Sorry, Daddy," said Athena, "we returned from the North of England in the last hour. Phoenix and I have been travelling for hours. What train? Where did this happen? Why did Mummy go on a train without you?"

"She visits Daphne, her old friend from Greenwich, most Mondays. They have coffee somewhere together, and then your mother comes home. Taxis in London cost the earth these days, and now we're eligible; we've picked up

Freedom Passes and Sixty Plus Oyster ID Cards. That provides free bus travel and concessions with the Senior Railcard on off-peak Oyster fares."

Athena was incredulous; that didn't sound like Daddy. He always travelled first-class everywhere. She couldn't have helped the Olympus Project without her share of the family fortune she inherited when reaching twenty-five.

"I don't know why you two are scrimping and saving, Daddy. Forget that for the time being. Tell me what's happened."

"Mummy takes the bus to Tower Gateway and then travels to Greenwich, with one change of line. The whole trip takes her fifty minutes. On her return trip, she was due to change at Westferry from the Lewisham-Bank line. When she reached Tower Gateway, it was only a fifteen-minute walk home. Walking has been part of her exercise regime these past weeks. However, the consultant still reckons she's overweight and putting too much strain on her heart."

"So, where did this accident happen?" Athena asked.

"The train derailed at Heron's Quay just before noon. It wasn't an accident, darling. On the news, they said there was a bomb; someone left an IED on the tracks. I'm watching the latest news now. Emergency service people are scrambling over the train and the tracks. It's a mess. It had to be a terrorist attack, but nobody has claimed responsibility yet. If Mummy was in the first car...."

"Phoenix and I will be there by six o'clock; if we can get hold of our helicopter pilot at such short notice. You stay by the phone. We'll find out where they are transferring the survivors. As soon as we know something, either Phoenix or I will call. I love you, Daddy. Try not to worry. Mummy will be fine."

Geoffrey replaced the phone and walked into the

lounge. On the screen, there were wide-angle shots of the three-carriage EMU. Paramedics hustled three stretchers along the track carrying casualties. Those poor beggars must at least be alive, though Geoffrey thought, or they would move much slower.

It was fast approaching four o'clock. The live feed ended, and in the studio, the newsreader updated the confirmed number of casualties.

"Seventy-three passengers are continuing to receive treatment at the A&E departments. A further one-hundred and three have been released with minor lacerations and bruising. Those that remain in the hospital include twenty-eight with serious, life-altering injuries. Eight of those twenty-eight are critical. At this time, the death toll is eighteen. Screens are being erected by the track to allow the removal of the bodies of the deceased. That operation will start in a few minutes."

The programme switched to one of the hospitals, where a senior doctor confirmed the number of fatalities and sent his condolences to the families. The leading causes of death were severe trauma associated with crush injuries. As for those on the critical list, the next twenty-four hours were vital. When pushed on whether the number of deaths might rise, he said it unlikely that the eight would make it through the night.

Geoffrey sank into a chair and waited for the call he hoped never came.

Three Weeks in September: Chapter Two

Meanwhile, at Larcombe Manor, Athena and Phoenix confirmed their plans. Biggles was en route from Filton airfield. He would land on the grounds in ten minutes. They were to fly to Fairoaks, a small airfield southwest of London. Forty-five minutes after take-off, an Olympus driver would drop them in Vincent Gardens one hour later.

Athena rang her father.

"We'll be with you by six, Daddy. Any news?"

"Nothing yet, darling. All the survivors are out of the train. Only body bags to bring out now."

Even though she tried, Athena couldn't hold back the tears. She wanted to hold her father and take away the pain. Where was Phoenix? He had gone to the ice-house to find out what information Giles and Artemis had gathered. Athena could hear Biggles approaching.

Athena stood, drying her eyes by the window. Phoenix was standing on the lawn waving to her as Biggles came in to land. She waved back and headed for the nursery door. Maria, Elena and Hope were inside playing.

"We need to shoot off again," she told the nanny, "can you feed this one and put her to bed? I've no idea when we'll be home again."

Athena gave their daughter a quick cuddle and kissed her forehead.

"Night, night, poppet," she said and dashed away before the tears returned.

"Something's up," thought Hope.

Athena emerged from the main building onto the lawn and ran towards the helicopter. Phoenix was already seated. Biggles waited until she had fastened her belt, and then he was up and away, heading for Surrey.

"Any news?" asked Phoenix.

"Daddy was in a state," she replied. "He knows the casualties are now out of the train, no matter how major or minor their injuries. The bodies are leaving as we speak. He said there were eighteen fatalities. What did you learn?"

"Artemis had details of those recorded as having left the hospital after treatment. Your mother's name wasn't among them. She was still checking on the rest. Several will stay in overnight."

"Did Giles have any clues this was imminent? Who might have carried out the attack?

"Nobody has claimed it so far," said Phoenix, "but it has certain hallmarks that point to Islamic State. Giles is monitoring the usual websites and forums. As I left, he had captured feed from CCTV cameras in Canary Wharf. He may find something. I asked him to investigate what trackside stretches are picked up by nearby cameras. Maybe we can identify who planted the device. Giles reckoned it had to be a remote detonation, which means hunting for the best vantage points and finding out who was in them when the bomb exploded. The problem is that vantage points are in the hundreds. That's why people pay big bucks to live or work there."

"You haven't asked the obvious question yet," said Athena.

"What? Why was Grace using the DLR?" asked Phoenix.

"Precisely," said Athena, "you need to have a serious talk with Daddy when this is over."

"Look, we've more urgent things to confront," said Phoenix, taking hold of Athena's hand. "Let's pray we find your mother sat up in a hospital bed, wondering what the fuss is."

"I have a bad feeling, Phoenix," sighed Athena. "Daddy will fall to pieces without her."

The flight with Biggles lasted the time he had told them at take-off. The private airfield was well-equipped, and the driver in the limousine was waiting for them to arrive. Within a minute of touching the tarmac, the car was gliding through the gateway from the airfield. They joined the flow of traffic travelling the three miles before joining the M25. Sixty minutes later, they arrived at Vincent Gardens,

Athena stood on the doorstep with Phoenix and rang the doorbell.

Geoffrey Fox answered, his face grey with worry. Phoenix thought he'd aged a decade since he saw him at the christening seven days ago.

"Come along in, you two," he said. "I've been by the phone, listening to the radio, but I've heard nothing. Surely, they'll send a police officer around, won't they? Or will they send an automated message to my phone?"

Athena led her father through to the lounge and got him seated.

"Tea or coffee?"

"Tea, please," replied Geoffrey.

"Right, I'll get drinks organised. While you and I keep one another company, Phoenix will make the phone calls."

Phoenix joined his wife in the kitchen.

"Get the relevant numbers from Giles," she said. "We can't call him in the ice-house and give Daddy an insight into what goes on at Larcombe. Find out what progress he's made on the CCTV leads. Then you can find which hospital Mummy went to; there's still time to visit this evening. If we're looking at the worst-case scenario, we need to face it tonight. We have important operations to see carried out over the next few days."

"Either way, you must stay here at least for tomorrow," said Phoenix. The kettle had boiled; Athena made the drinks and carried them to the lounge. Geoffrey sat with his head in his hands.

"God knows how I'll cope if she's gone," he said.

"We could have lost her on several occasions in the past four years, Daddy," said Athena, wrapping her arms around her father. "We'll get through it together if we must."

Phoenix was in the hallway calling Giles.

"I need the contact details for each of the A&E departments involved. If other numbers are necessary for morgues, or what have you, then can you provide those too, please?"

"Of course," said Giles, "are you ready?"

Phoenix wrote the numbers for each of the hospitals where they transported casualties.

"The emergency services commandeered only one morgue," said Giles and relayed the number.

"Thanks, Giles. Anything new?"

"Our eagle-eyed former police officer caught sight of a possible bombing suspect. Artemis saw a man on a side street parallel to the DLR, four hundred yards from the blast site. He carried a rucksack over his shoulder. He was a Muslim dressed in European-style clothing. The surrounding crowds were animated, alerted by the explosion thirty minutes earlier, but he passed by without a glance. I agree with Artemis; the guy looked too calm."

"I'll leave you to carry on the search," said Phoenix, "he may not have been working alone. If we can place this man, or any companions, near the exit to a high-rise building in the locality, then we can eliminate the time difference. The vantage point is what we're seeking. Find that, and no doubt they will have spent those minutes super-cleaning the flat or office they used; this wasn't a random attack by a lone bomber. On the contrary, it has all the signs of being highly organised. Ask Artemis to identify this man. I want to know who we're dealing with."

"Will do, Phoenix," said Giles. "I hope you hear good news about your mother-in-law. She's a lovely lady. Maria Elena and I enjoyed her company at the christening. Mrs Fox was so happy, and we could tell she doted on little Hope."

"Thanks, Giles," replied Phoenix. "I'll start by ringing the last number you gave me. Let's hope the others aren't redundant. Grace and Geoffrey are the only grandparents Hope will ever have, so they're doubly precious."

Phoenix dialled the number for the morgue.

"Darling, you're back," said Athena as he re-entered the lounge three minutes later.

"I'm sorry, Geoffrey...." Phoenix began.

Geoffrey clung to his daughter and burst into tears.

Athena was sobbing on his shoulder. Phoenix knew how much she loved both her parents. She was heartbroken. The morgue had confirmed the terrible news that Grace Fox was among the eighteen fatalities.

Phoenix wanted to hold his wife, to comfort her. But she and her father sat together, consumed by their grief, and now was not the time. Phoenix had never experienced unconditional love, nor had he grieved when his parents died. He liked to think he was a different person now, over twenty years later, but he had never regretted his actions.

He sat across the room in silence until Athena looked up at him.

"What happened, Phoenix? Do we know how she died? Where is her body?" she asked.

Geoffrey composed himself somewhat and, still clinging to his daughter, listened as Phoenix told them what he had learned.

"Grace was on the right-hand side, two-thirds of the way up the front car. It's thought she hit her head on the seat in front when the train decelerated immediately following the blast. The autopsy will provide the final answers, but her head injury doesn't appear to have been severe enough to cause her death. Initial examinations suggest she may have suffered a cardiac arrest."

"Poor Mummy," said Athena. "If she had a heart attack in many other circumstances, she might have lived, despite the problems we know she had. But, it would take too long for anyone to get to her in a crash like that."

"We can only hope it was quick," said Phoenix.

"Where did they take her?" asked Geoffrey.

"I'll call the driver," said Phoenix, "and ask him to return here. We can go to see her. The autopsies will take place over the next few days; it might be too early to make funeral arrangements. I'll ask what timetable they think we're using. We can stay here tonight. I'll return to Larcombe in the morning. Darling, you need to be with your father. Stay as long as you both need."

Athena nodded. She wanted to return home to her daughter, but Phoenix was right. She was needed here. Maria Elena would cope, and Phoenix could take the opportunity for father-and-daughter time. For her part, she had her heart set on getting her father through the ordeal and preparing him for the future. Athena didn't want to lose him for many years yet. He was only in his late sixties and enjoyed good health.

"The car's outside," said Phoenix.

"I'll grab a coat," said Geoffrey, and he hustled out into the hallway.

Athena took the tray of cups and saucers through to the kitchen. She glanced at the His and Hers calendar by the fridge. It held appointments for the hairdresser, the chiropodist, the dentist, and the doctor. The flowers in the bowl on the window sill were her mother's favourites.

As she followed the two men to the waiting car, she realised that although the little things her mother had done to make this house a home remained, nothing would ever be the same.

After they arrived at the morgue, they confirmed who they were. Then Geoffrey was taken through to make a formal identification of the body. Phoenix and Athena accompanied him. Grace looked serene, apart from the wicked-looking bruise on her forehead. It was as if she was merely sleeping.

Phoenix watched as Athena and her father wept. The glass between them and their loved ones made the situation even more painful. However, he understood they must observe protocol. The autopsy came first. When they returned to reception, two other couples were waiting. Two more families were going through the same nightmare.

"Go ahead, darling," whispered Phoenix. "I'll ask when we might expect to collect your mother's belongings and get information from a staff member before I leave. Wait for me in the car."

He joined them five minutes later, and they drove to Vincent Gardens. Once inside the house, Phoenix ensured Geoffrey was comfortable in a chair. Athena took a seat beside her husband.

"Her belongings will be released within forty-eight hours. So it might be a week before we know an exact date for the body to go to whichever undertaker you choose. We're looking at two weeks from today before any funeral can take place."

Phoenix then left Geoffrey and Athena alone, discussing what until then had always been a taboo subject. Athena had never asked what funeral service her parents wanted. Along with many others, it was something she hoped she didn't need to worry over for ages. He went into the hallway and called Giles again.

"It was bad news, Giles. It seems Grace died of a heart attack. The shock of the explosion was too much for her already weakened heart. She didn't suffer any traumatic injuries, thank goodness. At least she was spared that."

"I'm so sorry, Phoenix," said Giles. "I'm sure my colleagues here at Larcombe wish me to send their condolences. What will you do now?"

"I'm returning tomorrow. There are things I need to do. Athena will stay here for the time being."

"Right, I'll warn Maria Elena to keep Hope occupied

until you're free to care for her," said Giles. "Leave that with me. I'll ask Artemis to tell Rusty that you'll be back in time for the missions planned."

"Thanks, Giles," said Phoenix. "I'll catch up with you tomorrow to hear what you've discovered. Yes, Rusty and I are heading north again on Wednesday. Athena and I posed as day-trippers over the weekend, checking the lay of the land around Rotherham."

"I can give you the latest figures in the morning, Phoenix," said Giles, "but your initial thoughts were correct. The number of men charged with child sexual abuse offences is only a drop in the ocean compared to the true scale of what has gone unchecked for a decade."

"Rusty and I will head to Rotherham and Rochdale on Wednesday morning. We will meet with our colleagues from the nearest Olympus groups and carry out our reprisals. Unfortunately, we can't rely on the police to be quick enough off the mark to stop hundreds of potential suspects fleeing the region or even flying back to Pakistan."

Phoenix returned to the lounge, where he found Athena and her father looking through photographs he had taken at the christening. The last happy occasion they shared. Little did they know. Phoenix's mind drifted to events leading to direct action in the North.

Twenty years ago, care-home managers had investigated reports children in their care were being picked up by taxi drivers. Over a decade ago, names of alleged perpetrators, several from one family, were passed to the authorities. Four years ago, the first group conviction occurred when they convicted five British-Pakistani men of sexual offences against underage girls. They never arrested the ringleaders. Two years ago, the Times newspaper reported that sexual exploitation in the town was widespread, and the authorities had known about it for over a decade.

That same year the trial of a Rochdale child sex abuse ring took place. Nine men went to jail for several offences against up to fifty young girls over the previous three or four years. At long last, someone in government thought action was required. The report from the resulting independent inquiry was discussed in the morning meeting at Larcombe last Tuesday.

The report's conclusion showed that the council had a bullying, sexist culture of covering up information and silencing whistle-blowers and was not fit for purpose. The report's writer attributed the council's failure to address the abuse to factors revolving around race, class and gender. Phoenix had read the article and despaired of any real justice for the fourteen hundred victims.

The apologists would have a field day. There would be a good deal of hand-wringing for the TV cameras. A few officials would do the decent thing, resign and then walk away with an obscene gold-plated pension. Another inquiry would follow in time. The horrors would get swept under the carpet once the spotlight fell on another sector of society.

Sometimes the Olympus way was the only way.

"Do you want a hot chocolate, darling?"

It was Athena; she had interrupted his train of thought.

"I don't think so, thanks," he replied.

"Daddy will try to get a few hours' sleep," said Athena. "I won't be long behind him. What time are you leaving in the morning?"

"I asked the driver to collect me at seven, sorry. I have to get back."

"Well, you had better have a word with Daddy now while I find the cocoa. I doubt he'll be out of bed early in the morning."

Phoenix nodded. Athena headed to the kitchen; he sat closer to Geoffrey.

"What a day, Phoenix," the old man said with a deep sigh.

"We're all going to miss her, Geoffrey," said Phoenix, laying his hand on his father-in-law's arm. "Do you mind if I ask you a question?"

"Fire away," said Geoffrey.

"What sparked this change of routine? The taxi firms around Belgravia have made a roaring trade, with trips to restaurants, theatres, railway stations, and airports. Why was Grace using the bus and train combination to visit her Greenwich friend?"

"I don't want Annabelle to worry," said Geoffrey, "but our investments have taken a hit over the past few years. I understand we're not alone, and thousands of couples would love to be in our position. They offered us these concessions when we reached sixty, but we always refused them. Grace agreed with me that there were far more deserving cases across the capital. Then, on our last visit to the chap in Harley Street, the chap warned us Grace was risking her health by not being more active and not exercising to reduce her weight. So, I contacted the authorities and took every card and concession going. Then we planned how to get Grace to visit her friend and organise a trip to the theatre, etcetera. It saved a good deal of money. We walked further, which helped us get fitter, and using the brain to find devious ways to get the most out of the system exercised the brain cells. We thought it was a 'win-win' situation. Sadly, it didn't last as long as we planned."

"I get it now. Geoffrey. When you feel ready, carry on with what you are doing. Use your brain, stay fit and healthy, and who knows? You might see Hope learn to drive, reach a university, even get married."

"Might Hope have a brother or sister?" the old man asked.

"It's not out of the question," replied Phoenix.

"Annabelle's forty this year," said Geoffrey, "time's not on her side. Especially with the two of you so involved in this charity business."

"We'll see, it's very much in our plans, but unforeseen events may overtake us."

"The best-laid plans and all that? Today has been a stark reminder of that, Phoenix. I'm glad you're here with Annabelle. She's in safe hands. I'll not keep her fussing over me for any longer than necessary. You and little Hope need her more than me in the long run."

"I'm away first thing tomorrow," said Phoenix, shaking the old man by the hand. "I've got business to attend to up north, but I'll be back by the weekend. How long I stay will depend on what emerges in the next few days. Never fear. I'll attend Grace's funeral. I had grown very fond of her in the brief time we knew one another. I was never fortunate enough to have a loving mother."

"Charity business up north, is it?" asked Geoffrey, probing for the truth, as always.

"Missing person cases," replied Phoenix.

Athena had returned to the lounge and caught the end of the conversation. Her father hugged her and wished them both goodnight. After the door closed behind him, Athena asked what Geoffrey's response had been to the question of why they had been saving the pennies.

Phoenix gave her father's reasoning as best he could

without disclosing the under-performance of her parents' investments. Geoffrey hadn't gone into any detail. The banking crisis and subsequent recession had been a testing time. Athena seemed satisfied enough with his explanation.

"What did you mean by missing person cases?" she asked.

"OK, I admit the men involved don't know they will be missing in a day or two, but it was the best I could come up with at short notice. Your Dad is always keen to trip me up, to trick me into revealing too much on what goes on at Olympus."

"We had better get to sleep," yawned Athena, "that driver will bang on the door before we know it."

"That wouldn't do in Vincent Gardens, would it?" said Phoenix as he followed Athena out of the lounge to the stairs. "The neighbours would have an attack of the vapours if he rolled up, and tooted his horn, to let me know he's arrived."

"You're incorrigible," said Athena.

"How much did you overhear?" Phoenix asked, "your Dad wondered about the chances of an addition to the family."

"Not tonight, sunshine," Athena replied.

They had reached the landing. The light under the door to Athena's parent's bedroom suggested Geoffrey was still awake. She raised a hand to knock. Phoenix shook his head.

"He won't thank you," he whispered.

Sleep didn't come to either of them for what seemed forever. Grace Fox had been taken from them far too soon. Geoffrey couldn't imagine life without her. Athena worried that her father felt so alone he would follow his beloved wife before long.

Phoenix was thinking of the suspect they had spotted.

Was he part of a cell? What were their future targets? How long before he could take his revenge on the men who murdered his mother-in-law?

Sweet dreams.

Grab your copy…
vinci-books.com/three-weeks-september

About the Author

Ted Tayler is the international best-selling indie author of the Freeman Files and Phoenix series. Ted lives in the English West country, where his stories are based. He was born in 1945 and has been married to Lynne since 1971. They have three children and four grandchildren.

His thought-provoking mysteries appeal to readers of Sally Rigby, Joy Ellis, Pauline Rowson, and Faith Martin. His action-packed thrillers are a must for fans of Mark Dawson and J C Ryan.

Gus Freeman's cold case investigations are carried out with reasoned deduction rather than bursts of frantic action. In each of the 24 books, unsolved murders are accompanied by romance, humour, and country life. The core message in the 12 Phoenix novels is that criminals should pay for their crimes. Unfortunately, the current system fails to deliver the correct punishment, so Phoenix helps redress the balance.

Acknowledgments

The love and support of my family; without them, this would have been impossible.